Pam
EVANS

Dance Your
Troubles Away

HEADLINE

First published in 2017 by
HEADLINE PUBLISHING GROUP

First published in paperback in 2017 by
HEADLINE PUBLISHING GROUP

1

Cataloguing in Publication Data is available from the British Library

ISBN 978 1 4722 3827 6

Typeset in Bembo Std by Palimpsest Book Production Limited,
Falkirk, Stirlingshire

Printed and bound by CPI Group (UK) Ltd, Croydon CR0 4YY

HEADLINE PUBLISHING GROUP
An Hachette UK Company
Carmelite House
50 Victoria Embankment
London EC4Y 0DZ

www.headline.co.uk
www.hachette.co.uk

To my beautiful granddaughter Millie and lovely Richard
on the occasion of their wedding.

Acknowledgements

My heartfelt thanks to my editor Clare Foss who continues to be a joy to work with, always enthusiastic and warm hearted. A mention for Hannah Wann who helped me through a digital problem recently and all the team at Headline who make my manuscripts into lovely books. Thanks too to my agent Barbara Levy who continues to work on my behalf. Warmest wishes to Tony Faure for his invaluable help with research.

Chapter One

So here we are again, thought Polly miserably, back in the Anderson shelter, which seemed even darker and more depressing after two bomb-less years.

'I thought we'd finished with this flamin' lark when the Blitz ended,' said Flo Pritchard to her daughter as they settled into the chilly, damp abyss dug deep into the back garden of their home in Hammersmith, west London.

'I think we all did, Mum,' said Polly, tucking a blanket over her three-year-old daughter Emmie, who was sleeping in a makeshift bed on the bench.

'I hope this isn't going to be a regular thing like the last lot,' said Flo, lighting a candle and standing it on a saucer on an upturned metal box they used as a table.

'With a bit of luck it'll just be a one-off,' said Polly, who usually tried to have a positive attitude.

Polly was outwardly calm as she concentrated on Emmie, but she was actually very frightened. She was trying to remember how she'd coped during the long London Blitz, when they were ensconced in the shelter every night and the bombing had been relentless.

1

The drone of an enemy plane grew nearer and, as it roared overhead, Polly automatically braced herself. 'Hold tight, Mum. We'll be all right.' That was what you did: you waited and hoped.

Flo nodded, and they were both silent, weak with relief when it passed over.

'What's the matter, Mum?' asked Polly after a while.

'I'd have thought that was obvious,' said Flo, a small woman with faded brown hair in a hairnet, and a crossover apron over her dress.

'Apart from the air raid, I mean,' added Polly, who sensed that her mother had something else on her mind. She'd noticed it earlier. 'I know something is worrying you.'

'Compared to the possibility of being blown to bits any minute, it's nothing.'

'Let's assume that our luck holds and we survive. You might as well tell me what's bothering you, if only to fill the time while we're waiting for the all-clear.'

'Nothing for you to worry about,' Flo said. 'It's just that I heard on the wireless earlier that the government have raised the age that women are required by law to register for war work. It's now gone up to fifty. So at forty-seven, I'm eligible.'

This news was potentially a problem for Polly too. 'But you look after Emmie so that I can work, and that's a contribution to the war effort,' she reminded her mother. 'Surely they'll take that into consideration, won't they?'

'I only look after Emmie in the mornings,' Flo said. 'They might make me do an afternoon shift somewhere.'

'I thought the rules about war work applied to women without domestic responsibilities, and you have plenty of those.'

'It isn't that I don't want to do my bit,' Flo said, obviously

2

Dear Reader

Thank you so much for selecting DANCE YOUR TROUBLES AWAY. I do hope you find it a good read. It was a pleasure to write, because dance halls were such lively places during the war, full of fun and romance.

When I was researching my last book, WHEN THE LIGHTS GO DOWN, set against a cinema background, I learnt a lot about wartime dance halls too because dancing was as popular as film-going in those hard times. So I thought it would make an interesting backdrop for my next story.

Social events were vital to people's morale in those dark days. With the bands playing popular songs and servicemen from all over the world filling the dance halls in their smart uniforms, it was no wonder young women flocked to the halls, managing to look glamorous despite clothes rationing and the shortage of absolutely everything. While the air raid sirens wailed outside, inside these palaces of fun people carried on dancing and enjoying themselves. People worked long hours, but it didn't stop them from getting dressed up and going out to have a good time after a day's work.

American servicemen taught British girls to jitterbug and jive and they loved it. Many romances began on the dance floor but hearts were broken too, especially when the war ended and the men went home to the other side of the world.

I hope you enjoy reading about Polly and Emmie and their family and friends, and that you like the setting I have created for them. Every reader is important to me and I very much enjoy hearing from you. So if you would like to get in touch, or are interested in knowing more about my books, please visit my website at www.pamevansbooks.com

Very best wishes

Pam

PAM EVANS was born and brought up in Ealing, London. She now lives in Surrey, near to her family and five beautiful grandchildren.

For more information about Pam and her novels visit
www.pamevansbooks.com

By Pam Evans and available from Headline

A Barrow in the Broadway
Lamplight on the Thames
Maggie of Moss Street
Star Quality
Diamonds in Danby Walk
A Fashionable Address
Tea-Blender's Daughter
The Willow Girls
Part of the Family
Town Belles
Yesterday's Friends
Near and Dear
A Song in Your Heart
The Carousel Keeps Turning
A Smile for All Seasons
Where We Belong
Close to Home
Always There
The Pride of Park Street
Second Chance of Sunshine
The Sparrows of Sycamore Road
In the Dark Street Shining
When the Boys Come Home
Under an Amber Sky
The Tideway Girls
Harvest Nights
The Other Side of Happiness
Whispers in the Town
A Distant Dream
On Her Own Two Feet
The Apple of Her Eye
When the Lights Go Down
Dance Your Troubles Away

agonising about it. 'Just that I haven't been out to work for so long, I don't know how to do anything. I'd be hopeless.'

'You would never be hopeless at anything, Mum,' Polly assured her. 'You'd be taught what to do and you'd soon get the hang of it. But I don't think you should be forced out to work at your age if you don't want to do it.'

'If I'm needed, I shall have to answer the call, but there's a lot of protests about this latest age change apparently,' Flo said. 'They're calling it "the grannies' call-up". Even some politicians aren't happy about it, and there's been arguments in Parliament.'

'I'm not surprised. It is taking things a bit too far when people are forced out to work in their later years. But I'm sure that when you tell them you look after Emmie, and that Dad is in essential employment at the docks and you like to make sure he has a hot meal when he gets home, they won't make you do it.'

'Let's hope you're right,' said Flo, but she had mixed feelings. So many women she knew were now in paid employment for the war effort, she sometimes felt lacking because she stayed at home. She did enjoy being a full-time housewife, though, and had no wish to go out to work, unlike some women who saw it as liberating and couldn't wait to get out of the house.

Twenty-three-year-old Polly was aware of how difficult it would be for her personally if Mum was forced into war work and couldn't choose her hours. As a widow, Polly needed to be able to earn money, and relied on her mother to look after Emmie. She only worked mornings because she thought time with her daughter essential, especially as Emmie was quite delicate. Having a child under fourteen meant that Polly wasn't obliged to be employed outside the home. It was a matter of financial necessity for her with no husband to support her.

Deciding to change the subject for the moment, she said, 'Where's Dad? Is he out on ARP duty?'

'More likely to be propping up the bar in some pub or other,' said Flo without rancour.

Polly gave a wry grin, fully aware of her father's fondness for a drink or two with his mates at the local. He was rarely the worse for alcohol, but he enjoyed company and wasn't the sort of man to sit at home of an evening.

She wondered how she and George would have fared as a middle-aged couple like her parents. It was hard to imagine George as the homely type. Blessed with good looks and the gift of the gab, he'd been sociable, funny and probably every parent's last choice as a husband for their daughter, as he was a bit of a wide boy and kept dubious company. Even as a lad he'd been in trouble with the police.

But Polly had thought he was the most beautiful boy she had ever seen when, as a schoolgirl, she'd passed him in the streets around Hammersmith. When he'd later sought her out at a dance, she'd fallen for him and had felt blessed when he'd reciprocated. Even if George did sometimes sail close to the wind as far as the law was concerned, she had known instinctively that he would never break his marriage vows. She had been the love of his life, as he was hers.

Anyway, Hitler had seen to it that they wouldn't grow old together, because George had been killed at Dunkirk. It was nearly three years since she'd received the devastating telegram; enough time for her to get used to it, though she knew she never would, not really. The wound was too deep. She put on a brave face so that people wouldn't worry about

4

her, nodding at the platitudes but knowing that, although time would heal, there would never be another man for her.

Emmie was her *raison d'être* now, a permanent reminder of George. While Polly had auburn-tinted blond hair and blue eyes, Emmie had inherited her father's beautiful dark eyes and black hair, though she wasn't as robust as her father. Although an exuberant and cheerful child, she was pale and slight of build, and suffered a great deal with minor ailments. If there was a bug going around, Emmie would get it. Polly couldn't afford the doctor often, but when she had taken Emmie to see one, she had been reassured that there was nothing actually wrong with her daughter, and she would probably grow out of it.

Polly was recalled to the present by her mother saying that there was another bomber on the way. After it had passed over and the explosion had sounded quite close, Polly said, 'I hope Auntie Marian is all right.'

'I don't think we need to worry too much about her,' said Flo dismissively. 'She knows how to look after herself.'

'But she doesn't go to the shelter, Mum. She carries on working during raids,' Polly reminded her.

'Yeah, I know, and it's very silly of her.'

'I suppose she feels the show must go on as people have paid to get into the dance hall.'

'She should get herself a job where she isn't out half the night,' Flo declared.

'But she really loves working there,' said Polly, who adored her mother's younger sister. 'Entertainment of all kinds is considered essential for morale in wartime, which is why she hasn't been forced to go into a factory. Someone has to run the dance halls, and they are all packed every night, so I've heard.'

5

'It isn't the right sort of work for a woman of her age, especially a spinster,' said Flo primly.

'I don't see what difference her age or being single makes.'

Ignoring both issues, Flo said, 'You need a man to keep order in a place like that.'

'There aren't any men available to do it. Anyway, Auntie really enjoys what she does,' said Polly, who would never forget the fact that she had first got together with George at the Cherry Ballroom, where her aunt was manager. 'And she makes a very good job of it.'

'She's never run with the pack, that one,' said Flo, as though thinking aloud. 'Always has to be different.'

'Women are doing all sorts of jobs nowadays,' Polly reminded her. 'In the factories and the services; working as plumbers and electricians. Running a dance hall isn't all that different in comparison. If Auntie was younger, I expect she would be in the forces.'

'Yes, I think you're probably right.'

The conversation was halted by a voice from above. 'Are you two all right down there?' It was Polly's father, Wilf. 'I'm coming down.'

'The all-clear hasn't gone yet,' said Flo in an admonitory manner when her husband climbed in to the shelter. 'You should have waited. It's dangerous out there on the streets during a raid.'

'And there was I thinking you'd be pleased to see me.'

'I am, of course, but preferably alive.'

'Well here I am, all in one piece,' said Wilf, a grey-haired man with greenish-brown eyes, who was a skilled metalworker at the docks.

'And with a good few pints under your belt, too.'

'A pint and a half actually, dear,' corrected Wilf. 'You know me. I never have more than that, except on special occasions.'

'Every night is a special occasion to you,' Flo retorted.

'That isn't true and you know it.'

'What's it like out there, Dad?' asked Polly, hoping to stop their niggle from developing into a full-blown row. 'Some of the explosions sounded quite close.'

'I didn't see any new damage, though some of the bangs did sound a bit near,' he said. 'They say that the Luftwaffe are on the Russian border, which is why we've had it quiet for a while. They must have visited us tonight to let us know that they haven't finished with us yet.'

'Mum's worried that she might have to get a job,' Polly mentioned. 'The government have raised the age, so she's eligible now.'

'Over my dead body,' he bellowed. 'I'm not having my wife going out to work.'

'If the government say I must, there won't be anything you or I can do about it, Wilf,' said Flo.

'You're forty-seven years old,' he reminded her with his usual lack of tact. 'A bit late in the day to go gallivanting off to work.'

'I'm not in my dotage yet,' she pointed out.

'No, but neither are you a spring chicken,' he said. 'We're both knocking on a bit now.'

'Thanks for reminding me,' she said sardonically. 'I really needed to hear that.'

'Just stating facts,' he said bluntly. 'Anyway, I didn't think you wanted to go out to work.'

'I don't, but I don't like being written off by you either.'

'I'm not writing you off, love,' he said. 'You do a good job here at home, and there's young Emmie to consider.'

'Emmie is my responsibility, Dad,' Polly reminded him quickly. 'If Mum can't look after her, I'll have to find someone else.'

'I'm not going out to work unless I am absolutely forced to, and I will make sure I'm still available in the mornings to look after Emmie whatever happens, so will the two of you shut up about it,' said Flo forcefully.

'All right, Mum,' said Polly as the all-clear sounded and relief surged through her. 'But if you ever do feel you want to venture out into the workplace, you mustn't let my need of you stand in your way.'

'Emmie is my only grandchild and I adore her,' Flo stated. 'I enjoy looking after her and I am not planning on stopping, so you can just stop worrying about it.'

'Thanks, Mum,' said Polly gratefully. She'd hate to have to leave her daughter with a stranger.

Despite the fact that her parents bickered their way through their life together, Polly thought they were probably devoted to each other in their own way. The other love of her mother's life, Polly's brother Ray, was in the navy and had been away for most of the war with only the occasional period of home leave. She'd heard it said that there was often a special bond between mother and son. Ray was certainly Flo's favoured child, but Polly didn't resent it, because she adored her brother too.

Apart from the usual sibling squabbles when they were little, they had always got on well and she'd missed him terribly when he first went away. She'd got used to his not being around, of course, but she loved it when he came home on leave.

★   ★   ★

The Cherry Ballroom was an imposing building on the outskirts of Hammersmith. It had a large sprung dance floor, a cafeteria at one end, a sitting area at the other, the stage midway between and a standing area all around. There was an abundance of gilt, red velvet and coloured lighting, which created a glamorous ambience in contrast to the drab streets outside.

On an office door at the back of the building were printed the words MISS MARIAN ATKINS – MANAGER. On hearing the all-clear, the occupant of the office swung the door open and made her way down the corridor to the ballroom, which was crowded with people jiving and jitterbugging to the Glenn Miller hit 'Chattanooga Choo Choo' under the coloured lights. A pall of cigarette smoke hung over everything, along with an amalgam of perfume, Brylcreem and sweat. The uniforms of many nations were here tonight, with a predominance of Americans, who had brought the jitterbug to the British Isles.

A tall, attractive woman approaching forty with bright red hair fashionably swept up at the sides, her white blouse and black skirt set off nicely by high-heeled court shoes, Marian was full of admiration for the dancers, who were determined to enjoy themselves whatever the risks of staying in the ballroom during a raid. Without them she would be out of a job.

Making her way around the edge of the dance floor, she spoke to the bandleader at the front of the stage, who stopped the music briefly and announced that the all-clear had sounded.

A short cheer went up and then everyone carried on dancing.

'They don't care if there's a raid or not,' said the bandleader, stepping aside to talk to Marian while the band played on. 'It'll take more than a few bombs to stop them enjoying themselves. While we turn up, so will they.'

'They come to see you, I reckon, Ted,' she joked.

'To hear my music,' said Ted, a man of middle years with dark hair and a neat moustache. He was dressed in a black jacket and dark trousers with a white shirt and maroon bow tie. The bandleaders she hired were usually charismatic types and able to connect with their audience, an essential part of the job. 'I'm a bit long in the tooth now to be a heartthrob. Even the boys in the band are getting on. All the young musicians are away at the war.'

'It hasn't stopped yours being one of the best and most popular dance bands around.'

'Thank you,' he said graciously. 'We try to keep up with the times by playing all the latest numbers. The dancers come to look at each other, not us, but we like to appear smart.'

'And you always do.' Marian looked towards the dance floor. 'There are men in the forces from many different countries here tonight and they are united in their determination to enjoy themselves.'

'Yeah, it's good to see it, and all nationalities seem to like the jitterbug.'

'I don't blame them. I'd have a go myself if I wasn't on duty.'

'I bet you would,' he said with a friendly smile.

'Anyway, I must get on,' Marian said. 'Is your wife well, and the kids?' She valued everyone she hired and was always interested in their lives.

He nodded. 'They're fine, thanks. The kids are all bigger than me now.'

'I suppose they must be.'

As Marian made her way back to the office and sat at her desk, she allowed herself a moment of pleasant reflection. She knew that she wouldn't have this job if it wasn't for the shortage of men due to the war. Very few ordinary women had been in managerial positions in peacetime. Now the sky was the limit and she revelled in it. After years of doing as she was told at the wrong end of a mop and bucket or a shop counter, at last she had a job she enjoyed, and was able to use her abilities fully.

Someone had once told her that a good manager should be willing to do every job themselves if the need ever arose, and she agreed with that wholeheartedly. She couldn't actually take over from Marge, the bookkeeper, because she didn't know how, but everything else she turned her hand to if necessary: selling tickets, sweeping and polishing if one of the cleaners didn't turn up; she'd even stopped a fight once when her security people had been slow on the uptake.

But officially she was paid by the owner to manage the place. She hired and fired all the ballroom staff, brought in electricians and decorators when needed, booked the bands, made sure the Cherry was always within the law as regarded the number of people in the hall at any one time, and enforced the rules about no alcohol on the premises. It was a very responsible position and she thrived on it.

She hadn't had the life she'd wanted when she was young, and she still occasionally felt disappointed about that, but she made the very best of the life she had now. Like most women she would have liked marriage and children. But it hadn't worked out for her and she'd learned to accept it.

Her only close relatives were Flo and her family, and she saw them all as often as she could. As a child she had worshipped her big sister, even though Flo had never seemed to want her around, which was often the case with older siblings. It had hurt then and Flo still had the power to wound her now. But Marian would never give up on her because she loved them all: Ray, Polly and Emmie. Even Wilf was like a brother to her.

Whilst Marian saw herself as a capable single woman with aspirations, the rest of the world, especially Flo, perceived her – and all unmarried woman of a certain age – as a sad spinster, an old maid. Even though she made an effort with her looks, wore smart clothes, was clever with make-up and brightened her hair with a bottle of something from Woolworths, she was missing that gold ring on her finger, and that made her inferior in many people's eyes. Still, she was respected at work and that meant a lot.

There was a knock at her door and Dolly the ticket clerk came in.

'I hope you've left the ticket office covered,' said Marian. 'People are still coming in.'

'Yeah, Marge is looking after things,' Dolly said. 'I thought you should know, there's a bit of trouble in the foyer. Some soldiers have had a few too many in the pub across the road. I've told them I can't let them in because they're drunk, but they won't accept it.'

'Where are the security men?'

'Someone's been taken ill in the ballroom and they're dealing with that.'

'All right, I'll see to it,' said Marian, rising.

Soon after the Pritchard family had gone back to the house after the air raid, the key turned in the front door and a voice said, 'You didn't have to put on a firework display for me, you know.'

'Ray!' said Flo joyfully, rushing over to her son and flinging her arms around him. 'Oh, it's so good to see you.'

'Likewise,' he said, grinning broadly. They were used to him just appearing without warning, but it was always a lovely surprise. He hugged his sister, shook hands with his father and lifted a sleepy Emmie up and kissed her head.

'I thought the raids had finished here,' he said when he was sitting in an armchair with a cup of tea and a sandwich. 'I had a shock when I heard the siren.'

'It's been quiet until tonight,' said Polly. 'We haven't had one for ages. I hope it isn't going to be a regular thing.'

'Me too,' he said. 'I hate to think of you having to put up with bombs every night.'

They chatted for the rest of the evening, and after their parents had gone to bed, Polly stayed up to talk to her brother alone.

'So how have you been, little sister?' he asked. 'Any romance in your life?'

'Of course not.'

'Why of course not?' He sounded puzzled. 'George has been gone a long time.'

'That doesn't mean I have to look for someone else.'

'I thought perhaps someone else might have just come along,' he said. 'It's a shame for you to be on your own.'

'I don't want anyone else, Ray. George was the only man for me. I'd sooner be single than just be with someone because it's the expected thing.'

She seemed rather sensitive about the matter, and since it was really none of his business, he nodded and changed the subject. 'Mum and Dad are on fine form.'

'The same as ever, still managing to disagree over most things,' she said.

'It wouldn't be the same if they didn't.'

'Mum's worried she might have to go out to work,' Polly told him. 'A little job might be the making of her, though.'

'In what way?'

'Well, she never seems truly happy, does she? She's full of beans when you're around, but in general she seems to be harbouring some sort of resentment, though she never says what. She isn't really a joyful woman.'

'That's just her way, I think.'

'Yeah, she's been like it ever since I can remember, and the other day I found myself wondering why. Then, when the subject of her going to work came up, it struck me that a part-time job might take her out of herself, give her another interest apart from us lot. I haven't told her my thoughts on the subject, of course. Telling Mum what to do isn't a good idea.'

'It certainly isn't,' he said with affection for his mother in his tone.

'So, what's the situation on the woman front?' she asked. 'Have you got anyone writing you love letters at the moment?'

'Not one.'

'All the nice girls love a sailor; it says so in the song.'

'I shall have to have a night out at the Cherry to find one then, won't I?'

'Good idea.'

Ray was a younger version of their father, with a shock of light brown hair and greenish eyes. Polly adored him and knew the feeling was reciprocated. As there was only a year between them, they had played together as children, and often fought as kids do. But they had remained close, and she knew that he would always be there for her, as she would be for him. Maybe only in spirit while this awful war was still on, but he would never let her down.

'Oh it's so good to have you home, Ray.' Suddenly overcome with emotion, she got up, went over to him and hugged him, tears in her eyes.

'Steady on, sis,' he said, patting her on the back. 'I'm not going anywhere, not for a few days anyway. But I'm very pleased to be home too.'

It was one of those rare moments that she knew would linger in her memory.

'Well, chaps,' said Marian to the four young soldiers in the attractive foyer, all Axminster and gilt-edged mirrors on the wall. 'You've put me in an awkward position. I want you to come in and enjoy yourselves, but it's more than my job's worth to let you into the Cherry in that state.'

'We've only had a couple,' said one of them.

'And the rest,' said Marian.

'We just wanna have some fun,' said another.

'Find some girls,' added a third.

'We're only in London for the night; we've got to get the late train back to camp.'

They were so young, thought Marian, noticing the fresh bloom on their cheeks. They looked barely old enough to shave, let alone fight for their country.

She tried to assess their condition and decided that they were merry rather than blind drunk, and unlikely to cause trouble. 'I'll do a deal with you,' she said. 'I'll let Dolly sell you some tickets, but you must go straight to the café and have some coffee, and stay there for half an hour or so until you've sobered up a little. I shall tell our security team to keep an eye on you; any sign of trouble and you're out, without your money back.'

'Thanks, miss,' said one of them.

'We don't have an alcohol licence, so there must be no drinking on the premises. Can you promise me you don't have any bottles hidden on you?'

'We don't.'

'Better turn your pockets out to ease my mind.'

This done, she turned to Dolly, who was back at the ticket desk. 'All right, love, you can go ahead and take their money.' She turned to the lads. 'I'm trusting you, so don't let me down.'

'We won't, miss, promise,' said one of them, his face wreathed in smiles.

'I really don't know how you did that,' said Dolly after the soldiers had headed for the ballroom. 'You had those boys eating out of your hand. All I got was a load of cheek when I was dealing with them.'

'It's all down to age and experience,' Marian said. 'You're young so they think of you as one of their own, whereas they probably see me as a mother figure.'

'I can't imagine my mum being able to control a bunch of lads like that.'

'It's part of my job,' Marian said.

'Yeah I suppose so,' agreed Dolly. 'Oh, and while you're here, Miss Atkins, I might as well tell you now that I have to leave the Cherry. They want me to do more hours at the factory, so I won't finish in time for my shift. I've been working here to pay off a debt to my dad, but the extra factory hours will cover that. My boss has made it clear that I don't have a choice in the matter. War work gets preference, you see.'

Marian cursed silently. Getting decent staff was the most difficult part of her job. 'I'm sorry to lose you, Dolly. When will you be leaving?'

'Saturday night will be my last night,' she said. 'I start my new hours at the factory on Monday. Sorry it's short notice. They sprung it on me.'

Part-time casual staff like Dolly didn't have to give the standard one week's notice, so there was nothing Marian could do about it except smile and wish her well.

'We'll miss you,' she said.

'I shall miss being here,' said Dolly. 'I'd much rather be dishing out tickets in a lovely place like this than working at a machine in a noisy factory. But we have to do what we're told in wartime, don't we?'

'I'm afraid we do,' Marian agreed.

'Sorry to leave you in the lurch, Miss Atkins.'

'Don't worry about that,' said Marian, thinking miserably that it only needed the girl who looked after the coats to quit and she really would be in trouble. 'I'll make sure I see you before you go.'

'Of course,' said Dolly, smiling brightly as a crowd of girls appeared at the window of the ticket office.

Polly called at her Aunt Marian's on the way home from work the next day. 'Guess what, Auntie,' she said excitedly.

17

'You've got a date,' said Marian jokingly.

'No, much better than that,' said Polly. 'Ray is home on leave for a few days. He walked in last night out of the blue.'

'Lovely. I bet that's cheered your mum up.'

'I'll say. She's like a dog with two tails when he's around. He's always been her pride and joy.'

Polly was such a sweet-natured girl, thought Marian. It wouldn't ever occur to her to be jealous of Flo's obvious favouritism for Ray.

'I'll pop around to see him a bit later on, before I go to work,' she said.

'I was hoping you might,' said Polly. 'He would have come to see you before he goes back if you hadn't, but he's only got a few days. Anyway, it'll give Emmie a chance to see you. You know how she loves her Auntie Marian.'

The older woman smiled, touched by Polly's thoughtfulness. She'd always been warm hearted, even as a child, and the two of them had a long-standing close relationship.

'Everything all right, Auntie?' asked Polly. 'Is your landlady behaving herself?'

Marian gave a wry grin. For years she'd rented two rooms in the house of a widow, an arrangement that suited them both, though they did sometimes have their differences, mostly because Mrs Beech was so different to Marian. 'We had a little disagreement the other day because I washed a few things and wanted to hang them on the line.'

'Why was that a problem?'

'It was a Saturday, and she doesn't like putting washing out at the weekend because it might lower the tone of the neighbourhood and upset the neighbours. The way she carries on, anyone would think this was Park Lane. A few trees and privet hedges and she reckons she's Lady Muck.'

'It's not much more than ten minutes' walk from ours, and no one cares when you hang washing out in our street.'

'They probably don't here either, but she's got this bee in her bonnet about it. Still, it's a roof over my head and Mrs Beech does have her good points. She doesn't charge the earth for rent, and she'd be there for me if I ever needed help, I'm sure of that. It's just these snobbish ideas of hers that are sometimes a bit irritating.'

'Why don't you move in with us?' suggested Polly.

Marian couldn't think of anything worse than losing her independence and being at the mercy of Flo's sharp tongue full time, but she just said, 'You don't have enough room.'

'We'd make room if you needed it,' said Polly.

'It's a sweet thought, but I'm all right here,' said Marian. 'I'm quite comfortable.'

Polly felt sad for her aunt suddenly. Most women of her age had a home and a family of their own, even though many had lost their husbands to the war. Her aunt had never had that. Polly didn't know why, because no one ever spoke about it. But Marian was an attractive woman who must have been stunning when she was young, so she would have had her chances.

Still, she seemed happy enough with her life. She had a good job and her rooms were comfortable and well furnished, even though the decor had seen better days.

'It's a nice place, Auntie,' she agreed.

'I'm lucky to have somewhere to live at all with this terrible housing shortage.'

Polly nodded. 'Anyway, I'd better be on my way,' she said. 'I can never wait to get home to Emmie after work.'

'I'm looking forward to seeing her later too,' said Marian as she showed her niece down the stairs and out of the front door, which was Mrs Beech's pride and joy because it had a panel of patterned coloured glass at the top. She thought this was the ultimate in class.

'Still enjoying your job, Auntie?' asked Ray later on when Marian called at the house. Greetings had been exchanged and she'd heard all his news.

'Very much, thanks,' she replied. 'It suits me down to the ground.'

'I can just imagine you swanning around telling everybody what to do,' he said, teasing her.

'I don't swan around anywhere,' she corrected amiably. 'And as for telling everyone what to do – well, staff are so hard to get these days, I sometimes feel as though they're the ones in charge. I've got staff problems at the moment, as it happens. One of my ticket clerks told me last night that she's leaving, and I'll be hard pressed to find someone by the end of the week. She only does four nights, but that's enough to create chaos.'

'What will you do?'

'I'll ask the other girl to do extra nights until I find someone, and if she can't help out, I'll have to go in the ticket office myself and stay late to catch up on my own work.' She sighed and gave a wry grin. 'But it will get sorted, I'll make sure of it.'

'If it wasn't for Emmie, I wouldn't mind the job myself,' said Polly casually. 'I could do with the extra cash. She grows out of her clothes so fast, it isn't easy to keep up.'

'You wouldn't have to get there until seven, so she'd be in

bed, wouldn't she?' said Marian, keen on the idea of her adored niece working with her. 'And you'd finish by ten.'

'Yes, but Mum already has her while I work in the mornings. I can't ask her to babysit evenings too.'

Marian looked at her sister, whose face was expressionless. 'No, I suppose you can't,' she said. Flo wasn't the sort of woman you took advantage of.

Flo's thoughts were racing. She had seen a way of ensuring that she didn't have to go out to work. If she looked after Emmie in the evening as well as the morning, surely she wouldn't be expected to get a job too? Caring for a child must be considered a priority by the authorities in these troubled times.

Looking after her granddaughter was a pleasure to her, and certainly preferable to working in a factory, especially as the child would be in bed anyway. And since she'd be doing this for Polly, she would have no need to feel bad about staying at home.

'I'll look after Emmie if you want to take the job at the Cherry,' she said, looking at her daughter.

'Are you sure, Mum?' asked Polly with a half-smile, not quite able to hide her delight at the idea of being able to earn some more money.

'Positive,' said Flo, light headed with relief now that the threat of outside employment had been removed.

'Looks like you've got yourself a new ticket clerk, Auntie,' said Polly, beaming at Marian.

'Excellent,' said Marian. 'Thanks for that, Flo.'

'No trouble,' said Flo, pleased with the way she had handled things.

★　　★　　★

That evening, a man walked into a back-street pub in Hammersmith and ordered a pint of bitter at the bar. He was in his early forties, tall and handsome, with fair, slightly greying hair and warm brown eyes.

'Good evening,' he said to an elderly man standing beside him.

'Wotcha, mate,' said the man. 'Haven't seen you in here before.'

'No. It's many years since I've been in these parts.'

'You visiting, then?'

'I'm working round here, in Shepherd's Bush,' said the stranger. 'I live in Essex.'

'That's a bit of a trek to work.'

'Not really. I live near the tube and it's straight through.'

'Can't you get a job closer to home?'

'I did have, but I've been sent over this way by the government,' he said. 'I'm a toolmaker, and they need someone with my skills at the aircraft factory. So I don't have a choice. That's how it is in wartime. You go where you're sent.'

'Still, at least you're not in uniform.'

'Too old, mate,' he said. 'I'd be deferred anyway because of my trade. Mind you, if the war goes on much longer, they'll even be calling up pensioners.'

The old man laughed. 'Let's hope it doesn't come to that. I don't think I'd be much use to them now. I did my bit in the last war and I'm past it now.'

The stranger thrust his hand out. 'Archie Bell,' he said.

'I'm Syd,' said the other man, shaking his hand.

'Nice to meet you,' said Archie.

'Likewise.'

The two men drank their beer in silence for a while, then

Syd said, 'What made you come to a back-street boozer like this rather than the bigger ones near the Broadway? I'm surprised you even knew it was here.'

'I spent a lot of time around here in my youth,' Archie replied. 'But back then I wasn't old enough to go into a pub.'

'Did you live here then?' asked Syd.

Archie didn't answer right away; he seemed thoughtful. 'No. I knew a family who did, though.'

He knew he shouldn't have come. The place was so full of memories, it was acutely painful. All these years he'd never been near; then, finding himself in the area, he'd given into temptation. But why? What did he think he would find here? He couldn't rewrite the past. The sensible thing to do was finish his beer and leave. There was nothing for him here.

'Who were the family?' asked Syd chattily. 'I've lived here all my life. I probably know them.'

Archie stared at him in silence. He wanted to walk away, but the need to know something, *anything*, was just too strong, and he knew that he couldn't resist. He opened his mouth and heard himself uttering the words.

Chapter Two

As a member of the typing pool in the offices of a large muni-
tions factory, Polly was no stranger to hard work. She was used
to tough targets, a strictly observed no-talking rule and a vigilant
supervisor who could spot the tiniest lapse in a typist's concen-
tration and relished the opportunity to exercise her authority.

She was also accustomed to the working mum's guilt for
not being with her child and the regret of missing a chunk
of her day that she could never have back.

So it was a surprise to her to find that paid employment
could be fun. She had to earn her pay, of course, but the
atmosphere at the Cherry Ballroom was sociable, and once
she got the hang of the ticket machine, she thoroughly enjoyed
greeting the punters and taking their money, all done against
a background of friendliness and popular dance music drifting
from the ballroom.

Such was the nature of motherhood, she felt even guiltier
for enjoying the job, and regularly reminded herself that she
was here so that she could give her child the things she needed.
At least she had the comfort of knowing that she had put
Emmie to bed, read her a story and kissed her goodnight

before she left the house. The recent air raid had proved to be a one-off, so that was a relief.

The Cherry clientele was mostly young; the girls surprisingly glamorous despite the shortage of clothes and cosmetics and the men smart in uniforms of a variety of nations. Everyone was ready for a fun night out and possibly a spot of romance.

For the first time since she'd learned of George's death, Polly felt like a young woman in the swing of things again, partly reminded by the casual flirting that came her way from some of the male customers. Maybe some women would have been offended, but Polly saw it as a bit of fun and enjoyed it.

'So what do you think?' asked Marian when her shift ended. 'Are you coming again tomorrow?'

'Try and keep me away,' Polly replied. 'I adore the musical background, it makes me want to dance. I'd love to do the jitterbug.'

'Why don't you go into the ballroom, then?' suggested Marian. 'We don't finish until half past eleven, and I'm sure there will be plenty of chaps only too happy to teach you. It's high time you had some fun.'

Polly was surprised by the suggestion, given her circumstances. 'I have to go home to my daughter, Auntie,' she reminded her in a serious manner.

'Emmie is tucked up in bed and doesn't know if you're there or not,' Marian pointed out.

'I can just imagine what Mum would say if I stayed,' said Polly with a wry grin.

'She won't hear about it from me,' said Marian. 'Anyway, I can't see the harm in it.'

'No, it wouldn't feel right.'

'I wasn't suggesting that you go on the game, love,' said Marian drily. 'I just thought it might be nice for you to have a dance, or at least watch the others and enjoy the atmosphere. Just for half an hour or so.'

'I'd better not,' Polly said reluctantly. 'I need to go home.'

'How much longer are you going to stay in mourning for George?' asked Marian.

'I'm not in mourning.'

'You're not dressed in black, but you're still grieving for him,' Marian observed. 'It's been more than three years.'

'I can't help the way I feel, Auntie. I always try not to be miserable so as not to upset other people.'

'And you never are miserable,' Marian assured her. 'But you don't seem able to move on. You're a young woman, Polly. Please don't let life pass you by.'

'Just because I don't want to pick up some random man in a dance hall doesn't mean I'm letting life pass me by. I'm a mum and that's my priority now.'

'All right, love,' said Marian patiently. 'But if at any time you do want to go into the ballroom after work, it will be on the house. One of the staff perks.'

'Thanks, Auntie. I'll be off now. Goodnight, see you tomorrow.'

'Night, love,' said Marian, and watched her hurry away down the corridor, a trim figure in a white blouse and floral skirt.

It was high time that girl had some fun in her life, thought the older woman. She'd been an anguished widow for far too long. Still, at least now she was spending her evenings in a sociable environment. Maybe that would have an uplifting influence on her and encourage her to take a step forward from George.

Much to Polly's astonishment, when she told her mother about Marian suggesting that she call in to the ballroom after work, Flo was in agreement.

'I thought you'd disapprove,' said Polly.

'Why would I do that?'

'Well, because you look after Emmie while I work, not while I'm out dancing.'

'The child is fast asleep, and I'm quite capable of dealing with her if she was to wake up,' said Flo, who also thought it was time her daughter put George behind her. 'I'm not saying I'd like you to come rolling home in the early hours, but I can see no harm in your calling in after work for a little while, especially as it's free.'

'I only want to watch because the jitterbug looks such fun,' Polly said. 'But if a chap sees a woman on her own, he thinks she's looking for a man.'

'Just tell anyone who asks that you're just watching,' suggested Flo.

'It doesn't work like that, Mum.'

Up went Flo's brows. 'I was your age once, you know,' she reminded her sternly. 'I do know how these things work. What would be the harm in dancing and being friendly anyway?'

'It might give them ideas.'

'One dance?'

'Yes, one dance. Most people go to a place like that hoping to meet someone.'

'I know that, but you might enjoy speaking to some new

people,' suggested Flo. 'Just because you talk to them doesn't mean you want to go out with them or anything.'

'What is it with you and Auntie?' asked Polly. 'Anyone would think you want me to find someone new. I will never, *ever* replace George.'

'Of course we don't want that, but neither do we want you to spend the rest of your life clinging on to someone who isn't there any more.'

Polly was quiet for a moment. 'You didn't like George much, did you, Mum?' she said.

Flo hesitated, choosing her words carefully. 'I didn't dislike him. He was a very jovial fella and was always good to you.'

'I sometimes had the idea that you didn't approve of him, though.'

'I worried about the company he kept and the way he earned his living,' Flo admitted. 'But I had nothing against him personally.'

Polly sighed heavily. 'I'm glad about that, but it doesn't matter now anyway, does it?'

'No, I suppose it doesn't.'

'Anyway, I might have a look in at the dance one of these nights, since you're happy about it,' Polly said vaguely. 'But I won't be staying long and I definitely won't be looking for a man.'

'Of course not, dear,' Flo said patiently.

'Is it just one ticket you want, sir?' Polly asked the man waiting at the ticket office.

'I'm about twenty years too old for one of those,' he said,

grinning, and she thought how handsome he was, though he looked to be middle aged.

'What can I do for you, then?'

'I'd like to see Marian Atkins, please.'

'Are you a sales rep?'

'No.'

'May I ask what it's about, then?'

'Absolutely not!'

'It's part of my job to enquire, because Marian doesn't usually see anyone when we have a dance in progress. She has a lot of work to do.'

'It's personal, and I'd like to surprise her.'

'Oh, I see.' Polly noticed a queue forming behind him. 'Well, if you wouldn't mind standing aside while I serve the people waiting, then I'll go to her office and tell her. Who shall I say wants to see her?'

'An old friend,' he said.

'That's all?'

'Yep, that's all.' His manner was friendly, but it was not one that invited argument.

'All right,' she said. 'I'll go and speak to her as soon as I have a moment. But I can't promise anything.'

'An old friend,' said Marian, not looking pleased. 'Surely you could have got more information than that for me, Polly. You know I don't see random callers when we have a dance in progress.'

'I told him that and he just said it was personal,' Polly explained. 'I knew you wouldn't be happy about it, but he seemed determined.'

'Well whoever he is, he's got a bloomin' cheek, waltzing in here demanding to see me.'

'He didn't really demand,' Polly pointed out. 'He just has a way with him somehow. He seems very nice, Auntie.'

'We'll soon see about that,' said Marian briskly. 'Send him through and I'll pack him off with a flea in his ear.'

Polly nodded and headed back to the ticket office.

'Come in,' said Marian in reply to a knock on her office door. 'This had better be good,' she added, without looking up from her paperwork. 'I'm running a business here, not some sort of old pals' club.'

'Don't you recognise me, Marian,' said a voice. 'It has been a very long time.'

She looked up and studied him for a moment, the blood draining from her face. Then she stood up slowly. 'Archie?' she said hoarsely.

'Of course it's me,' he said, sounding emotional. 'Surely I haven't changed that much.'

'You were just a boy the last time I saw you,' she said thickly. 'Of course you've bloody changed.'

'So have you, but I would still have known you anywhere,' he said. 'You're looking good.'

'You're not so bad yourself, for an old boy,' she said, smiling and offering him a seat, her legs trembling so much she was glad to sit down.

The band was playing one of her favourites, 'In the Mood', when Polly finished work, and she was very tempted to go into the ballroom; she knew the jitterbuggers would be in their element with this number. But walking into a dance hall on your own wasn't easy, especially as she didn't want to be misunderstood. She really did just want to watch.

If Auntie was around, she would have given her courage. There was an air of reassurance about her somehow. But Marian had appeared with the mystery visitor, introduced him as her old friend Archie, and said she was taking the rest of the evening off to go for a drink with him. Most unusual for her to take any time out, so he must be special. Polly hoped she would find out more in due course.

But for now she wanted to be on the other side of the swing doors and closer to the music. Taking her courage in her hands, she pushed open the door.

'So why now, after all these years?' asked Marian after a large gulp of gin and tonic in a nearby pub.

'I'm working locally and I suppose I just finally gave in to temptation,' Archie said. 'I figured it wouldn't matter after such a long time.'

'It doesn't, of course,' she assured him. 'It was one hell of a shock, though.'

'Sorry, but I wanted to surprise you.'

'You did that all right.'

'I made a few enquiries at the pub near your sister's place and found out that you weren't married. I wouldn't have come anywhere near if you had been. The chap I was speaking to didn't know your address, but he knew where you worked, so here I am.'

'Are *you* married, Archie?'

'No. I wouldn't have come if I had been,' he said. 'I've been close to it once or twice, but it didn't happen. It was never right.'

'After all these years, it's almost like meeting for the first time, isn't it?' Marian remarked. 'We don't know each other now. We were just kids back then.'

'I never forgot you, though,' he said.

'Likewise but the people we are now are strangers.'

'We could do something about that if you fancy it,' he said. 'We could start from the beginning and see what we think of each other now that we're all grown up. If we don't like each other, we can leave it at that. We've certainly got some catching-up to do, regardless of anything else.'

'We certainly have, and I think we should get cracking on it,' she said.

'No time like the present,' he agreed.

The atmosphere inside the ballroom was electric, the music behind the doors loud and exciting. Most people were on the dance floor, but a few were standing around; all of them seemed to be men. Taking a deep breath, Polly went closer to the dance floor to get a better view.

Oh, the jitterbug looked such fun; so different and slick. There were legs flying, bodies twirling, feet moving fast and neat. Some of the women were lifted into the air by their partners.

'Would you like to dance?' said a male voice with a strong accent and, turning, she found herself looking at a blond-haired soldier with a broad grin and greyish-blue eyes.

'Thank you, but I'm not actually dancing. I just came to watch,' she said.

'That seems like a waste of your ticket money.'

'I work here so I don't have to pay,' she explained. 'I've just finished my shift and I thought I'd call in and have a look.'

'Seems a shame not to dance as you're here.'

'I can't do the jitterbug anyway.'

'I'm not an expert, but I could teach you what I know,' he offered.

She was sorely tempted. 'I suppose one dance wouldn't hurt,' she said. 'But I have a little girl at home so I can't stay long.'

His gaze moved towards her left hand. 'Oh, so you're married,' he said. 'I didn't realise.'

'A widow,' she explained. 'I still wear my wedding ring. It seems only right even though it's been a while.'

He nodded. 'Well, if you've got time for a dance, I'd be honoured.'

'Are you American?'

'Canadian.'

'Oh. The accent is similar.'

'Non-Canadians seem to think so, but we don't think we sound alike at all,' he said.

'Oh dear, did I say the wrong thing?' Polly was embarrassed. 'I've never been outside of England so I'm not good with anything foreign. Until the war, the only time we heard an American accent was on the films.'

'There are so many different nationalities in your country at the moment, you'll be a lot more familiar with foreigners by the time this war is done,' he said. 'But there is always a bit of competition between us and the Americans. Some people don't realise that Canada is a country in its own right.' He looked at her and smiled. 'Anyway, that's enough about that. Shall we head for the dance floor?'

'Well you've certainly introduced some glamour to the word spinster, Marian,' observed Archie.

'I do my best,' she said. 'I've always liked to look smart, so I just carried on the same as when I was young. I have the advantage of not caring what people say about me, so the mutton and lamb remarks are like water off a duck's back.'

'Good for you,' he said. 'I suppose you had plenty of chances to get married.'

'The subject came up once or twice,' she said. 'I've taken some knocks, though. A chap I was going out with turned out to be already married; another one just disappeared.' She smiled, her blue eyes twinkling. 'These things hurt, but I'm a tough old bird. I won't allow myself to be destroyed.'

'I can see that.'

'I was toughened up at an early age, wasn't I, Archie? We both were,' she added, her expression becoming serious. 'Not pleasant at the time, but good grounding for later.'

He nodded and put his hand on hers in a comforting gesture, and they both lapsed into a sad kind of silence.

Polly was enjoying herself so much, she was disappointed when the music ended.

'I really do have to go now,' she said to her partner, who'd told her that his name was James.

'Aw, can't you stay for one more dance? It might be another fast one and we can jitterbug some more.'

'I'd love to, but I have to get home,' she said. 'I've really enjoyed myself, though. Thank you for teaching me.'

'Can I see you home?'

'The thing is, James,' she began, turning to him as they walked towards the exit, 'I'm not looking for a boyfriend.'

'I was offering to see you home, not proposing marriage.'

'I asked for that, didn't I?' she said, embarrassed.

'I guess.'

'I just wanted to be straight with you,' she said.

'I appreciate that,' he replied. 'How long since you lost your husband?'

'It's over three years now.'

'Oh.' He sounded surprised. 'I didn't think it would be as long as that.'

'Because I'm not looking for a boyfriend yet?'

'Well, yeah.'

'He was the love of my life,' she explained. 'No one could ever replace him, so it wouldn't be fair to start something with anyone else.'

'He must have been a great guy.'

'Yes, he was.'

'I'd still like to see you home, though.'

'But you'll miss the rest of the dance, and there's still quite a while to go.'

'I can ask for a pass to get back in.'

'Of course you can. I didn't think of that,' she said, smiling. 'I'll get you one from the office.'

'So what do you do in Canada when you're not away being a soldier?' Polly asked as they walked through the warm summer streets, James's army torch showing them the way in the blackout.

'I work on a farm,' he said.

'Really? I've never met a farmer before. Do you enjoy it?'

'I've never done anything else to compare it with,' he said. 'But yeah, I guess I do.'

'Are you stationed near here?'

'Aldershot,' he replied. 'When you go into the town, there's a sign that says "The Home of the British Army", but it's more like the home of the Canadian army at the moment. There are such a lot of us stationed there. Guys have been arriving since the beginning of the war. We're mostly here for training and to defend the UK.'

'We're glad to have you,' she said. 'We need to get this flaming war finished, but it just goes on and on.'

'Things are beginning to look better lately, though,' he said. 'The Americans had a victory in Sicily the other day, and the British are doing good things around that area too.'

'Dad was saying something about that,' Polly said vaguely. 'But I don't really follow the technicalities.'

'The barracks are full of it,' he said. 'There's always a lot of military talk.'

'I suppose there would be in that sort of environment,' Polly mused. 'I haven't been to many places outside of London, but I've heard of Aldershot and imagine it to be a long way out. Us Londoners do tend to think that anywhere else is the back of beyond.'

'We come in to London on the train and it doesn't take all that long.'

'Wouldn't it be more convenient for you to go to local dances?' she asked.

'Sure, and we do go out locally sometimes, but we like to come into London if we can.'

'You don't take your leisure in the West End, then?'

'Sometimes we do,' he said. 'We originally came this way for the Hammersmith Palais. We'd heard all about it.''

'Everyone has heard of the Palais,' she said. 'It's our biggest rival.'

'When we were there, we heard about the Cherry, so we thought we'd give it a try.'

'I'm very glad you found us,' she said. 'You've given me a taste for the jitterbug. It wasn't around when I used to go out dancing before I got married. We've got the Americans to thank for that.'

'Sure.'

'Do you like England?'

'I sure do, especially London,' he said. 'At first it seemed strange because there are so many people everywhere. Where I live, in the countryside in Ontario, you can walk for miles and not see another soul. Here you can't go more than a couple of paces without bumping into someone and it took me a while to get used to it. Now I enjoy the buzz, the fact that you see so many different faces. At home you see the same people when you go into town. Everybody works on the land, except the shopkeepers, of course. In London there are crowds, and I doubt if you would ever see the same person twice.'

'In the West End that's true,' she said. 'Here in the suburbs there's more of a local community.'

'I suppose there would be,' he agreed.

'Oh well, at least the war has given you the chance to see something of the world,' said Polly, slowing her step as they reached her gate.

'Yeah, that's true.'

'Well, this is where I live,' she said. 'Thank you for seeing me home.'

'It's been a pleasure.'

There was an awkward moment when she wondered if he was expecting her to invite him into the house. Perhaps they did that in Canada, but not here in London, not when you'd just met someone anyway.

'Maybe I'll see you again if you go to the Cherry,' she said casually. 'I'm there Wednesday to Saturday.'

'I might see you then,' James said.

'Goodnight.' Polly leaned towards him and kissed his cheek. 'That's for being such a gentleman.'

'Goodnight,' he said, and turned and walked away.

Gentleman he might be, but James wasn't prepared to give up at the first hurdle. The instant he'd seen Polly, she had stirred something in him, and he was darned if he was going to lose that without at least investigating it further. Aldershot wasn't on the doorstep and he couldn't always get to London, but that wasn't going to stop him keeping in touch. He had tried to appear nonchalant about walking Polly home, but on the way he had taken the precaution of making a note of her street name and house number.

The following afternoon the Pritchards' living room was ringing with music and laughter. Polly was teaching her daughter to jitterbug as 'Deep in the Heart of Texas' played on the wind-up gramophone.

'That's right, Emmie, step back, then sideways, then twirl . . . around you go, that's right,' she encouraged. 'Oh well done, love. You're a natural.'

'Again!' cried Emmie when Polly tried to stop, having been at it for a while.

'Just one more time then,' said Polly, loving to see her daughter's exuberance as they twirled and twisted.

'Last time,' said Flo, who was winding the gramophone.

'Phew, you've worn me out,' said Polly at the end of the song, flopping into an armchair.

'How did you learn that, Polly?' asked her mother.

'A chap at the Cherry taught me a few steps after work last night,' she explained.

'A chap. That sounds promising,' said Flo.

'Nothing like that, so don't get excited,' said Polly.

'Who was he, Mummy?' asked Emmie.

'Just a man I got talking to,' said Polly.

'What's his name?' asked her daughter.

'James.'

'Does he live in this street?'

'Oh no, darling, he lives in an army camp a long way from here,' said Polly, who had her daughter happily ensconced on her lap. 'And his real home is even further away, across the sea in a place called Canada.'

'Canada,' Flo burst out. 'There's no point in getting involved with him, then. There'll be no future in it, because he'll be on the other side of the world after the war.'

'As I have no intention of getting involved with him, that won't affect me,' Polly said. 'I made it very clear to him that I'm not looking for a boyfriend, let alone a husband.'

'It's time you did have someone, Polly. I want that for you

and Emmie. But not someone who lives halfway across the world,' said Flo. 'I'm not having you going somewhere so far away. We'd never see you again.'

'Honestly, Mum, you don't half get ahead of yourself,' said Polly. 'I had one dance with him and he walked me home. I'll probably never see him again.'

'I bet there will be a lot of women who'll go to live overseas after the war with men they've met from other countries,' said Flo in a more serious tone.

'Well I won't be one of them and that's for certain, Mum, so you can relax.' Polly gave a wicked grin and added, 'I wouldn't mind a bit more jitterbug practice, though, and it would be nice to learn some other steps.'

'Can we do some more dancing tomorrow?' asked Emmie sweetly.

'Of course we can, honeybun,' Polly said, wrapping her arms around her daughter and holding her close. She cherished the time she spent with her between jobs.

Marian wanted to speak to her sister privately, so she went to see her one morning when she knew she would be on her own with Emmie.

She came straight to the point. 'I'm seeing Archie Bell,' she announced.

'Archie Bell!' gasped Flo. 'You never are.'

'I am,' confirmed Marian in a firm tone. 'I wanted you to know; I didn't want to be secretive about it.'

'I'm absolutely amazed.' Flo sounded disapproving.

'Me too, but I'm very pleased,' Marian said. 'I've been on my own for long enough.'

'Archie Bell, though . . .'

'Yes, Archie Bell,' she said determinedly. 'There'll be no trouble and there's no need for you to meet him if you'd rather not. But I shall definitely be seeing him.'

'Well I'm sure it's none of my business who you go out with,' said Flo with a sniff.

'No it isn't, Flo,' Marian agreed.

'Did you just run into him?' asked Flo.

'No. He tracked me down and came to see me at work. He's working locally, so we'll see each other now and then and see how it goes.'

'It's your life,' said Flo dismissively.

'Yes, it most certainly is.'

There was a brief hiatus; the threat of awkwardness. Then Flo said, 'Do you fancy a cuppa?'

'I wouldn't mind, if you can spare your tea ration,' Marian said, following her sister to the kitchen.

The two women sat down at the table to drink their tea, chatting pleasantly. But not another word was said about Archie Bell.

There was someone else Marian needed to have a serious word with, and the sooner the better. As soon as she got back, she knocked on her landlady's sitting-room door.

'Can I have a word please, Mrs Beech?' she asked.

'Of course you can,' said the other woman, who was grey haired and frumpish. 'Please take a seat.'

Marian perched on the edge of a mustard-coloured armchair with an embroidered antimacassar on the back. Mrs Beech sat on a matching chair opposite.

'I hope you're not unhappy with the accommodation, Miss Atkins,' she said.

'No, nothing like that, Mrs Beech.' Marian had been living here for more than ten years, but they still never used Christian names.

'What's on your mind, then?'

'Well, I have a friend, a man, and I may want to bring him here to my rooms sometimes.'

The other woman shot into a stiff upright position, looking worried. 'Oh no, Miss Atkins,' she said sternly. 'That won't do at all, not on my premises. A man. Oh no. Absolutely not!'

'Hm, I see,' said Marian. 'He wouldn't be staying overnight or anything.'

Mrs Beech's eyes bulged and her mouth turned down. 'I should hope not,' she said. 'A woman of your age. The very idea.'

'I'm not pushing up the daisies yet, and I do pay a decent rent for the rooms,' Marian pointed out calmly. 'I think I should be able to bring friends home.'

'I have never stopped you bringing women friends here,' said the widow.

'I hardly think a gentleman caller will bring your house into disrepute. In fact it might cheer the place up a bit. He's a very nice man.'

'I'm sorry, but the answer is no.'

'So be it.' Marian knew she was going to have to take a risk. Affordable rented rooms weren't easy to come by, and Mrs Beech knew that. But she would also be aware that quiet, considerate lodgers, who were out a lot of the time and always respected their landlady's privacy, weren't around in huge numbers either. 'In that case, I shall have to think about giving notice.'

Mrs Beech flushed angrily. 'Oh, I see,' she said. 'You won't find anywhere as reasonably priced and nice as this.'

'Maybe not, but I'm sure I'll find a place where they don't mind visitors of either sex,' she said.

'If that's your attitude . . .' said the landlady.

'It is, I'm afraid,' said Marian. 'I've paid the rent in advance so I have time to find somewhere. It's a pity, though, because you and I have rubbed along quite nicely together for a very long time. Giving each other space and minding our own business.'

'Indeed,' agreed Mrs Beech, who had red anxiety blotches around her throat, despite her calm manner.

Marian rose. 'Anyway, I'll find somewhere else as soon as I can and be out of here at the earliest opportunity. I'll leave you in peace for now,' she said, and left the room.

She'd taken a chance and it hadn't worked, dammit. Oh well, she'd have to start looking for somewhere right away, because she wasn't going to back down. She might be a single lady of a certain age, but she wasn't ready to be bullied just yet.

Mrs Beech stayed sitting in her armchair, feeling sorry for herself and wondering why life was always so difficult now. First her husband had died and left her to fend for herself; then she'd been forced to rent out half her house to make ends meet. If that wasn't bad enough, the war had come and made life even harder, and now she was going to have to look for a new lodger.

There would be no shortage of applicants, but what would the new tenant be like? Mrs Beech wasn't good with people, and now she was going to have to get to know a complete stranger. There were all sorts of strange people out there. Could be someone noisy, or even dishonest.

Miss Atkins had been here a long time and Mrs Beech was used to her. She could be a bit flighty at times; often overly friendly towards the tradespeople who called at the house, the baker, greengrocer and so on. But she always kept her part of the house spotless and never overstayed her time in the shared kitchen and bathroom. In fact, Mrs Beech couldn't recall her ever having taken any liberties at all.

If this man friend of hers wasn't going to stay overnight, maybe it wouldn't be too bad. She could always force herself to turn a blind eye. The thought of having a stranger living in her house was far worse than the idea of a man in her lodger's rooms. In fact, it was too much to bear. Mrs Beech hurried up the stairs and knocked on Miss Atkins' sitting-room door.

Chapter Three

James didn't appear at the Cherry again. Polly found herself feeling disappointed but guessed he'd been looking for more than she had to offer. She did venture into the ballroom again after work, and even managed a little more practice in the jitterbug. But none of the men were as understanding as James had been about her limited availability. She realised it was naive of her to expect otherwise; after all, most single people went to dance halls in search of more than just a dance partner. So she went straight home after work now.

'Surely you don't want to spend the rest of your life on your own,' said her mother one night.

'I haven't really thought about it, but I'm only twenty-three, Mum,' Polly reminded her.

'Exactly. You're far too young to give up on men altogether. George has been gone a long time,' said Flo tactlessly. 'You should be looking to the future now.'

'Honestly, Mum, you don't half go on. I don't suppose anyone ever really gets over losing the love of their life, though I must admit that awful aching feeling of grief seems to have eased off.'

'That's something, anyway. So why are you so against getting fond of anyone else?' asked Flo.

Instead of giving the stock answer she used whenever her mother was quizzing her in this irritating manner, Polly gave the matter some thought. 'Probably because George was so special I could never replace him. Also, I don't ever want to feel that vulnerable again,' she said.

'We're all vulnerable, from the day we're born,' declared Flo dismissively. 'And even more so in wartime. You can't let that stop you living your life.'

'I live my life in the way I want to,' said Polly, clinging to her severely tried patience. 'Let's just see what happens, shall we, though I can understand it if you want me off your hands.'

Flo looked as though she had been slapped. 'How dare you say such a thing?' she blasted, her cheeks flushed with anger. 'I love having you and Emmie here. Surely you must know that. It's you I was thinking of.'

'I wouldn't blame you if you wanted us gone,' Polly said. 'Children grow up and leave home. That's how it's supposed to work.'

'In normal times perhaps. But not in wartime, when there's a shocking housing shortage,' pronounced Flo. 'So let's have no more of that sort of talk. You're welcome here for as long as you want to stay.'

On impulse, Polly stepped forward and gave her mother a hug. 'Thanks, Mum. I don't know what I'd do without you and Dad.'

'God willing you won't have to,' Flo said, drawing back. 'Not for a very long time, anyway.'

Her mother wasn't comfortable with displays of physical affection. Polly had accepted that years ago. Except when it came to Ray, of course, and then she was all hugs and cuddles. Some people might have been hurt by this, but it didn't seem to touch Polly. Probably because her parents had always been good to her, and she didn't feel the need for anything more.

As August progressed, incipient autumn began to tinge the evenings with its cool ambrosial scent. The nights remained bomb-free and there was a sense of optimism in the air as people waited for news of the Allied invasion, which was generally referred to as the Second Front and which everyone hoped would end the war.

In late September, something happened that took Polly's mind off the war. She had a letter from James. He'd been away on a training exercise apparently, but was back now and had a pass next weekend. He was planning on coming to London and hoping to see her at the Cherry. *I know you don't want a boyfriend but thought you might like a dancing partner when you finish work on Saturday night. Maybe you could even stay a bit longer this time. I won't deny that I was rather taken with you but am quite happy to be just a friend if that's what you want, and I won't pester you.*

'Well hurray for James,' approved Flo when Polly told her. 'There's a man with a bit of go in him. I like him already. So long as he doesn't have any ideas about whisking you off to Canada after the war, he and I will be good friends. And if you want to stay a bit longer at the dance as he suggests, Emmie will be fine here with us.'

'Thanks, Mum, but don't get too carried away; it's only a few dances.' Polly, though, was quietly delighted. In fact, rather more pleased than she'd expected.

*   *   *

By the time Saturday night came, Polly had that pre-date mixture of excitement and nerves, even though seeing James wasn't a date as such. It seemed so long since she had felt like this, fully alive and self-aware. She'd forgotten how nice it was!

'You're looking particularly pretty tonight, Polly,' remarked her aunt when she arrived at work and removed her coat to reveal a pale blue blouse with a lace trim, smart black skirt and high heels. She was wearing a little make-up, too.

'Thanks, Auntie.'

'Someone special coming in?'

'Yeah, James, the Canadian chap I told you about,' she said. 'I'll see him after work.'

Marian chose her words carefully, because her niece always insisted that she wasn't looking for a replacement for George and tended to be sensitive about it. 'It'll be nice for you to have some young company. I know how you love to dance.'

'I really do.'

'You've got some work to do before then, though, so let's open up and earn our wages.'

'Right you are,' said Polly, smiling.

Because this was a prearranged meeting and she knew that James was keen, Polly hoped she wasn't going to get that feeling of wanting to escape that did sometimes happen on such occasions. Even more worrying, would she even recognise him? She had only seen him once before, for a short time. She needn't have worried. She had to keep her eyes and mind on the job, but she recognised his voice immediately.

'One, please, Polly,' he said, and there he was with his twinkling eyes and wide smile.

She returned his smile, gave him a ticket and his change, said, 'See you soon,' and moved on to the next customer. But she was looking forward to the end of her shift, excited about having fun after such a long time.

It took no time at all for Polly to get completely caught up in the atmosphere; the lights, the music and the company made her forgot all about the war, her horrid supervisor at the typing pool and her grief for George. She danced the next hour or so away, jiving and jitterbugging with the odd slow dance in between.

'I'll have to be going soon,' she said as the evening drew towards its end.

'You can't stay for the last waltz, then?' James sounded disappointed.

She knew her mother wouldn't mind if she stayed longer but she didn't want to take liberties; neither did she want to give James the wrong idea, because the last waltz had romantic connotations. 'I'd better not,' she told him. 'I've had a good time and really enjoyed myself, but I need to go.'

'I'd like to see you home.'

'I'd like that too, James,' she said, and realised that she meant it.

They talked non-stop all the way home. He told her he was twenty-four and had been in Britain for three years, initially in Scotland, then Sussex, and for the last few months in Aldershot.

'Have you been in action at all?' she asked.

'Sure. I was involved in a cross-Channel operation back in '42.

It was meant to be one of the biggest raids of the war, but it ended in disaster for our division because there was deadly enemy fire waiting for us on the beaches of Dieppe. The operation failed and we lost a lot of men. More than half of those who went were killed.'

'That's awful.'

'Yeah, it was. I felt pretty bad for surviving when others didn't, but you have to get used to that sort of thing when you're a soldier. You can only do your best and you have to try not to feel guilty because you stayed alive when your buddies didn't.'

'Oh James,' said Polly, shocked. 'How awful to burden yourself with those sort of feelings. It's bad enough having to kill people without adding that to it.'

'I guess so.'

'Still, perhaps this invasion they're planning will help bring the war to an end,' she said.

'Yeah, I think that's the general idea.'

She suspected that he knew more than he was allowed to say, so she changed the subject.

'I've really enjoyed myself tonight thanks to you,' she said. 'It's nice to have fun again.' She paused. 'Mind you, there's an element of guilt there too, because I'm enjoying myself and poor George didn't even live to see his twenty-first birthday.'

'That's really tough, but you're a young woman, Polly,' he said. 'You must live your life, and I'm sure George wouldn't begrudge you some enjoyment.'

'So everybody keeps telling me, and I know they're right. George enjoyed life and he'd want the same for me,' she said. 'I think maybe I've made a start tonight.'

'Good. I hope this will be just the beginning for you.'

'It's hard when you've lost your other half,' she confided.

'But you've helped to show me the way forward. You've reminded me of what it feels like to have a nice time.'

They reached her house and stopped at the gateway. 'Are you going back to Aldershot tonight?' she enquired companionably.

'That was the plan, but I'm not sure now if I'll make it in time for the last train.'

'So what will you do?'

'Wait for the first one in the morning,' he said casually.

'But where will you sleep?'

'On the station.'

'You can't do that,' she said, astonished at the suggestion.

'Sure I can,' he said. 'It won't be the first time, and I'll have plenty of company. My buddies and I regularly miss the last train when we come to London. I'll find a bench, and if there isn't an empty one, I'll bunk down on the floor. I've slept in worse places since I've been a soldier.'

'Well this is one night you're not going to rough it,' Polly said, making a sudden decision. 'The sofa in our living room isn't exactly a feather bed, but it's a damned sight more comfortable than the floor at Waterloo station.'

'I'll be fine,' he insisted. 'I'm young and healthy; I can sleep anywhere.'

'Look, James, you've missed your train because of me, so it's the least I can do.'

He shrugged. 'Okay,' he said casually and followed her up the path to the front door.

The next morning, Flo went downstairs as usual and put the kettle on for tea. When she went into the living room to draw the curtains, she let out a shriek.

'Sorry to have startled you,' said James, sitting up with a start, a blanket around him. 'I'm Polly's friend James.'

'Oh thank Gawd for that,' Flo said. 'I thought we had a burglar.'

James was struggling to compose himself. He was glad he had slept in his clothes. 'I missed the last train back to camp,' he explained.

'That's all right, dear,' said Flo, who had enormous respect for all servicemen. 'What sort of person would I be if I minded a soldier sleeping on the sofa? You Canadian lads are doing a good job helping to keep our island safe. I expect you'd like a cup o' tea.'

Actually he preferred coffee, but the British were fanatical about their tea so that was what he'd have. 'Thank you,' he said. 'I'd love one, but what about your rations?'

'Never mind that,' she said. 'You stay there and I'll bring it in.'

Despite James's concerns about the Pritchards' rations, Flo persuaded him to stay for breakfast, which was porridge and toast with margarine.

'So I suppose you're not allowed to tell us anything about this invasion they've got planned?' said Wilf.

'They don't tell us much, but there are always rumours flying around the barracks. You're right, though, we're sworn to secrecy about anything we hear,' said James, who was enjoying the luxury of home comforts enormously. Flo had told him that he was welcome to sleep on their sofa any time.

'Will you be stationed here in England for the rest of the war?' she asked.

'I have no idea, Mrs Pritchard,' he replied. 'You never know with the army what's going to happen from one day to the next.'

'You must miss your family,' said Flo.

'I sure do.'

'Do you have a big family?'

'A sister and three brothers,' he replied.

'Any of them living at home?'

He nodded. 'My sister, and one of my brothers didn't pass the medical so he isn't in the military.'

'I expect your mother is pleased about that.'

'I guess so.'

Polly felt comfortable having James here. Mum and Dad seemed to like him, and he was a hit with Emmie. He chatted to her and after breakfast made her squeal with laughter piggybacking her around the house.

As it was Sunday and she wasn't working, Polly offered to go to Waterloo with him.

'I'd like that,' he said.

'He seemed a nice young fella, didn't he?' Flo said to Wilf after they'd gone.

'Yeah, I thought he was a decent sort of a bloke,' agreed Wilf. 'Easy to get on with.'

'I'm pleased to see her enjoying herself, but nothing can come of it in the long term.'

'Why not?'

'Because he'll go back to Canada after the war, of course,' she reminded him.

'Mm, there is that,' he agreed. 'But that could be years away. Anything could happen before then.'

'Exactly. We have to live in the moment in wartime.'

'I thought you might have wedding bells in mind,' Wilf said with a smile.

'And have him whisk her off to Canada? Not likely!' Flo declared. 'It's good for her to have a boyfriend, though, and I like him. He'll always be welcome in this house, whatever happens between the two of them.'

'Because he's a soldier?'

'Exactly. And as you say, he's a decent bloke.'

The station was noisy and crowded, mostly with servicemen and women and civilians seeing them off. The concourse was hectic, with travellers moving in all directions, and the noise deafening: the hiss of steam, the roar of human voices and the crackly and barely audible announcements over the loudspeaker.

'Well, I've enjoyed our time together, James,' Polly said after they'd found out which platform he needed.

'Me too.'

'Thanks for coming.'

'No need to thank me. I wanted to come and I've had a good time,' he assured her. 'I don't know when I'll be able to get to London again, but I'll be in touch.'

She smiled. 'I'll look forward to it.'

He leaned down and kissed her on the lips. Much to her surprise, she enjoyed it.

'Well, I'd better be on my way,' he said. He smiled briefly and headed off through the crowds towards the platform.

She watched until he disappeared, then walked slowly in the direction of the tube, engrossed in thought. She didn't have the same depth of feeling she'd had for George, when even parting overnight had been painful. But she did enjoy being with James and was hoping that he would contact her again soon.

'This is ridiculous, Marian,' said Archie. 'We're both over forty, for Gawd's sake.'

Marian put her hand to her mouth to stifle a giggle. 'I know I'm being silly, but I can't help it. My landlady is down there listening to every movement, and it puts me off.'

'But you pay for these rooms; what you do behind closed doors is none of her business.'

'You're right, but just knowing she's down there makes me feel embarrassed.'

It was a Sunday evening, Marian's night off. They were in her sitting room and Archie was feeling amorous. Having gone to the trouble of persuading Mrs Beech to let her have Archie here, Marian felt awkward now that he was.

'I think I'll go into your bedroom and jump on the bed a few times to make the springs squeak; that'll shake her.'

'She'd probably give me notice, if she doesn't have a heart attack first.'

'I think you should leave if you aren't relaxed here, Marian,' Archie suggested.

'I was relaxed until you started coming round.'

'Well I don't intend to stop. Where else can we go to be on our own?' he asked. 'I think we're a bit past shop doorways and back alleys.'

'Don't be coarse, please, Archie.'

He laughed. 'Don't knock something you were grateful for once.'

'That was back in the dark ages. I like to think I'm a bit more dignified now.'

'You always had bags of dignity, Marian,' he said. 'Back alleyways or not.'

'Why thank you, Archie.'

'Come and sit on the sofa with me, love,' he said, patting the space beside him. He gave her that crooked smile of his that she'd never been able to resist.

'All right then, but no funny business,' she said. 'I don't want to give Mrs Beech palpitations.'

She sat down beside him, his arm going around her, the wireless turned down low.

'If you aren't comfortable with me coming to your place, we'd better change it to you coming to mine.'

'But you live out in Essex and we're both at work all week,' she said. 'You're already in London, so it makes sense for us to see each other here.'

'Perhaps I should move back to London,' he suggested thoughtfully. 'That would be the sensible thing to do.'

'Yes, it would,' she said, mulling it over. 'If you're willing to take such a step and can find a place, the housing shortage being as it is.'

'I'm earning good money at the moment, especially with all the extra hours, so I could afford to pay over the odds for rent,' he told her.

'That would make a difference,' she said. 'It would be lovely if you lived nearer.'

'I'll look into it tomorrow,' he said. 'Meanwhile, come here.'

She melted into his arms and suddenly didn't care what Mrs Beech thought.

*   *   *

Polly had a letter from James a few days after he went back to camp, saying that he'd had a wonderful time with her and couldn't wait to see her again.

As the mellow autumn days darkened into winter, their romance progressed and strengthened. James couldn't come to London every weekend, and sometimes he had to get back to camp the same night, so they made sure he caught the last train. Other times he slept on the Pritchards' sofa. Sometimes he telephoned her at the Cherry from a call box in Aldershot. It was a very exciting and romantic time for Polly.

When he was at the Cherry waiting for her to finish her shift, he sat in Marian's office to save him hanging around in the ballroom, and the two of them struck up quite a friendship. The older woman loved hearing him talk about Canada and said it was just as well he didn't come every night, as she would get no work done at all.

When James told Polly that he was in love with her, she was able to say truthfully that she felt the same. Neither of them mentioned the long-term future because they both knew they might not have one together. But they lived in the present and enjoyed every moment they managed to spend with each other. James took Emmie to his heart and she adored him.

As Christmas drew near, James broke the good news that he had two days' leave over the holiday. When Polly told the family, her mother made an astonishing suggestion.

'He can sleep in Ray's room as it's Christmas and it's going to be for two nights,' she said.

Polly stared at her in amazement. Her brother's room was sacrosanct, the bed made up and the room regularly cleaned in anticipation of Ray's return. No one was allowed to even sit on the bed, let alone sleep in it.

'Are you sure, Mum?' she said. 'You keep it nice for Ray.'

'It's only a couple of nights, and I don't suppose Ray would mind. He said in his last letter that he definitely won't make it home for Christmas,' Flo said. 'James is a good lad. He deserves a decent night's sleep over the holiday.'

'Thanks, Mum.'

Emmie picked up the magic word 'Christmas' and said, 'Is Uncle James coming?'

'Yes he is,' replied Polly.

'Whoopee!' she cried. 'How long to go now?'

'Two weeks,' said Polly.

'Is that long?'

'Fourteen sleeps; quite long enough for you to try and forget about it for a while,' said Polly without much hope.

Polly was almost as excited as her daughter, but Emmie would probably explode if she had any encouragement, so it wouldn't be wise to show it.

'Auntie Marian's boyfriend lives in London now,' Polly mentioned to her mother one afternoon a week or so later. 'That will be better for them, won't it?'

'Yes, I suppose it will.'

'I'm really pleased she's got someone, aren't you?'

'Mm.'

'It must have been lonely for her before.'

'Your aunt has had plenty of chances,' said Flo crisply.

'Has she?' asked Polly, interested. 'Was she a bit of a girl in her day, then?'

Flo was silent for a while. 'I don't know about that,' she

said at last, 'but she was good looking and always very outgoing, so she never lacked for male interest.'

'Yet she never married.'

'No.'

'Seems a bit strange if all the blokes were after her.'

'Probably preferred to stay single.'

'Was Archie one of her boyfriends back then?'

'For a while, yes.'

'Quite romantic, isn't it?' said Polly. 'Him coming back to find her after all these years.'

'I'm not sure about that.'

'Oh Mum, of course it is,' said Polly with enthusiasm. 'Will he be coming to ours with Auntie at Christmas?'

'I don't know,' Flo replied. 'The subject hasn't been mentioned yet.'

'I do hope so,' said Polly. 'She can't leave him on his own. They're both local to us now, so they can walk round.'

'I'll mention it to her,' said Flo.

'I can tell her when I see her at work if you like,' offered Polly.

'No, I'll do it,' Flo said in a determined manner.

'Just as you like,' Polly agreed, realising she had hit some sort of raw nerve.

'I've told Marian she can bring Archie Bell at Christmas,' Flo said to Wilf as they got into bed.

'Who?'

'Archie Bell,' she repeated. 'I did tell you she was seeing him again.'

'Oh yeah, I vaguely remember you saying something about it,' he said casually.

'I don't know if I should have invited him.'

'It's not as though you've asked him to move in,' Wilf said drily. 'The more the merrier at Christmas as far as I'm concerned.'

'I might have known you'd be no help,' she said.

'What is there to help with?'

'You know very well.'

'You're making a mountain out of a molehill, as usual,' he told her.

'I don't know why you married me,' she said, sounding put out. 'You never give me any moral support.'

'Give over, woman,' he said, his voice rising. 'I always give you plenty of support if it's necessary, but in this case it really isn't. One more for Christmas dinner is no big thing.'

She came back at him and there was a war of words for a while, then they kissed goodnight and settled down to sleep. Arguing was as natural as breathing to them, and neither of them fretted about it afterwards.

'My sister Flo has invited us round for Christmas Day,' Marian told Archie.

'Oh no.'

'Have you got relatives you need to be with?' she asked.

'Nothing I can't get out of,' he said.

'Why the long face, then?'

'I was looking forward to us having some time on our own.'

She looked worried. 'That's very flattering, and I'm touched, but you know me better than that, Archie,' she said. 'As much as I love you and want to be with you, I like to be with other people too at Christmas.'

'But we don't get much time off to be together.'

'That's true, but Christmas Day is for being sociable,' she said. 'I always go to Flo's. Polly's boyfriend James is going to be there as well, so it should be lots of fun. I couldn't bear to miss being with Emmie at Christmas.'

'Mm, I can understand that. It's a time for the kiddies.' He paused. 'Has Flo specifically invited me? Without any arm-twisting from you?'

'Yes, of course she invited you,' Marian fibbed. Flo had needed more than a little persuasion.

'I haven't seen her since I've been back, and she's never been my greatest fan, has she?'

'No, that's true, but Christmas can sometimes be a time for reconciliation.'

'It's also known to be a time for arguments,' he said. 'People have a drink or two and sparks fly.'

'No arguments, please,' she said. 'Promise me. I know my sister can be difficult at times, but can you let it go this once, just for me?'

'I'll do my best,' he said.

'Thanks, love. You always got on well with Wilf, and you like James, don't you? So you'll have plenty of male company. The three of you might manage to slope off to the pub for half an hour in the evening, if you can find one open.'

'Yeah, all right. I'll come and I'll be on my best behaviour,' he said. 'Honestly, the things we do for love.'

'And you'll be nice to Flo?'

'I will be charm itself.'

'In that case, roll on the big day,' Marian said excitedly. 'Oh, I do so love Christmas.'

Chapter Four

'You're nothing short of a genius, Flo,' said Marian as they sat down to Christmas dinner. 'You've done wonders with the meat ration.'

'Thank you,' said Flo, who was rather proud of her prowess in the kitchen under trying circumstances. She had made a small piece of lamb look like a banquet with the generous use of vegetables, especially potatoes and swede, everything endlessly queued for. 'Everybody chipped in with the ingredients, so I had plenty to work with.'

It was normal practice for ration books to be supplied when visiting for meals, and James had made his contribution by bringing chocolate, biscuits, boiled sweets and a large tin of ham from the camp.

'I don't know how you do it, Mum,' said Polly truthfully. 'I can't wait to start.'

'Come on then, Wilf,' said Flo. 'Get carving.'

Polly was enjoying herself enormously. This was the first Christmas she'd felt even remotely festive since she'd lost George. But sitting here with Emmie one side of her and James on the other, she felt truly blessed. She'd been given a second chance at love and she was making the most of it.

Emmie had had them up early and had been delighted with her presents, which had been hard to come by because toys were in such short supply. But by queuing and sewing and cutting and sticking, there had been a decent pile of packages for her to open. Everything felt special on Christmas Day; even the house smelled different. There was less of everything, and things were not necessarily made from genuine ingredients, but the place was still fragrant with the aroma of freshly baked mince pies, sausage rolls and Christmas pudding.

Polly felt something under the table and was about to squeal when she realised it was James reaching for her hand. When she turned to him, she could see tears in his eyes, and she smiled and squeezed his hand, guessing that he was feeling homesick.

'Hey, you two, no canoodling at the table,' said Flo, who didn't miss a thing. 'There'll be plenty of time for that sort of thing later on.'

'Sorry, Mrs Pritchard,' James said thickly.

'That's all right, dear,' Flo said cheerfully. 'I was young myself once.'

'She was all over me in those days,' said Wilf, teasing her. 'It didn't matter where we were: dinner table, teatime, anywhere. She couldn't get enough of me.'

'Take no notice of him,' Flo said, but she was laughing – they all were – and the meal continued in similar jocular vein.

'Were you feeling homesick at dinner?' Polly asked James later when they went for a walk to the river. 'You seemed to be in a sentimental mood.'

'Not homesickness,' he said. 'I'm a bit overwhelmed by your family's hospitality.'

'Oh, that's so nice,' she said. 'It's Christmas. A time to make people welcome.'

'It isn't just because it's Christmas,' he said. They were standing on Hammersmith Bridge, the river dark beneath the steel-grey sky. 'It's the same every time I come, and has been since the very first day.'

'They like you,' she said. 'Which isn't surprising; you're a likeable sort of bloke.'

'I'll never forget it,' he said.

'You make it sound as if it's going to end.'

'It will eventually.'

'The war probably won't be over for years yet,' she said.

'Maybe not, but when it is, I'll be going back home.'

'Yeah, you will,' she said, staring ahead of her at the landscape she knew so well. The day was very still, smoke curling from chimneys, everywhere eerily silent, the river empty of traffic for the holiday. 'And I'll become a distant memory.'

'You will never be that.'

'There's no point in thinking ahead, James,' she said. 'Anything could happen. We're still at war, even though we haven't had any raids lately. All we have is now, so let's enjoy it and just be thankful that we're together.'

'Yeah, sure,' he said, slipping his arm around her as the sky darkened towards evening.

As well as having produced such a fine Christmas dinner, Flo also came up with a lovely tea: wartime sausage rolls, mince pies, fish-paste sandwiches and cheese straws. She'd even managed to get hold of a tin of pineapple and some evaporated milk.

'Well, everybody,' announced Wilf, 'I think my wife has excelled herself today, putting on a marvellous spread despite the rationing. She deserves some appreciation. Three cheers for Flo . . . hip hip hooray!'

Polly was rather moved by her father's gesture. It was good to see, as he did sometimes seem to take everything for granted – as they all did up to a point. Mum ran the household so efficiently, and hated interference, so it was easy to forget the hard work that went into it: the daily shopping that was heavy to carry home, the queues at every shop and the delicate art of making the rations go around.

True to form, though, after tea her father said to Archie and James, 'Well, chaps, is it time for us to take a walk to see if the local is open?'

'Oh Wilf, surely not on Christmas Day?' said Flo.

'Only for half an hour, love,' he said. 'You know I don't like to be indoors all day.'

'There's plenty to drink here,' she reminded him.

'It isn't the same as a pub,' he said. 'But I'll only have one and we won't be long, then we'll all have a few drinks together when we get back.'

Polly and Marian exchanged a look. Every Christmas Day they listened to this identical conversation.

'Go on then,' said Flo predictably. 'But don't stay out all evening.'

James looked at Polly. 'A British tradition?' he surmised.

'A Pritchard tradition,' she explained. 'Dad always likes a break; he usually escapes about this time. Boys will be boys and all that.'

'Come on, James,' urged her father. 'Get your coat.'

'Hurry up, or you won't be one of the boys,' said Polly, smiling at him.

She'd grown up with this sort of male attitude, so it didn't bother her one bit.

'You can't beat a pint in a pub, can you, lads?' said Wilf, having taken the top off his pint of beer. 'It just doesn't taste the same at home.'

'It's the atmosphere, mate,' said Archie, glancing around the bar, which was bereft of females but crowded with men.

'They only open for an hour or so on Christmas Day, but it's just long enough for a break,' said Wilf. 'Flo does a cracking Christmas and she works hard at it, but I have to have some time out or I can't sleep.'

Archie laughed. 'Even I can see that's a feeble excuse, Wilf,' he said. 'So I don't suppose Flo buys it.'

'Course she doesn't, but she doesn't really object either, even though she pretends to as a matter of course,' said Wilf. He turned to James. 'What about you, lad?' he said. 'You're too young yet to want to escape. You still can't get enough of Polly.'

James nodded politely. 'I'm enjoying being out with you fellas, though,' he said.

'So what about this invasion, then?' said Archie. 'Will you be going?'

'I guess so, but I haven't been told yet.'

'He wouldn't be able to tell us even if he did know,' said Wilf. 'It's bound to be hush-hush.'

'As it should be,' said Archie.

The three men chatted easily. It was a very pleasant interlude.

'It's nice to have you around again after all these years, Archie,' said Wilf.

'Likewise,' said Archie.

'Things have a way of working themselves out, don't they? I'm glad you and Marian are back together after such a long time. It worked out for the best for all of us really, didn't it?'

'I suppose it did,' said Archie politely, hoping that what he said was true.

'I shall get so used to your family's hospitality I won't want to go home after the war,' said James later when he and Polly were alone together downstairs.

'I don't believe that,' she said lightly.

'I do feel very welcome here, though.'

'That's because you *are* welcome,' she said. 'We love having you and it has been a really good day.' She looked at him. 'You must miss your home and family, though.'

'I guess so, but I'm too caught up with you to feel homesick.'

'Ah, that's so sweet.' Polly kissed him. 'But don't forget our golden rule. For us there is only today. All the rest we'll worry about when the time comes.'

'I'll try to remember,' he said, holding her close.

'Wilf said something that struck me as odd when we were in the pub,' Archie mentioned to Marian as they walked home.

'You know Wilf. He's the master of indiscretion. What did he say?'

'Something about things working out for the best for all of us,' he said.

Marian was silent for a moment. 'I suppose he must have been talking about us getting back together after all these years,' she suggested. 'People are always pleased when things go right for members of their family, aren't they? I expect he and Flo are glad to have me down off the shelf at last.'

'Yeah, I suppose that must have been it,' Archie said, taking her hand in his.

The new year didn't bring news of the invasion. Instead there were air raids, and plenty of them.

'I don't think anyone was expecting this,' said Flo as she, Polly and Emmie climbed into the shelter. Wilf was working late. 'It's downright ridiculous the way this war is dragging on.'

'The bombs won't hit us, will they, Mum?' asked Emmie anxiously.

'Course not, darlin',' said Polly, relieved that it was her night off and she didn't have to leave her daughter. 'How can they when I'm here to defend us?'

'That's what I thought,' Emmie said. 'But it is very noisy.'

'It certainly is,' said Polly. 'You get under the blanket and I'll tell you a story.'

'Goody!' whooped the little girl.

'That's better,' said Flo when she'd lit the candle. 'A little bit of light does make a difference. I came in in such a rush

I didn't have time to make any tea. I'm not properly back into the air-raid habit yet.'

'And I forgot Emmie's storybook, so I'll have to make one up,' said Polly.

'I like made-up ones best,' said Emmie.

'Once upon a time,' began Polly, and concentrated on dragging up some sort of tale from her imagination, which was not easy but at least it took her mind off the bombers that just kept on roaring overhead.

'How are ticket sales, Polly?' asked Marian, standing behind her niece's desk.

'Very good, Auntie,' she replied. 'Numbers haven't dropped since the raids started again. We're almost up to full capacity. And it isn't even a weekend. I shall have to shut up shop soon.'

'All quiet so far tonight,' Marian said. 'No siren yet.'

'Fingers crossed it doesn't come at all.' The raids were even more traumatic for Polly when she was at work, because her daughter was at home and that really was frightening.

'Keep up the good work,' said Marian as more people came to the ticket window and she headed back to her own office.

Since the raids had started, Polly didn't linger at the Cherry to watch the dancing; her maternal instincts had magnified and she wanted to be at home to do her job as protector. The siren had been mercifully silent tonight, but she was just finishing the cashing-up when its horrible wail sounded over the building.

'Bugger,' she said under her breath as she bagged the money ready for the night safe, her hand trembling slightly. Forcing herself to stay calm, she finished the job, cleared the desk, put her coat on and headed for Marian's office with the bags.

Suddenly there was a loud crash and she was knocked to the ground. Shocked, she scrambled up, still carrying the money, and carried on, but the door of her aunt's office had been blown off and the whole area was thick with dust.

'Auntie!' she yelled. 'Auntie!'

'I'm trapped under the desk,' called Marian weakly. 'It's my leg. Something's on it and I can't move.'

Mercifully, Archie had just arrived; he came every night to go with Marian to the bank safe then walk her home. 'It's all right, Polly,' he said. 'I'll take care of it.'

'Polly,' called her aunt weakly. 'Go into the ballroom and see what it's like in there. If no one is hurt, ask Ted to keep playing and tell the punters the dance will carry on.'

'Will do, Auntie,' said Polly through dry lips.

'So as long as you want to stay, the band will play on,' announced Polly to loud applause. 'Please enjoy your evening if you can.'

The band struck up with 'That Old Black Magic', and people went back out on to the floor, some doing a slow jive, others a more traditional foxtrot. Polly couldn't tell if anyone had taken flight and left, but the dance floor seemed as crowded as ever. She was moved almost to tears and very proud to be a part of this place.

Back at Marian's office, the rescue workers had arrived and were trying to remove the weight from Marian's leg.

'Is everything all right in the ballroom?' asked her aunt.

'Yeah, most people have stayed,' Polly said. 'But don't you worry about this place. You worry about yourself.'

'It's taken me years to get a job like this and I'm buggered if I'm gonna let Hitler take it from me.'

Polly and Archie laughed. 'I'll take over from here, Polly, if you want to get off home. Your aunt isn't seriously hurt and I'll look after her,' said Archie.

'Are you sure?'

'Positive,' he said. 'Emmie and your mother need you more than we do.'

'Goodnight then,' Polly said.

Much to Polly's shame, she cried all the way home, presumably a reaction to the night's events, but there was no evidence of it when she got to the house and found the family safe in the shelter, Emmie fast asleep.

'Thank God you're home,' said Flo. 'We've been worried sick about you.'

'We heard the Cherry had taken a hit,' explained Wilf. 'I was going to come over to see if you were all right, but—'

'But I stopped him,' interrupted Flo. 'I didn't want to lose both of you.'

'You haven't lost either of us,' said Polly, and went on to explain what had happened to her aunt.

'Poor Marian,' said Flo. 'I'll go round and see her first thing in the morning.'

When they finally heard the all-clear, they were all too

exhausted to rush back to the house and instead made their way slowly, Wilf carrying the sleeping Emmie.

When Polly got home from work at the typing pool the next day, she found her mother in a black mood.

'It's that sister of mine again,' she explained. 'She'll be the death of me.'

'What's Auntie done this time?' asked Polly with a sigh.

'I went round to her place this morning to see how she was, and was told by her stuck-up landlady that Marian had stayed the night at her boyfriend's place.'

'Oh. I suppose Archie thought she might need some support after last night,' suggested Polly. 'I think it will be best for her, Mum. It can't be very nice being on your own when you're off colour.'

'They aren't married, so she's no right to be staying there,' Flo said adamantly. 'And I can't even go and see her to tell her so because I don't have Archie's address and neither does Mrs Beech.'

Polly thought that was probably just as well at this stage. The last thing Auntie would want after being hurt was her sister reading the riot act.

'I expect she'll only be there for a couple of days,' she suggested. She could see no wrong in it personally, though she knew it was against the rules of decency. 'There might be an address for Archie in her office somewhere. I'll see what I can find later on when I go to work.'

'Why does she do these things?' wailed Flo. 'She and I had exactly the same upbringing, so she knows right from wrong. Why does she always have to cross the line?'

'It isn't anything wicked she's done, though, is it, Mum?' Polly tried to reason. 'Not something that will do any harm to anyone.'

'Of course it will do harm: to our family reputation,' Flo declared. 'My mother will be turning in her grave.'

'But Grandma isn't around any more, so she can't be hurt by it,' said Polly.

'That isn't the point,' raged Flo. 'I've tried to help her. All her life I've tried to do my best for her. But some people just can't be helped because they're too selfish.'

'Auntie isn't selfish, Mum.'

'Of course she is, or she would have a little more respect for other people's feelings.'

Polly could see that her mother wouldn't be comforted, so she just said, 'I'll see if I can find Archie's address, then perhaps we can go and see her tomorrow afternoon.'

'She'll get a piece of my mind, I can tell you,' said Flo.

Polly didn't doubt it for a moment.

When Polly arrived at work that evening, she was surprised to see her aunt there.

'I thought you'd take things easy for a few days at least,' she said, looking around. The place had been cleared up. The roof was still there, so the damage must have been caused by the blast from the explosion.

'Not likely,' Marian said. 'I'm not going to risk losing my job by staying at home.'

'I'm sure you wouldn't lose it, Auntie.'

'I'm not taking the chance just because of a bruised leg,' she said.

'But isn't it painful?' asked Polly.

'Nothing I can't cope with,' Marian said, swinging around from the desk so that Polly could see the large dressing. 'Bruised and grazed, that's all. I can walk and it'll be healed in no time. Meanwhile, you and I have a job to do.'

'Just so you know, Auntie, Mum went round to yours this morning to see if you were all right.'

'Oh Lord. Mrs Beech told her where I was, I suppose.'

Polly nodded.

'I'll go and see your mother in the morning,' Marian said. 'But for now, let's open the ticket office and let business commence.'

'I don't know how you've got the nerve to show your face around here,' blasted Flo when Marian called to see her next morning.

'Thanks for the sympathy,' said Marian sarcastically.

'Well, you must be all right or you wouldn't be here,' said Flo, glancing at her sister's bandaged leg. She wasn't normally devoid of compassion, but in this instance her kind side had been outweighed by her dedication to respectability. 'What's actually the matter with it anyway?'

'Bruised and grazed.'

'You'd better take the weight off your feet, then.'

Sitting down on a chair in the Pritchards' living room, Marian said, 'I understand that you called to see me yesterday.'

'Yeah, for all the good it did me,' said Flo. 'Honestly, Marian, do you have no shame?'

'I would if I did something bad,' she said. 'If I committed an offence.'

'You stayed the night at Archie's; is that not bad enough?' raged Flo.

'It isn't against the law, as far as I know.'

'It's against all the laws of decency; morally wrong. Everyone knows that.'

'I'm not thick, Flo,' Marian objected. 'I do actually know how things work.'

'But you change the rules when it suits you.'

'If I can see that no one is going to get hurt by it, yes, I do, especially if it's the sensible thing to do,' she said. 'Archie came to the hospital with me and I was a bit shaken up, so he suggested I went to his for the night.'

'And I suppose you slept in his bed.'

'That is my business,' said Marian.

Flo sighed dramatically. 'I'll take that as a yes, then,' she said.

'You can do what you like,' said Marian. 'My sleeping arrangements are nothing to do with you.'

'Why can't you just stick to the straight and narrow like me?' asked Flo. 'It can't be that difficult, surely.'

'Not everyone is lucky enough to have things work out exactly as they want,' Marian said. 'You met the man of your dreams when you were young, and lived happily ever after. It doesn't happen like that for all of us. If Wilf hadn't been "the one", you'd have married him anyway, because that's what people do and you don't like to be different.'

'Neither do most people.'

'I have never set out to be different,' said Marian. 'My life has taken another course, that's all. We all have to make the best of what comes our way. I'm nearly forty Flo; too old to be worrying about what people think.'

'You really have no idea, have you?' said Flo, sounding emotional. 'It actually physically hurts me when you break the rules of common decency.'

Marian looked at her. 'Why, Flo?' she asked. 'I can understand why you might have felt that way when we were young, and Mum and Dad were alive. But we're middle aged now, and I don't live with you. None of your friends and neighbours know where I live or what I do, apart from the fact that I work at the Cherry. So they won't be gossiping about my spending the night with Archie, that's for sure.'

'It isn't about other people,' said Flo. 'All right, I don't like our family being the subject of gossip, I admit that, but it goes much deeper than that with me. I feel it inside. You and I had a good upbringing and it seems to count for nothing with you. That's what hurts.'

'I'm sorry that the way I live upsets you,' said Marian. 'I don't want to do that.'

'Stop doing these awful things, then.'

'They aren't awful things to me, Flo,' she said. 'They're matters of the heart. I don't have the husband and the family life that you have. When it comes down to the nitty-gritty, I'm on my own. No one to answer to or turn to for advice.'

'You have me.'

'That isn't what I meant and you know it, or have you been sheltered by your married status for so long that you've lost sight of how it is for someone like me?'

'I hadn't thought—'

'Wilf earns the money and takes all the responsibility,' Marian cut in. 'He's always there if you have a problem or just want to talk something over. You don't have to earn a living or find somewhere to live. I don't have that sort of security. So the things that worry you are mere trivialities to me.'

'But—'

'Yes, I am aware of the way society works, and that I fall off the straight and narrow now and then,' she continued. 'I admit I'm not a saint, but I try not to hurt anyone unnecessarily. I'm a single woman of a certain age trying to make the best of things. It's easy for you to look down from the moral high ground when you're surrounded by security. It isn't as simple as that for me.'

'I understand that—'

'Do you, Flo?' asked Marian. 'I don't believe you do, not really. How could you when you've been sheltered by Wilf for most of your adult life?'

'So I'm in the wrong now for being happily married?' said Flo.

'Don't be ridiculous,' said Marian. 'You know that I'm happy for you. But I wish you would realise that things aren't so easy for me and be less disapproving of everything I do.'

'I could try, I suppose.'

Marian gave a wry grin. 'I hope you actually mean that, because the perfect opportunity has arisen to put it to the test.'

Flo's brow creased. 'What do you mean?'

'Well, it worked so well my staying at Archie's last night that we have decided to make it a permanent arrangement. I'm moving in with him.'

Flo flushed. 'Oh no,' she gasped.

'Oh yes,' Marian confirmed. 'It makes perfect sense. Just one lot of rent instead of two, and shared household expenses. The closest thing I have had to security since I left home as a girl.' She looked at her sister, aware how deeply this sort of thing affected her. 'Sorry, Flo. I hope it isn't too painful for you. I promise to be very discreet.'

'Other people get married before they move in together; that's the way things are done in a civilised society.'

'We don't have the time for that at the moment, and we want to see if it works out,' Marian explained.

Flo shook her head, looking very downcast. 'I give up. You do what you like. Just don't tell me about it.'

'But we've always told each other things,' Marian said.

'Not any more; not when it comes to your immoral goings-on,' said Flo. 'What I don't know can't hurt me.'

'All right. If it will be easier for you, I'll avoid talking about my life with Archie.'

'I'd appreciate that,' said Flo, tight lipped. 'I suppose you'd like a cuppa while you're here.'

'I'd love one if you can spare it,' said Marian.

'It'll be a sad day when I can't give my sister a cup of tea,' said Flo, stiffly.

'Flo,' began Marian in a softer tone, 'why don't you just try to accept the fact that I'm not like you? It will be a lot less painful for you.'

'Can we change the subject, please?' said Flo. 'There are other people in the world besides you.'

'Of course,' said Marian, feeling the barb. 'How is Wilf? I haven't seen him lately.'

'He's fed up with the air raids, the same as the rest of us, but other than that he's fine.'

'Good,' said Marian.

She supposed it was the way her life had gone that had made her different: feistier, less worried by convention than her sister. She'd had to stand on her own two feet from a very early age. Now, for the first time in many years, she felt as though she had someone looking out for her, and she was looking forward enormously to moving in with Archie.

No more Mrs Beech watching her every move in the hope that she would see something to disapprove of. No need to creep in when she got home from work. Archie had a proper flat, too. It was over a shop and it had its own front door, so there would be much more privacy.

They had agreed to give it a try, and if it didn't work out, they would go their separate ways. But Marian was going to work hard to make sure it did, because she knew this was her last chance to have the sort of life she'd always wanted.

Chapter Five

The Little Blitz, as the latest period of air raids had become known, had petered out by the end of March. Though shorter than the earlier Blitzes, it had been very frightening and damaging, so people were thoroughly relieved to see the back of it.

The skies were far from quiet, though, as spring got under way. But nobody minded now because they were filled with Allied planes, which everyone presumed had something to do with the much-vaunted but still undated Second Front.

One night in April, when Polly had just finished her shift, James appeared unexpectedly at the Cherry.

'I can't stay long as I have to get the train back to camp tonight,' he told her. 'But I just had to come and see you. All leave is being cancelled from tomorrow, so I don't know when I'll get to London again.'

'Oh James. That's awful news,' she said. 'Is it because of the invasion?'

'We haven't been told officially, but we're all assuming that's the reason,' he said. 'We're sworn to secrecy about everything, so I wouldn't be able to tell you even if I knew.'

'Will you be taking part?'

'Not sure.'

She gave him a quizzical look.

'I'm being straight with you, Polly. I really don't know.'

'Surely there must be training . . . wouldn't you know through that?'

'There is training, lots of it, but we still don't know the details of who will actually be going, or when. We'll be told later, I guess,' he said. 'The army has to be secretive for all our sakes. What we don't know we can't repeat.'

'I suppose that makes sense.' She perceived a new energy about him, a curious kind of excitement. 'You want to go, don't you?'

He made a face. 'I wouldn't say that exactly,' he said. 'I guess I just want to do something positive to help get this war over and done with. And yeah, maybe the prospect does seem like an adventure. It's what we've been trained for.'

Polly knew she must be supportive, but having lost her husband to the last big invasion, she feared she might lose James to this one. 'Since you don't have a choice in the matter, it's just as well you're enthusiastic,' she said. 'I shall miss you like mad, though; your lovely visits to London to see me at the Cherry, and those wonderful weekends together.'

'We'll do all that again, honey,' he said, determinedly optimistic. 'I might not be gone for long, or even at all, in which case I'll see you as soon as they reinstate leave.'

But they both knew he was clutching at straws.

'As long as you come back safe, I can put up with anything,' she said.

'I'll do my very best,' he said. 'And before I rush off back

81

to the station, let's go into the ballroom and have a dance to keep us going until we see each other again.'

'What a good idea, and this one will be on the house,' she said. 'Special staff guest.'

The ballroom was vibrant with fun, excitement and romance. Polly and James jived to 'Comin' in on a Wing and a Prayer', then smooched to 'Moonlight Becomes You'.

'Sorry I can't stay for the last waltz,' he said. 'I really will be in trouble if I'm late back.'

'It was very good of you to come all this way for such a short time,' she said.

'It was worth it because I was so desperate to see you,' he said. 'You'll always be in my heart, Polly, no matter what happens or where I am.'

'Ah, that is so sweet, James. I'll be thinking of you all the time you're away from me.'

They had their farewell kiss in the foyer, and she stood outside and watched, wet eyed, as he hurried down the street towards the station, his shadowy figure just visible in the moonlight. As she walked home alone shortly afterwards, she felt very tense, and realised that it wasn't only the fact that he was probably going into action, though that was worrying enough. She was also reminded of the ephemeral nature of their relationship, knowing that whatever happened, they would go their separate ways when the war was over.

There was a general feeling among people now, fuelled by news from abroad, that the war was in its final stages. So that would be it for her and James when it finally ended. There simply was no way that they could stay together. Still, there were more important things to worry about for the moment: the invasion, and James staying alive . . .

One day in May, Polly returned home from her typing job to find her mother frantically cleaning. She was on her knees, polishing the hall floor as though her life depended on it.

'Hello, Mum,' Polly said warily.

'Oh, you're home, are you?' Flo got up, looking strange. She was pale, but her cheeks were flaming, and there were pink anxiety blotches suffusing her neck. 'There's a casserole in the oven and vegetables simmering. It won't be long.'

'What's the matter?' asked Polly.

'I've got to finish cleaning,' she replied. 'I have to do all the floors.'

'You can stop for lunch, though, can't you?'

'I don't want anything to eat,' she said, her voice sounding odd. 'I'll just serve up yours and Emmie's, then I'll go back to my work.'

This was very strange behaviour indeed. Flo normally ran her day like clockwork, and cleaning was always finished by lunchtime.

'Has something happened, Mum?' asked Polly.

Flo looked at her daughter for a moment, then put her hand in her apron pocket and took out a piece of paper, which she handed to Polly shakily. It was a telegram to say that Ray had been lost at sea.

Polly ran all the way to Marian's with the terrible news.

'Oh Auntie, I don't know how Mum will ever get over this,'

she sobbed. 'She's always idolised Ray. His bedroom is all ready for when he comes home. She's devastated. Please will you come?'

'Of course I will,' Marian said without hesitation.

'I can't stop her cleaning the house,' said Polly as they hurried through the streets. 'She won't stop for lunch or even a cup of tea.'

'It's probably therapeutic,' suggested Marian, choking back the tears. 'If cleaning makes her feel better, we should let her get on with it.'

'It doesn't seem very normal to me,' said Polly.

'It isn't a normal time.'

'Oh Auntie,' wailed Polly. 'Our lovely Ray, gone just like that. Twenty-five years old.'

'It's awful, I know, love,' said Marian. 'It doesn't make any sense at all.'

'I daren't let Mum see me cry.'

'Why not?'

'She's upset enough,' said Polly. 'She doesn't need to be worrying about me.'

'It won't hurt her,' said Marian. 'It's a family bereavement. She'll expect you to be upset, as I am. We'll weep together.'

'Dad will comfort her, but he won't be in from work until late,' said Polly. 'I don't think I'll be able to come to the ballroom tonight, Auntie. I can't leave her with Emmie for any length of time. Not in the state she's in. Dad doesn't get home until after I've left.'

'Don't you worry about work,' said Marian. 'That's the least of our problems.'

* ★ ★

When they reached the house, they found Emmie sitting at the table calmly eating her lunch, and Flo busy cleaning the living-room windows.

'Terrible news, Flo,' said Marian, dabbing her eyes with a handkerchief. 'I'm so sorry, love.'

Her sister grunted.

'Will you come and sit down?' Marian asked. 'If you don't want anything to eat, just have a cup of tea.'

'These windows are a disgrace,' was Flo's response. 'It's the dust from the bombing. I thought I'd got it all off.'

'Come and sit down with us, Flo,' said Marian again. 'We're all hurting. Your daughter needs you. She's lost her brother, who she adored.'

'The paintwork is filthy too,' Flo said, as though her sister hadn't spoken.

Marian marched over to her and took hold of her arms. 'Right, Flo,' she said in a firm voice. 'You're normally the bossy sister; you've been telling me what I should do for the whole of my life. But today I'm the one giving the orders. So come and sit with us, please.'

Flo stared at her for a long time, and Polly's stomach churned as she waited for an outburst. But then her mother's face crumpled and she started to cry. Marian led her towards the sofa and sat down next to her with her arm around her while she sobbed.

'Why is Grandma crying?' asked Emmie.

'Because your Uncle Ray has gone to heaven and it has made her very sad.'

'Is Uncle Ray the man in the picture?' Emmie asked, glancing towards the photograph on the mantelpiece of Ray in his naval uniform.

'That's right.'

'As he's gone to heaven, does that mean he won't be coming home?' asked Emmie innocently.

'Yes, it does mean that,' said Polly, feeling as if her heart would break. But with her mother in pieces and a small child to look after, she knew she must be strong.

Having given in to her feelings, Flo was in tears for most of the afternoon. Marian had to leave to go to work, but Polly felt in control now. She had never thought her mother and aunt were close, but she knew now that behind their cool attitude towards each other, which often seemed so full of hostility, some sort of a bond existed. She also realised that she couldn't have brought her mother through this crisis on her own. In those early moments, Mum had needed her sister more than her daughter. Maybe it was a generational thing. Now Polly was able to comfort her mother, and that was helping her to cope with the devastating loss herself.

Later on, after Polly had given Emmie her tea, something extraordinary happened. Her mother stopped crying, washed her face, combed her hair and said, 'Isn't it time you got ready for work, Polly?'

'I won't be going tonight, Mum, obviously.'

'Why obviously?'

'Because we've had terrible news and I wouldn't dream of leaving you alone.'

'In normal times we would all stay at home in mourning; that would be the right and respectful thing to do,' Flo said. 'But this is wartime, and life must go on. Besides, your dad will be home before too long. So you get Emmie ready for bed as usual and leave the rest to me.'

'If you're sure?' Polly said.

'I'm positive,' Flo replied. 'Anyway, I want to give the kitchen floor a good do.'

Polly realised that her aunt was right: obsessive cleaning was her mother's way of coping, and she had to let her do it, however much it hurt. Somehow they all had to get used to life without Ray, though at this early stage Polly didn't know exactly how.

'Come on, then, Emmie,' she said. 'Let's get you washed and into your jim-jams, and I'll read you a story before I get ready to go to work.'

'Be a good girl for your mummy,' added Flo.

Polly looked at her mother, the dullness of her eyes, the dejected stoop of her shoulders, and she knew that a part of Flo had died today. The light of her life had gone out. She would carry on and learn to live with it because she had no choice, but she would never be quite the same again.

Everyone was talking about the Allied invasion. People saw it as the forerunner to the end of the war and were anxious for it to get under way. When it finally happened, on 6 June, Polly heard the news on the wireless as she was getting ready for work at the typing pool. It was officially confirmed later that morning, and there was jubilation in the office. 'D-Day at last,' said her colleagues. 'Our boys are over there again. Hooray!'

Polly didn't feel like cheering. The invasion was necessary to end the war, but how many more lives would be lost on the other side of the Channel before that happened? Somewhere in the fray, James and the other boys would be giving their all so that the rest of them could be free. She offered up a silent prayer and hammered away on her typewriter at a speed to delight the supervisor.

News of victory following D-Day didn't come. Instead, Londoners found themselves under attack again, this time by lethal unmanned rockets that fell out of the sky at all times of the day and night, causing death and destruction. The V-1s – or doodlebugs as they became known – came over so frequently that people just had to carry on with their lives, so while they took cover when they could, sometimes all they could do was dive on to the ground or into a shop doorway when caught in the path of one of the awful things.

Polly had a letter from James.

'Does he say anything about what's happening wherever he is?' asked her mother.

'Not a word. They're not allowed to,' replied Polly. 'It's more of a note really, just to say that he's all right.'

'Still, at least we know he's alive,' said Flo. 'He was when he wrote that letter, anyway.'

Polly nodded. She suspected that her mother was wishing it was Ray who was alive, instead of James, but Mum was coping in her own way with Ray's death. She still found solace in activity, and the house gleamed from her energetic therapy.

One evening in July, when Polly arrived for work at the Cherry, her aunt had news for her.

'Ted's singer has been injured by a doodlebug and can't

come in to work for a few nights, and Ted can't get anyone to fill in for her at such short notice.'

'Oh that's a shame,' said Polly. 'Still, as long as the punters have the music to dance to, they won't mind.'

'We're having a talent show tomorrow night to make up for it,' announced Marian.

'What a good idea, Auntie.'

'You're in it.'

'I most certainly am not.'

'You and I will be singing together.'

'I can't do that,' Polly protested. 'I don't have any kind of a singing voice.'

'You're no Judy Garland, it's true,' admitted Marian. 'But you can hold a tune if you put your mind to it. You're always singing around the place. Anyway, I'm not brilliant either, but it doesn't matter because the idea is to encourage other people to join in and do a turn.'

'They come here to dance, not make fools of themselves,' said Polly.

'They come here to enjoy themselves, and a talent show will be a bit of fun,' Marian said. 'If you and I start the ball rolling, it will encourage others to join in, especially as we won't sound like the Andrews sisters. If we were too good they might be put off coming forward. Come on, Polly. Where's your wartime spirit?'

'It must have deserted me, because I'm not doing it,' she declared.

'I'm the boss around here, and I think you'll find you are,' said Marian.

'And *I* think you'll find that I'm a ticket clerk and I will be busy doing that,' retorted Polly.

'The talent show will be after the interval, when you'll have nearly finished at the ticket desk apart from a few latecomers, and they won't mind waiting.'

'Even so, I'm employed to sell tickets not provide entertainment and make a fool of myself. People pay good money to come to the Cherry. They don't want to be fobbed off with amateur crooners.'

'Mm, you do have a point, I suppose, but it would only be a one-off,' said Marian thoughtfully. 'It's almost impossible to get singers at short notice because so many of them are away in the services. I thought if we provided the punters with a bit of fun for half an hour or so, they might enjoy it.'

'The idea is a good one, Auntie,' said Polly. 'It's me taking part that isn't. Can't you do it on your own? You've got the confidence for something like that.'

'Doing it alone wouldn't bother me in the slightest,' Marian said, looking downcast. 'I just thought it would be more fun with the two of us.'

Polly looked at her: the downturned mouth, the soulful eyes. She knew she was being blatantly manipulated. 'Honestly,' she tutted. 'Poor old Archie. That man doesn't stand a chance with you in his life. All right, I'll do it, but I'm not happy about it, not happy at all, and you'll regret forcing me into it.'

'Bless you,' Marian said, hugging her, all smiles now. 'I knew I could rely on you for support.'

Polly heaved a sigh of resignation.

Emmie thought it was terrific fun when her great-auntie Marian and her mother had a rehearsal at the house the following afternoon. Even Flo took an interest.

'The problem, as I see it, is that you don't have anything resembling a decent singing voice between you,' she told them straight.

'Don't be so mean, Flo,' said Marian. 'You're supposed to be encouraging us.'

'I'm only speaking the truth,' she said. 'Surely you must know that you can't sing.'

'We're doing it for a laugh,' said Marian. 'Anyway, we're not that bad.'

'That's a matter of opinion. But why don't you try a different song?' suggested Flo, who could see that Marian was determined to go through with it. 'What about the Bing Crosby number "Don't Fence Me In"? That doesn't sound too complicated, and we all know the words because we've got the gramophone record.'

'Flo, you might have a very good point,' said Marian. 'Let's have a listen.'

Flo got busy winding the gramophone, and singing along with Bing made it a whole lot easier for Marian and Polly, though they did rather drown him out.

'Not too bad,' said Flo. 'Except that you were out of tune for part of it.'

'It isn't about being good, it's about having a go,' said Marian. 'Encouraging other people to get up and do a turn. When they realise we're not brilliant, they'll feel less intimidated.'

'I'm glad I'm not going to be there to see it,' said Flo.

For once in her life Polly was grateful to Hitler when she heard the next day that a doodlebug had hit the building next door to the Cherry and the blast had damaged part of the ballroom's foyer. She assumed that this meant the place would be closed while repairs were carried out, and she called at her aunt's on the way home from work at the typing pool to confirm this.

'I heard about the damage to the Cherry,' she said. 'I'm guessing we won't be opening tonight.'

'Whatever gave you that idea?' said Marian. 'The glass has been blown out of the front doors, that's all. I've got people putting up plasterboard as a temporary measure. It's perfectly safe. All the glass has been cleared away, every last splinter. The foyer and the pavement outside are completely clear.'

'We won't have the talent show though, surely?' said Polly hopefully. 'People might stay away as news of the explosion gets around.'

'We'll have to wait and see about that,' Marian said. 'But if the punters come, the show goes ahead.'

'That's a pity,' said Polly gloomily.

'Think of it as a bit of a giggle,' suggested Marian. 'It'll be something to take our minds off the flying bombs.'

Polly put her hand to her head. 'Oh Auntie. Why can't you be one of those sweet old aunts who sit quietly in the background?' she asked.

'God forbid,' Marian responded. 'You wouldn't like me much if I was one of those.'

'I don't know about that,' Polly laughed.

'Oh, and by the way,' said Marian, 'can you come in a bit earlier this evening so that we can have a rehearsal with the band?'

'With the band?' repeated Polly worriedly.

'Of course. Obviously we need accompaniment.'

'You know I can't read music.'

'Neither can I, but Ted and the boys will get us through it,' she said. 'They're masters at their game. They can probably even make us sound all right.'

'They're musicians, not magicians, Auntie.'

'It's just a bit of fun,' Marian reminded her again.

It felt more like a disaster to Polly later that day when she and her aunt couldn't keep in time with the band. After a few run-throughs, the whole lot of them collapsed into laughter.

'Try it once more,' said Ted when they had recovered. 'Remember, it's just one song for a bit of a laugh. You're not auditioning for a singing job.'

'Just as well, too,' joshed the drummer, and the rest of the band roared with laughter.

Polly's last-minute hopes that no one would turn up so she would be spared the humiliation of the talent show were dashed when people flocked to the ticket window as usual. The interval arrived and the last ticket was sold. Archie, who had come to support Marian, noticed Polly's pallor while Ted was introducing the talent show and whispered to her, 'You'll be all right. It's only a bit of fun.'

'If I hear that phrase once more, I swear I'll strangle the person who says it,' she declared. 'It isn't a bit of fun for me; it's more like full-blown torture.'

'I don't think so, Polly,' he said in a serious tone. 'Real torture is a damn sight more painful than a spot of embarrassment.'

'I suppose so,' she admitted, feeling properly put in her place. 'I wasn't really being serious.'

'I know that.'

'I don't know what's got into Auntie, having a talent show when people come here to dance.'

'You know your aunt. She wants to give the punters that little bit extra,' Archie said. 'Let people have a moment in the spotlight. Running this place is more than just a job to her. It's more of a calling. She's endlessly trying to invent ways to give people a good time. The talent show won't last long, so the dancing will only be interrupted briefly.'

'I suppose so,' Polly agreed, and as they headed for the stage, she thought how protective he was towards her aunt. It was lovely, and she was so pleased for Marian.

'So, we'll kick off with Marian, our manager, and her niece Polly singing "Don't Fence Me In",' concluded Ted. 'Please give them a good old Cherry Ballroom welcome.'

As Polly walked stiffly on to the stage with Marian, the band struck up with the introduction. Much to her amazement, she was actually able to open her mouth and sing the words, and once she got going, she even began to enjoy it. She doubted if any of it was in tune, but at least it was soon over.

'Thank you, girls,' said Ted. 'It was something a bit different anyway.'

Roars of laughter from the crowd, then people began queuing up to have a go, obviously encouraged by the low standard of the opening act.

Marian had used the petty cash and her own sweet coupons to buy a box of chocolates for the winner, a girl from Chiswick who sang 'Moonlight Becomes You' rather nicely.

'Thank God that's over,' said Polly as the dancing resumed and she, Marian and Archie headed back to the offices.

'You enjoyed it, go on admit it,' said Marian.

'It certainly wasn't as bad as I'd expected,' Polly said.

'So I can put your name down for the next one, can I?' Marian said jokingly.

'Don't you dare,' laughed Polly. 'Honestly, Archie, this woman has a way of making people do things. I don't know how you put up with her.'

'She's the love of my life, that's how,' he said cheerfully. 'And I enjoy the manic energy that sometimes gives her dotty ideas. She keeps us both young and I wouldn't change a single thing about her.'

'Oh,' said Polly, taken aback by the strength of his emotion. 'What a lovely thing to say, isn't it, Auntie?'

'Yeah, and the same goes for me about him, though he doesn't have dotty ideas, of course. He's the sensible one. You need one of those in a relationship, and he's the best.'

'Should I make myself scarce, with all this love flying around?' said Polly jokingly.

'Certainly not, not just yet anyway,' her aunt told her. 'You're coming to my office before you go home for a glass of sherry to celebrate the success of our double act.'

'I wouldn't call it success exactly.'

'We did it and that's all I wanted, so it counts as success in my book.'

Finally Polly understood her aunt's motives in putting on what had seemed like a pointless exercise. The talent show had got people involved and talking. It wouldn't have mattered to anyone if it hadn't happened, but she was very glad that it had, and she guessed that the punters were too.

★　★　★

The doodlebugs continued to drop from the skies all summer, and although people got used to them and carried on with their daily business as usual, they caused a huge loss of life and widespread damage to buildings. In September, a new style of robot bomb called the V-2 arrived; these were even more lethal, because they arrived silently with no warning at all.

As time passed, Polly noticed that her mother stopped talking about Ray, though she still kept his bedroom like a shrine. She even laundered the bed linen regularly, even though it was never used. Polly, concerned, spoke to her aunt about it.

'It seems a bit strange, don't you think, Auntie?'

'Not really, love, not under the circumstances. I expect it's her way of keeping his memory alive,' Marian said. 'She'll stop doing it when she's ready, and if she doesn't, we'll let her carry on. She's causing no one any harm, just extra work for herself. If it helps her to cope with her grief, it can't be bad.'

Polly sometimes wondered if anything shocked her aunt, who seemed able to accept all types of behaviour. But she was always very reassuring, so Polly decided to stop worrying and just let her mother get on with it.

One thing that was noticeably different about her parents since they'd heard of Ray's death was that they had stopped bickering and were all sweetness and light to each other. It seemed odd and not entirely natural, but Polly supposed it was only to be expected.

Her father never talked about his feelings; Polly suspected he would see it as a sign of weakness. He didn't like to be asked how he felt, either, so all she could do was leave him alone. It wasn't an easy thing to do, though, when she knew he must be suffering.

★   ★   ★

One autumn morning, Polly came down for breakfast yawning and looking tired, and her mother commented on it.

'It's this little one here,' said Polly, turning to her daughter. 'She's sometimes a restless sleeper and gives me a few kicks during the night that wake me up.'

'I don't, Mummy,' denied the little girl.

'Yes you do. But you're asleep so you don't know you're doing it. You can't help it, so I'm not cross with you, darlin', honestly.'

Emmie started to cry. 'I don't want to kick you,' she sobbed. 'I don't want to do that.'

'It doesn't matter,' said Polly, wishing she hadn't mentioned it. 'We all do things when we're asleep. I probably snore and give you a kick or two now and then, but you don't know about it.' She looked at her mother. 'I bet you give Grandad a nudge sometimes, don't you, Mum?'

'Not half,' Flo said, catching on. 'Especially when he's had a few drinks. Arms and legs everywhere. He snores then too; as loud as a train.'

'There you are, Emmie,' said Polly kindly. 'You've got nothing to feel bad about.'

Eventually the little girl was pacified, but Polly was reminded of what a sensitive child she was.

'So it will be another wartime Christmas for us after all,' said Archie when he and Marian came to the Pritchards' for Sunday tea one day in November.

'Looks like it,' agreed Wilf. 'They certainly won't have got it sorted by then.'

After the success of the D–Day invasion back in June, hopes

97

had been high of an autumn victory and a peacetime Christmas, but they had faded when the airborne landing at Arnhem in September had failed. Now, with Christmas just weeks away, there seemed no chance of it.

'It's November now and here we are with bombs still raining down on us,' said Flo. 'They said it would be all over by Christmas 1939, and five years later we're still up to our ears in it and another wartime Christmas to look forward to.'

'Pile on the misery, why don't you, Flo,' said Marian. 'They're all doing their best to bring it to an end. The forces, the government, everyone who's involved.'

'I know that. I was just saying—'

'I don't think it'll be very long,' Archie cut in to avoid an argument between the sisters. 'Most of the news has been positive lately.'

'That's true,' said Marian. 'Have you heard from James, Polly?'

'I had a letter last week,' she said. 'He seems fine.'

'I'm sure he is, but even if he said he wasn't, the censors would scratch it out,' said Wilf.

Marian laughed. 'Cor, you're a right miserable lot today.'

'Yeah, let's change the subject,' suggested Polly. 'Let's talk about the celebrations we're going to have when the war does finally end.'

'We'll have one hell of a victory do at the Cherry, I know that much,' said Marian.

'There'll be parties everywhere,' Polly remarked.

'When are we having a party?' asked Emmie excitedly.

'Sometime soon, we hope,' said her mother.

'What will we do at the party?' Emmie wanted to know.

'We'll dress up fancy and have such fun; we'll play games and dance and there will be nice things to eat.'

The child's eyes were like saucers. 'What sort of things?' she asked.

'Cakes, jelly and blancmange, dainty little sandwiches – and as much of everything as you want.'

'One day soon you'll have ice cream,' added Flo.

'What's ice cream?' asked Emmie.

'Delicious white stuff. Creamier and nicer than custard, and very cold.'

As she was speaking, Flo realised how deprived wartime children were. Emmie hadn't even heard of half the things her mother had taken for granted as a child: bananas and ice cream and many other items that had disappeared for the duration of the war. She couldn't do anything about that until the hostilities were over, but maybe there was something she could do to make the little girl's life a little more comfortable. She needed to think some more about an idea that had come into her mind, because she had to make sure it was the right thing to do.

The atmosphere had lifted considerably with the talk of celebrations, and they were all still in a cheerful mood when the siren wailed.

'Have you got room for a couple of little ones in your shelter?' asked Marian.

'I'm sure we can squeeze you in,' said Flo.

Flo had intended to think about her idea for a few days, but the next morning over breakfast she unintentionally blurted it out.

'I've got something nice to tell you, Emmie,' she said as the child was eating her porridge.

Emmie stared at her, dark eyes bright with anticipation. 'What is it, Grandma?' she asked.

'Well, how do you fancy having a bedroom all to yourself, with your own bed and chest of drawers? Even a wardrobe for your clothes.'

The child's eyes were shining. 'Where is it?' she asked expectantly.

'Upstairs, darlin',' Flo replied. 'The room that used to be Uncle Ray's. It's yours now.'

Polly's eyes widened in surprise. 'Mum?' she said questioningly. 'Are you sure?'

'Yes, it's doing no good staying empty, is it?' Flo said. 'Ray would want it to be used.'

'Well,' said Polly, smiling at her daughter. 'What a lucky girl you are. Say thank you to Grandma.'

'Thank you ever so much, Grandma,' said Emmie dutifully.

During the day, Emmie's things were moved into her new bedroom, and she seemed thrilled about it. Bedtime came and the usual procedure was adopted, finishing with a story before she settled down, read by her mother, who wasn't working this evening.

Polly had just got downstairs when screams came from Emmie's room, and both she and her mother rushed out to find the little girl on the way down, sobbing her heart out.

'I don't like it,' she wailed, obviously beside herself. 'I want to go back to the other room with Mummy.'

'But why, love?' asked her mother.

'It's Uncle Ray's room and he'll be angry that I'm in there and he'll come out of heaven and get me.'

'Of course he won't,' said Polly. 'Uncle Ray would never hurt anyone.'

But the child was having none of it, so they took her downstairs to calm her, then put her to bed in Polly's room.

'It's my fault,' Flo said to Polly when Emmie was finally settled. 'I kept the room closed up and exactly as it was when Ray was around. Of course Emmie was put off by it.'

'You mustn't blame yourself, Mum. It was a lovely thought. Emmie is a sensitive child, that's all.'

'I'm not giving up on the idea,' Flo told her. 'But there will be changes. The room will be there for Emmie when she's ready, and she soon will be when I've finished with it.'

'What have you got in mind, Mum?'

'First of all, the door to that room stays open. Secondly, I'm going to have a word with Syd who works in the butcher's and has a mate who can get things for a price. I'm going to ask him to get me some paint. I doubt if wallpaper will be possible, but paint might be; I'll do the walls when things become available again.'

'Syd deals in the black market, then?'

'How else would he get stuff?' Flo said assertively.

'Oh Mum,' said Polly reproachfully.

'Yeah, yeah, I know it isn't right,' she said. 'But for once in my life I'm going to dip my toe into murky waters, and I won't be the only one around here. Lots of people are at it. Nobody admits it, of course, but we all know it goes on.'

'I suppose so,' agreed Polly.

'I don't think I'll be damned to hell over a couple of tins of paint, do you?'

'Of course not,' said Polly. 'I was surprised, that's all, because you're such a stickler about such things.'

'Well, it's time to let my halo slip,' Flo said.

'Good for you, Mum.'

'He might not be able to get me anything at all, but if he does, I won't be able to be fussy about the colour,' Flo went on excitedly. 'As long as it's light, though, it will suit me. And fresh paint won't be all of it. The rest will take a bit more imagination and will be well within the law. I've got big plans.'

'I can't wait to see the result,' said Polly, delighted to see her mother so full of enthusiasm. It was the first time she'd taken a real interest in anything since the news of Ray's death. A new purpose was just what she needed.

Flo had wrestled with her conscience long and hard over this whole thing, concerned about being disloyal to her son by handing his bedroom over to someone else. But it was just a room; a space surrounded by bricks and mortar. Ray would always be in her heart and that would never change, certainly not because she made a few material changes for the benefit of the niece he had been so fond of. She didn't feel good about her means of getting the paint, but she would just have to live with that.

Chapter Six

Although there were signs of approaching peace in the weeks leading up to Christmas – blackout restrictions were relaxed so that certain lights were allowed; on buses and trains, for instance – there was little else to inspire the public into thinking in terms of victory. The weather was cold and foggy, and people were run-down and suffering with aches and pains. Food and almost every other commodity was scarcer than ever.

Flo was too busy at her treadle sewing machine to complain much about all of this. The family was accustomed to her slipping off to her ancient Singer in her bedroom, as necessity had made her an able needlewoman. So no one was surprised when she went to the machine after dinner at night instead of listening to the wireless. The door of Ray's bedroom was firmly closed for the time being because Flo wanted its new look to be a surprise, but the smell of paint wafted out to the rest of the house occasionally.

Christmas passed pleasantly, with Emmie at the centre of things and Flo working wonders with meagre ingredients to produce a delicious dinner as usual. 'Well, Flo, you've done us proud again and cooked a meal fit for royalty,' said Marian.

'This should be the last wartime Christmas, so next year you'll have more stuff to work with.'

'Every year we say that,' said Wilf. 'Yet here we all are again in the same boat.'

'Stop moaning, Wilf, and let's raise our glasses to Flo,' said Marian.

Afterwards, they drank a more solemn toast to their lost war heroes Ray and George, and absent friend James. Polly had spent a lot of time thinking about James, wondering how he was, *where* he was, and hoping to see him again soon. But there was nothing to do but wait and hope.

Towards the end of January, Flo told the family she had something to show them and they were to follow her. They all trooped upstairs and she opened the door of Ray's bedroom, where there had been a complete transformation.

Gone was the sombre, masculine look. The dark curtains had been replaced by white ones, which Flo had apparently made out of some old sheets; the dismal wooden furniture had been painted pale yellow, the only colour Syd could get. She had knitted a pink pyjama case with the wool from an old jumper, and the bedspread was a colourful patchwork wonder made out of old clothes.

'It's beautiful, Mum,' said Polly emotionally. 'Absolutely lovely!'

'Thank you, dear,' she beamed. 'None of the colours match, but I couldn't manage that with the stuff I had to work with. It's bright and cheerful anyway.'

'Perfect for a little girl,' said Polly.

As Emmie walked around smiling and touching everything very gently, Wilf said to his wife, 'Well done, Flo. You're a ruddy marvel when you put your mind to something. I'm really proud of you.'

'The door to this room will be kept open in future,' Flo informed them. 'Unless Emmie wants it closed. It's her room and she gets to decide.'

'Mine?' said Emmie questioningly.

'Yes, yours, darlin', though it doesn't matter if you'd rather stay in the other bedroom with Mummy. No one will be cross with you. But if and when you want it, this room is yours.'

Polly put her arms around her mother. 'Thanks, Mum,' she said. 'It's wonderful.' She turned to her daughter. 'What do you have to say to Grandma?'

'Thank you, Grandma,' Emmie said, and this time she really meant it.

She only had a few dolls because they were so hard to come by, but her small collection and her teddy bear moved into the bedroom with her that night. And the rest of the family didn't hear a peep out of her until the next morning.

'My sister never fails to surprise me,' Marian said to Archie when they got home from visiting the Pritchards', where they had been shown Emmie's new bedroom. 'She can be as hard as nails and nasty to the point where I've hated her many times throughout my life. Then she does something like that and you know that she has a heart in there somewhere.'

'She's done a good job for Emmie, no doubt about it,' he agreed. 'But Flo's all right really. Her bark is worse than her bite and she isn't nasty to everyone. It's just you she has a problem with, I think.'

'And you.'

'That goes without saying,' he said with a wry grin. 'We're a team, you and me, both tarred with the same brush, and Flo has a very long memory.'

'She certainly has,' said Marian. 'But all that work she put into that room. The patchwork quilt alone must have taken ages. A labour of love, you might say.'

'It took a lot of skill, too.'

'She's always been very clever with her hands; knitting and sewing comes easy to her. I used to be hopeless, but I've got better since clothes rationing started. Being handy with a needle is essential these days if a woman wants to stay smart.' She paused in thought. 'It must have been very hard for Flo to move all traces of Ray out of that room. Sort of saying a final goodbye to him.'

'Her only son; it couldn't have been easy,' agreed Archie. 'But I think that was probably overridden by her fondness for Emmie. And there are photographs of Ray all around the house; plenty of evidence to remind us that he was here.'

'Yeah. She wouldn't need a room to remind her of him. He was always the love of her life and she didn't try to hide it,' said Marian. 'I don't think Polly ever minded, because she thought the world of him too.'

'Polly isn't the sort of girl to make a fuss about something like that anyway, is she?' Archie said.

'She doesn't seem to be, but you never know what's going on in someone else's mind, do you?'

'That's true,' he agreed, then added, deciding to lighten the atmosphere, 'no one would ever guess how much I hate you, would they?'

She laughed and gave him a playful slap. 'Don't push your luck, mate,' she said.

'I wouldn't dare.'

They were both smiling, each secure in the strength of their relationship.

As the new year progressed into spring, the sense of expectancy that the war would end soon was palpable everywhere. In April, the total abolition of the blackout was announced.

'Oh my Lord, it's very shabby behind there,' said Flo when she tore down the blackout material to see dust, dead insects and faded curtains.

'No more blackout, though, Mum. Isn't that wonderful?' Polly enthused. 'We can soon get it spick and span again, and make new curtains when we have enough coupons.'

Nobody could be too sad for too long about a bit of dirt and dust, because the ending of the blackout was such a significant and hopeful sign. When the lights were turned on again in the West End, Polly and her parents took Emmie to see them on Polly's night off. The little girl was overwhelmed at first, because she'd hardly ever been out after dark before except to the air-raid shelter. So this was a real treat, especially as the event was preceded by a ride on the tube.

There were crowds around Piccadilly and Leicester Square, and some of the small children were crying with fear at the sudden visual extravaganza. Emmie wasn't one of those; she was simply filled with wonder at the whole thing.

'The buildings could do with some smartening up, couldn't they?' remarked Flo.

'After nearly six years of bomb dust, they're bound to be shabby,' said Polly. 'But peace is on the way, Mum. That's the important thing.'

'It certainly is,' agreed her father.

The treat was further enhanced for Emmie when they went into Lyons and she had a glass of milk and a currant bun while the adults had tea.

'Good times are coming,' said Polly, infected by the atmosphere.

'Yes, I do believe they are,' Flo agreed.

'When victory actually arrives, I certainly won't be celebrating with tea and a bun,' said Wilf.

'Don't lower the tone, please, Wilf,' requested his wife primly. 'We all know how much you love the pub and your drinking mates, but you're out with your family now, so let's have no more talk about the seedy side of your life.'

'There's nothing seedy about a pint at the local.'

'Maybe not,' she conceded. 'But we don't want to hear about it now, thank you very much.'

'Would I dare to disobey you, my love?' he said drily, and Polly was pleased to hear it, because this was the first time since they'd lost Ray that her parents had even mildly bickered.

'You most certainly would,' said his wife, having the last word as usual.

If anyone had expected victory to immediately follow the abolition of the blackout, they would have been sorely disappointed, because just two weeks afterwards, floodlighting and decorative lights were banned again, this time to save fuel.

But the slow return to normality on the home front was well and truly under way. It now became legal to sound a factory hooter, buy a large-scale map and play a car radio, none of which affected the Pritchard family, but they were positive signs nonetheless.

Everyone listened to the wireless to keep up to date, and at last the news came that Germany had been defeated, but there was still no victory announcement. Flags and bunting were bought from street sellers and unearthed from dusty attics. Everyone was ready.

Reports came that Hitler had killed himself. All Germans in Italy and Denmark surrendered. Various other positive announcements were made. And still they waited. Everyone was excited. Finally the news came that Tuesday 8 May was to be celebrated as VE Day.

The long wait didn't detract from the joy of the day. Everyone was out on the streets, cheering and kissing, singing and dancing. Previously made arrangements for street parties were put in place. Polly had never experienced anything like it. It was a public and personal outpouring of joy. How could it be otherwise after nearly six years of war? Even indoors there was a party spirit, as on the wireless a cinema organ played all the wartime songs. The church services had an upbeat sound to them too, with rousing hymns.

They all helped put the flags and bunting on the front of the house, and Polly took a few quiet minutes to think about those who wouldn't be coming back. She guessed many other people would be having similar thoughts and prayers. Her own thoughts turned to James and she felt a stab of concern as she wondered what would happen to their relationship now that the war was over and he would go back to Canada.

The street party was scheduled to be held the next day, so when Auntie Marian and Archie came over, they all decided to go and join the crowds outside Buckingham Palace.

It would be a crush for Emmie, but there were plenty of them to look after her, and Polly wanted her to experience as much as she could of this momentous day. Maybe she was a little young to remember, but some memories might linger. Polly wanted her to be able to say when she grew up, 'I was there. I was a part of it.'

There were huge crowds in the West End, but Polly could see no rowdiness. Although there was a mass of people, it was possible to walk along quite easily. Emmie took turns with her grandfather and Archie to ride on their shoulders. Everywhere there were happy faces; people were so relieved to have the awful dark days behind them.

They walked to Buckingham Palace just as the floodlighting came on. The sight was so glorious it brought tears to Polly's eyes. It was as though the world had come to life again, but tinged now with magic. The palace balcony was draped in crimson with a gold and yellow fringe. Coloured rockets went up somewhere near where the Pritchards were standing, then the King and Queen and the two princesses came out on to the balcony. People yelled and waved and cheered. But there was a feeling of unity with the royals, because everyone had lived through the war and the relief was communal.

When the royals went back inside, Polly and the family ambled towards Hyde Park, where there was a huge bonfire. They walked by the lake, the coloured lights in the bushes shining on the water. After years of darkness, everything seemed to be lit up, and Big Ben looked magnificent.

Eventually Emmie was tired so they had to make their way home, but Polly felt enriched by the experience and was very glad they had come.

Back at the house, they drank a toast to Ray and George

with one of the bottles Mum had stashed away for the victory celebrations. It was achingly sad to think that neither of them would be coming back to enjoy the peace. But even that sorrow couldn't stem the huge relief that the war was finally over.

When Polly took Emmie up to bed, she stood at the window with the curtains drawn back, looking out.

'What are you looking at, Mum?' asked Emmie.

'The stars, darling,' she said. There were no searchlights out there, no barrage balloons; just the moon and stars. It was wonderful!

As if the child sensed her mother's emotional state, Emmie said, 'Would you like me to come in your bed with you tonight to keep you company?'

'That's a sweet thought, but I'll be fine,' Polly said. 'You stay in your lovely new room and enjoy it.'

Almost before the little girl said, 'All right, Mum,' her lids were drooping, and by the time Polly had left the room, she was fast asleep.

'Ah, there you are,' said her father when she went downstairs. 'I've poured you a glass of sherry.'

'Thanks, Dad,' she said, sipping it.

'Here's to the future,' he said, holding up his beer glass.

'I'll drink to that,' said Polly. 'To a beautiful, peaceful future with no more wars.'

They all raised their glasses.

'I'm thinking in terms of Saturday night for the victory dance at the Cherry,' Marian mentioned. 'I don't want to leave it too long because it will be nice to capture the current atmosphere of excitement. Does that suit you, Polly?'

'Lovely,' said Polly. 'I work on a Saturday night so I won't miss it.'

'You can stay a bit later if you'd like to join in after work,' said Flo. 'Emmie will be asleep so she won't miss you.'

'Thanks, Mum,' said Polly. 'I'll see how I feel at the time.'

There was already a long queue outside the Cherry when Polly arrived for work on Saturday, the front of the building decked in flags and bunting.

'The doors won't open for a little while yet,' she told the waiting revellers on her way to the staff entrance.

'We know; we just wanted to make sure we get in,' said someone.

'That's the spirit,' she said, and went inside to find Marian at the top of a ladder in the foyer fixing a huge Union Jack.

'Archie got it from a street seller in the West End,' her aunt explained. 'I just happened to mention that it would be nice to have a really big flag to greet people when they come in, and he goes straight out and finds one for me, bless him.'

'It looks lovely, Auntie,' Polly said. 'They're already queuing up outside, so I think it'll be a good night.'

'You'd better get the ticket office open then, hadn't you, kid, and let's get this party started.'

Although nothing could match the wonder of the VE Day celebrations for Polly, in terms of pure joy and emotion, the victory dance at the Cherry came a very close second. People were already smiling as they paid for their tickets; everyone was in the mood for a good time.

Ted and the boys in the band added to the atmosphere with jokes, and their singer was on fine form, belting out all the favourites. The second half of the evening had a distinctly party atmosphere. Marian emerged from her office to join in, and Polly took advantage of her mother's offer and stayed on to do the conga and the hokey cokey along with all the rest. She and Marian also danced an adequate foxtrot together, and even attempted the tango. As the evening drew to a close, the band played 'We'll Meet Again' and the singer did a marvellous job, getting the tears flowing among the dancers. Because the punters were happy, they were friendly too. If asked, Polly would have found it hard to describe the atmosphere, but it was as though the long-awaited peace had created an outpouring of communal goodwill.

'Oh, Polly, I do so love this job,' said Marian emotionally.

'Me too,' responded Polly.

Since the last waltz was generally accepted to be for couples, Polly left before then. As she walked home, still enjoying the fact that the streets were well lit again after the misery of the blackout, her thoughts turned to her late husband George and how bowled over by him she'd been when he'd asked her to dance at the Cherry that first time. He'd walked her home through these same streets and she had probably been in love with him before they'd even reached her front gate; it was that quick. With hindsight she could see that her initial attraction to him had been almost entirely lustful, because he'd been so physically gorgeous. A rough diamond, oozing good looks and charisma, but not the sort of man your mother would want you to marry, which only went to make him even more appealing.

George would give you his last penny but wouldn't tell you how he'd earned it. He would have you in fits with his hilarious sense of humour but discouraged talk of serious things like life insurance and saving for the future. She wondered what sort of father he would have made and knew instinctively that he would have adored Emmie. As for a roof over their heads and food on the table, she wasn't so sure.

James was different altogether, quieter, more serious, and instinctively she knew he was reliable even though she'd never had cause to challenge him. She'd liked him from the start and her feelings had grown over time. Whoever married him would have security. George had been her first love, but she cared for James deeply too, enough for it to be painful to know that their relationship could only ever exist in the short term.

She wondered when James would reappear and how long he would stay in England. Presumably the Canadian army would want to get their people repatriated as soon as possible, but it would probably take a while, so they should manage to have some time together. It would be lovely to see him again before he went home to Canada.

Her parents were still up when she got in.

'We're having a victory tipple,' explained her mother, holding a glass of something.

'Another one?' laughed Polly.

'It's only because we've got some left over from the VE celebrations,' explained Flo, almost apologetically.

'No need to explain, Mum,' Polly assured her. 'I like to see you relaxing.'

'I'm not normally a drinker,' she said, respectable to the nth degree. 'Your father drinks enough for the two of us, as you very well know.'

'I thought I'd get dragged into it somehow,' said Wilf. 'That woman never misses a chance.'

'Don't call me "that woman",' Flo objected.

'I'll call you what I like.'

'That's enough, you two,' admonished Polly, but she was smiling because everything was back to normal, as far as it ever could be without Ray.

As the summer progressed and the celebrations faded into the past, austerity began to bite and people started to wonder when they might see the benefits of peace. There were celebrations for VJ Day to mark the end of the war with Japan, but they were much less notable than those of VE Day. Everything was in short supply, nothing was done to start repairing the devastated city, and the housing problem remained as bad as ever.

Welcome Home banners to greet returning servicemen were already on show on many houses, and Polly guessed that her mother would be upset by the fact that there wouldn't be one outside the Pritchard house. She toyed with the idea of putting one up for James but decided that it would be insensitive. Anyway, he would have that sort of thing when he got back home to Canada. Even as the thought came, she felt saddened by it, but it was a fact of life. He lived there and she lived here.

The people of Britain showed their eagerness for housing and a fairer society for all by giving the Labour Party a landslide victory in the general election.

'After Mr Churchill brought us through the war, people

have abandoned him in droves,' said Flo the following weekend. 'It seems an awful shame.'

'He did a good job during the war,' said Wilf. 'But people want what's best for them in peacetime now. Repairing the damage, building new houses, schools and so on. Churchill is a toff, a member of the upper classes, and not short of a bob or two. Ordinary people think that the Labour Party will be better for them now that the war is over.'

'It must be a shock for him to be deserted like that, though,' remarked Polly.

'He's a politician; they're used to that sort of thing,' said her father. 'They have to be as hard as nails to do the job.'

The conversation was interrupted by Emmie coming in from the street for a drink of water. After which she did a handstand up the wall, then cartwheels across the room.

'Be careful you don't knock yourself on the furniture,' said Flo.

'I won't, Gran,' she said. 'The kids outside say I'm the best at cartwheels. I can do backbends too. Do you want to see?'

'Go on then,' said Polly. 'But be careful.'

They were treated to an acrobatic display all around the room. She really was very good and they were all smiling.

'No matter how hard life is, we have Emmie to cheer us up,' said Flo when the child had gone back outside. 'We are truly blessed.'

'We certainly are, Mum,' agreed Polly. 'There's a big change coming in September, though, when she starts school.'

A quietness crept over the room as they all reflected on the forthcoming event, which would be a new chapter in Emmie's life and a landmark for Polly. She intended to make the most of the rest of the time before her daughter was swept from under her wing.

★   ★   ★

Polly had rarely seen her aunt Marian shed a tear. So she was concerned to see her looking wet eyed when she came to the house one afternoon the following week.

'I've lost my job,' she announced to Polly and Flo.

'What!' Polly was horrified. 'You can't have.'

'I bloomin' well have,' she said. 'I went into work the same as usual yesterday and the owner of the Cherry was waiting to tell me. He's given me a week's money in lieu of notice so that my replacement can start right away. He started last night, in fact. I stayed on to give him an outline of the job. He's just back from the war, apparently.'

'I'm so sorry, Auntie.'

'Me too, love. I suspected it might happen when the men came home but I hoped I could somehow manage to stay on. This bloke is the owner's brother-in-law, so it's pure nepotism, but he's a man so he will be deemed the best person for the job anyway, just like used to happen before the war. He's been away fighting for his country so he deserves a job. I just wish he hadn't been given mine.'

'I'm sorry too,' said Flo dutifully.

'I'm more than sorry,' said Polly. 'I'm flippin' devastated. The place won't be the same without you.' She paused. 'I'm working tonight. I wonder if my cards will be waiting for me when I get there.'

'No, you'll be all right, kid. A part-time ticket clerk is considered to be a female job, so no man will want it. Mine was full-time management, so I was always going to be first to go.'

'But you were so good at it, Auntie,' said Polly.

'That counts for nothing now that the men are back. Working-class women aren't considered good enough for anything that takes a bit of savvy. I knew I would never have had that job in the first place if it hadn't been for the war, but I hoped that by working hard and making my mark I could somehow keep it. I wouldn't want to take a job from a man with a family to feed, but neither do I want to waste my experience.'

'Perhaps you'll have to accept a more ordinary job now that things are getting back to normal,' suggested Flo, who was always embarrassed by her sister's tendency to fly in the face of the status quo.

'Not without a fight, Flo,' Marian said. 'You know me better than that.'

Unfortunately, I do, thought Flo, but she said no more on the subject.

When Polly arrived at work that evening and went into the manager's office to get the float for the till and the keys to open up, she found the room full of cigar smoke and the new manager leaning back in the chair with his feet on the desk.

'Hello,' she said. 'I'm Polly. I work in the ticket office.'

'Nice to meet you, Polly,' he said, giving her an approving look. 'I'm Donald Wood. Mr Wood to you.'

He looked to be in his thirties and had short dark hair greased flat to his head, deep-set eyes and a thin black moustache that had obviously been enhanced with an eyebrow pencil. Polly took an immediate dislike to him, but managed to remain polite. 'If I could just have the keys and the float, I'll go and open up. They're usually kept in the top right-hand drawer.'

He opened the drawer and handed her the keys and a small bag of money.

'Thank you,' she said. 'If you need to know anything, you know where I am.'

'Thanks, but I doubt that will be necessary,' he said, puffing on his cigar and adding to the fog. 'I'm not new to this game. I was in it before the war.'

Polly nodded and left with the feeling that another war had just broken out.

'But you don't have to work, Marian, now that you have me,' said Archie that evening. 'They still need me where I am now that they're back to peacetime manufacturing, and I earn decent money. Certainly enough to keep the two of us.'

'Thanks, Archie, but I've been earning my own living since I was fourteen and I don't intend to be a kept woman at my time of life,' she said.

'Not even if I was happy to keep you?'

'Absolutely not.'

'You could always do the decent thing and marry me, then it would be my duty to support you.'

'I wouldn't marry you for that reason,' she said.

'Marry me for the right reasons then,' he suggested, not for the first time.

'One day, Archie,' she said. 'But not until I've proved to myself that I can hold down a decent job.'

'You'll always have something to prove, Marian,' he said. 'It's in your nature.'

They had often talked about marriage, but she wouldn't be pushed into it just for the sake of respectability. She loved Archie with all her heart, and she made sure he knew that, but she didn't believe it necessary to go through a ritual to prove it.

'Is that really what you think of me?' she asked.

'Yes, it is. You'll always find something that needs sorting,' he said. 'It isn't a criticism.'

'We will get married, Archie,' she said. 'But not just to save my good name or because I need supporting financially.'

'Do it to save *my* good name then,' he said jokingly.

'One day we'll just do it because we both want to,' she said. 'I promise.'

'Don't leave it until we're too old to enjoy it,' he said. 'We're both knocking on a bit.'

'You speak for yourself,' she joshed.

'Yes, of course, I forgot, you're never going to grow old, are you?'

'Not without a bloomin' good fight,' she said. 'But about this job business. I don't know how long it will take me to find work, so I might have to sponge off you for a week or two.'

'You can sponge off me for as long as you like,' he said. 'I'll be happy to help.'

She looked at him affectionately. His blond hair was greying now and there were a few feathery lines about his countenance. But he was still a handsome man in a rugged sort of way. She was lucky to have him and she thanked God that they had found each other again. She knew she wasn't always an easy person to be with because of her unequivocal views, which she didn't seem able to change. But that didn't bother him.

'You are a flippin' saint,' she said, putting her arms around him. 'We'll get married one day, I promise.'

Chapter Seven

Because Emmie was a sensitive child, Polly had been concerned as to how she would cope with school. But although she seemed a little daunted at the prospect of it being a regular thing, she settled in well and soon accepted the fact that going to school every day was what you did when you were five.

Polly missed her being around when she got back from her typing job, and was always eager to get to the school gate to meet her when she came out. It turned out to be rather a nice interlude, because she got to know some of the other mums and enjoyed a chat with women of a similar age.

Her job at the Cherry was no longer as enjoyable as it had been, because not only was Mr Wood unpleasant to work with, being moody and bad tempered, he was flawed as a manager. He seemed to like the idea of being top dog at such a well-known London venue, and made sure he was seen around, in the foyer and even in the ballroom itself, but he had no idea how to run the place properly.

Customers came to Polly at the ticket desk with complaints about the toilets needing attention, or their coats being creased and dirty when they collected them at the end of the evening, as though they had been on the floor rather than a hanger. She was also being told of rudeness from the men on the door.

Soon after Mr Wood had taken over as manager, he had sacked the cleaners, security people and other background staff and replaced them with contacts of his own, for a cheaper rate Polly assumed, though she didn't have access to the books so didn't know for sure. She apologised to the unhappy punters on behalf of the management and passed their comments on to Mr Wood.

'What do they expect when they come here, the Ritz?' he blasted at her when she went to see him in his office.

'They are entitled to a certain standard when they've paid for a ticket,' she said. 'It isn't exactly cheap to get in and they're mostly young people so they're not dripping with dosh.'

'It's only a bleedin' dance hall.'

'Maybe, but it's one of the best in the area and it does have a reputation to uphold,' she pointed out. 'People will stay away if the basics aren't looked after, and then where will we be? There are plenty of other halls they can go to in and around London, so we have to stay ahead of the competition.'

'Surely people come here to dance and have a good time. They won't care about the standard of the housekeeping,' he declared. 'And as for the facilities, I can't see any need for them to use them.'

'A dance goes on for four hours, Mr Wood. Of course they need to use the facilities. The ladies' cloakroom is very nicely done, with good-sized sinks and big mirrors for women to do their hair and touch up their make-up. But that's no use if people can't see clearly in the mirrors because they haven't been cleaned. And the ballroom could do with a thoroughly good going-over too. It's dusty and mucky.'

'All right,' he said grudgingly. 'I'll have a word with the cleaners when they come in tomorrow.'

On the way home that night, Polly was seriously considering the idea of leaving the Cherry. Work was work and she certainly didn't expect it to be a party, but she'd enjoyed the job when Marian had been in charge. With Mr Wood running the place, it was grim. Realistically, though, the extra money was vital to her and the hours were ideal, so she'd just have to grin and bear it. Anyway, she didn't want to be driven out of the job just because the owner had employed someone who was completely unsuitable. She would stick it out, for the moment anyway, and hope that things might improve.

'I want all the drawers tidied up, Miss Atkins,' said the senior assistant at the haberdashery counter of the department store in South Kensington. 'The press studs and hook-and-eye fasteners are in a terrible mess, so put that right, please, then get all the other drawers and cupboards spick and span.' She gave Marian a hard look. 'Right away, if you please.'

Because her manner suggested that Marian had been standing idle, she said defensively, 'I have only just this minute finished serving a customer.'

'Yes, but you are not serving anyone now, are you?' said Miss Harris. 'You are not employed here to stand around. Monday is usually a slack day, so that will give us a chance to get the department shipshape.'

Marian hated the other woman even more than she loathed the job, and could have cheerfully slapped her. It didn't help that Miss Harris was younger than Marian, probably mid-thirties, a stereotypical spinster with a scrubbed face and hair dragged back into a bun. It was her supercilious attitude that Marian found so hard to take, especially having been used to being the one who gave the orders. She hoped she had never treated staff at the Cherry the way Miss Harris treated her.

But as awful as the job was, it paid a regular wage, though she wasn't intending to stay any longer than she had to. She was hoping to get a better position when things settled down. It wouldn't be easy, because the role of women had returned to pre-war conditions, and any job with the slightest bit of responsibility was given to men.

Many married women had given up good jobs and returned to being housewives. Even most of those trained as engineers and pilots had been out of work at the end of the war. Marian thought it was a pity to waste all that training and experience, but that was the way things were. Men were the priority and that was that. She'd heard of a few women who had tried to fight through their trade unions to keep their jobs, but she doubted they would succeed. It was very definitely a man's world.

This store itself was depressing: dark wooden counters, dismal decor and old-fashioned goods for sale. There was nothing in the women's-wear department that Marian would be seen dead in, even if she could afford the high prices. The stock was far too frumpish for her to consider, though it would probably appeal to Miss Harris, who was the absolute mistress of the dowdy.

If Marian was in charge of this place, she would bring some light and colour in. But she wasn't, so she had to endure things as they were until she could find a position more to her taste. Meanwhile she would keep her eye on the situations vacant columns in the paper. And maybe there was something else she could do to improve her chances.

'Daydreaming won't get the job done,' Miss Harris was saying. 'Will you get started, please.'

'Yes, of course,' said Marian, jerking back to the present and the fact that she was having to take orders from a pompous little woman who didn't have a fraction of the savvy that she herself had.

She urgently needed to move on from this miserable job and she would do everything in her power to do so. Starting this very night, she thought, as her idea took root.

'Oh, Marian, you haven't,' said Flo that evening when her sister called at the house.

'Yes I have, and what's so terrible about it?'

'You're middle aged.'

'So what?' said Marian.

'Evening classes are for youngsters just starting out.'

'They are for anyone who wants to learn,' she corrected. 'As far as I know, there's no age limit. They certainly didn't say anything about one when I went to enrol.'

'You'll make a fool of yourself,' said Flo. 'The class will be full of school leavers.'

'So I'll be the odd one out. What does it matter as long as I learn something?' Marian said. 'I need to improve my chances of getting a decent job, because I don't intend to stand behind a counter selling buttons and press studs for the rest of my life.'

Wilf looked over his newspaper. He'd always rather admired

his sister-in-law's spirit. She was a bit of a loose cannon but a good sort, and would do anything for this family even though Flo was quite often horrid to her.

'What subject will you be taking?' he asked.

'Bookkeeping,' she replied. 'I thought that might come in handy in a management job. It's always an advantage if the manager knows how to do what the staff are doing, just in case it's ever needed. That often occurred to me when I was working at the Cherry.'

'Sounds sensible to me.'

His wife gave him a withering look. 'You're as bad as she is,' she said. 'Neither of you act your age.'

'There's no fun in that.'

'You should grow up, the pair of you.'

Marian could feel the heat rising. 'It's time I went,' she said.

'Good luck,' said Wilf as she got up to leave.

What she lacked in support from her sister, Marian had in abundance from Archie.

'What a cracking idea,' he said. 'Knowledge is power. The more you know, the better your chances. And that applies to everything.'

'That's what I thought,' she said. 'It's no good just sitting around waiting for an opportunity to come along. You've got to do what you can to make yourself more employable. Anyway, I enjoy learning new things.'

'Yeah, you do have an enquiring mind,' he said. 'And that can only be a good thing.'

'Honestly, Archie, I don't know how I can stand one more day in that awful store.'

'I've told you,' he reminded her. 'Leave and let me fund you until you find something better.'

'I can't be beaten by it,' she told him. 'So thanks for offering, but I'll stick it out and keep looking for something else. At least the evening class will make me feel as if I'm doing something to help my chances.'

'You're a one-off, Marian, you really are.'

'Not thinking of trading me in for a more conventional model, are you?' she asked lightly.

'Never in a million years,' he said, hugging her. 'There's no way I would let you get away a second time.'

He was such a comfort to her, she didn't know how she'd managed without him all these years.

Although the cleaning had improved a little since Polly's conversation with Mr Wood, the heart seemed to have gone out of the Cherry. It wasn't just that things had quietened down after the victory celebrations and some of the troops from overseas had gone home. That was balanced up by the slow return of British forces. It was more as if all the vitality and spirit had drained away; almost as though the Cherry had had its day.

'It just isn't the same now, Auntie,' Polly said to Marian when she was at the house one Sunday.

'Missing the wartime spirit perhaps,' Marian suggested.

'It's more than just that,' said Polly. 'It feels second-rate. It will be even worse now that Mr Wood has got rid of Ted and the band.'

'Oh no!' said Marian, shocked.

Polly looked miserable. 'It's his latest economy measure,' she said.

'Who has he got to replace them?'

'A dance band you'll never have heard of,' she replied. 'Very staid. I think the young people will stop coming altogether. The Cherry has always had a reputation for being up to the minute, and a lot of that is because of Ted and the boys. This new lot are keen on old-fashioned waltzes.'

'What on earth is Wood up to?' asked Marian. 'Is he trying to save money?'

'I suppose he must be,' said Polly. 'He's got rid of all the staff you employed and taken on people who don't do the job properly.'

'It just doesn't make sense. If the Cherry goes under, he'll go under with it.'

'I don't think he has a clue about management, that's the problem,' said Polly. 'Maybe he thinks that if he keeps costs down, he'll please the boss, but it's false economy because the place is going downhill fast.'

Marian tutted. 'I really don't know what he's playing at,' she said.

Polly was thoughtful. 'Sometimes it seems as if he doesn't even like the job. He's very tense the whole time. Lives on his nerves. Maybe all the showing off and being the big man is an act because he's terrified of the responsibility and scared the boss might find out, which he will eventually, of course. I know he's a war hero, and that's very commendable, but being a brave soldier is a damned sight different to running a dance hall.'

'Why doesn't he leave, I wonder?'

'The same reason as he was taken on, maybe,' said Polly. 'Family loyalty. Perhaps he doesn't want to upset his brother-in-law, or more importantly, his wife. She's the boss's sister.'

'Yeah, that's right.'

'I admit that I go around with a mop and cleaning cloth now and again because I can't bear to see the place looking scruffy, but I shouldn't have to do it.'

'You most definitely should not,' Marian agreed. 'And you must tell him that.'

'I have done, several times, and he says he'll talk to the cleaning staff and get things put right, but nothing ever changes. It isn't just the maintenance, either. I told him a good while ago that he needed to order more tickets, but he didn't do it, so I have to give people a till receipt instead so that they can get back in if they go out in the interval.'

'Oh, Polly, that isn't right.'

'I know. It's terrible.'

'The owner has several other business interests and is busy with them, so he lets the manager get on with it at the Cherry,' said Marian. 'I know that from experience. But he will get to know if the place really goes downhill, though by that time it will be too late and it will have to close down.'

'Exactly.'

'I'd work there for nothing to put the place back on its feet,' said Marian.

'I know you would, Auntie, but that isn't going to be possible,' said Polly.

'More's the pity. Of course, dance halls do go in and out of fashion, but the Cherry shouldn't have had its day yet, not by a long way. And it wouldn't if it was run properly.'

'Oh well, I'll just have to carry on as best as I can,' said Polly. 'If I create too much of a fuss, he'll give me notice. I have no influence at all. I have to sit back and watch the place deteriorate and not say a word. Mr Wood might be hopeless as a manager, but he does have the power to hire and fire.'

'That's true,' said Marian thoughtfully.

'I think the idea is outrageous, even for you,' said Archie when Marian told him about the plan that had slipped into her mind. 'Honestly, love. It spells disaster.'

'You're probably right,' she was forced to agree. 'But I can't just sit back and do nothing, can I? Surely anything is worth a try. And it isn't illegal.'

'No, but it isn't ethical either, and you might come out of it badly,' he said.

'What's the worst that can happen? So Mr Wood gets furious and gives me a right tongue-lashing. I can live with that. I don't think he's the violent type.'

'But what do you actually hope to gain from it?' he enquired with interest.

'That he'll confide in me, I suppose,' she said. 'He must know that things aren't as they should be and he might be glad of some advice.'

'And the King might come round here for tea tomorrow,' Archie said bluntly.

'Oh, Archie, why are you being so negative?'

'Because you set yourself up for trouble every time,' he said. 'The Cherry is nothing to do with you now.'

'I still care about it.'

'You'll go ahead and do it whatever I say, but make sure you don't drop Polly in it,' he warned. 'He'll be curious as to how you know things aren't going well.'

'I won't mention Polly or the fact that the place is going

downhill. If it carries on as it is she'll be out of a job anyway, so it's no more than my duty to try and help. I'll say I called in because I've mislaid an item of jewellery or something and wondered if I'd left it in the office. Once we get talking, maybe he'll let me give him a few tips. Christmas is coming up. Christmas Eve and New Year's Eve are big nights for dance halls. He'll need to get things up to scratch for that.'

'Don't count on it.'

'I got on well enough with him when I was showing him the ropes,' she said.

'But now the job is his,' Archie pointed out. 'And I honestly can't imagine you wanting advice from your predecessor when you worked there. Be honest.'

'Don't be such a pessimist.'

'Just worried about you,' he said. 'You jump right into things and make yourself vulnerable.'

'I'm a tough old bird, you know that,' she reminded him. 'It's half-day closing for me on Wednesdays. I'll go next Wednesday in the late afternoon. He'll be there then but Polly won't be, though there will be people there to let me in at the staff entrance.'

'I suppose no real harm can come of it,' Archie said. 'But just be careful.'

'Of course,' she said.

The main rush for tickets was over. People were coming to the window in dribs and drabs now. Even without doing any calculations, Polly knew the numbers were down, and she could feel knots tightening in her stomach.

'Hi, Polly,' said a deep voice, and looking up, her eyes widened in surprise and delight, the ticket sales forgotten.

'James,' she said, beaming. 'You're back. How wonderful. Welcome home!'

He waited in the pub across the road until she'd finished work, then they walked to her house together, arms entwined, but not before they had greeted each other properly.

'It's so good to see you again, James,' she said. 'It seems as though you've been away forever.'

'It felt like that to me too.'

'Still, you're here now and that's worth celebrating,' she said. 'Do you have to go back tonight?'

'No, not until tomorrow, so I was wondering if I could borrow your sofa for the night.'

'Of course you can. It'll be just like old times.' She paused, realising she needed to update him. 'Actually, James, something happened while you were away.'

He stopped walking and turned to her. 'That sounds serious,' he said.

'It is. Very,' she said. 'My brother Ray. He won't be coming home. He was lost at sea.'

'Oh, Polly, I am so sorry,' he said with feeling. 'You must all be devastated.'

'We are,' she said. 'I don't think Mum will ever be quite the same again.'

'Maybe I should get the late train back,' he said. 'I don't want to intrude.'

'You wouldn't know how to intrude,' she said. 'Mum will be pleased to see you. It will cheer her up. Both she and Dad are very fond of you.'

★　★　★

Flo and Wilf were still up when Polly and James got home, and he was given a very warm welcome.

'You should have let us know you were coming and we'd have laid on a spread to welcome you back,' said Flo. 'You missed all the victory celebrations.'

'I didn't know if I could get a pass until the very last minute,' he said.

'Next time you get a weekend off we'll have a bit of a do,' she said, seeming genuinely pleased to see him. 'I'll get Marian and Archie to come round and we'll have a few drinks.'

'I'd like that a lot,' he said.

'I suppose now that the war is over you'll be going back to Canada, won't you?' said Wilf.

James nodded. 'That's the general idea,' he said. 'But I don't know when it will be. There's a lot of us to ship home, so it will take a while.'

'The longer the better for me,' said Polly. 'But that's just me being selfish. You'll want to go home to your family.'

'Sure I will. I like being here as well, though,' he said. 'But none of that will be up to me. I'll be going home when they tell me.'

'We'll enjoy having you around while we can,' said Polly, and there was hearty agreement from her parents.

Because James had been abroad for a while, he was due some leave, so he became a regular user of the Pritchards' sofa and they had a celebration for him the following Sunday, when Polly and Marian weren't working.

Everything was still scarce, but they managed to get hold of a few bottles, and Flo baked cheese straws and sausage rolls.

It was still wartime sausage meat, and she used most of their combined cheese ration, but it all tasted good, as did the fish-paste sandwiches, their palates having become accustomed to basic food over the war years. Emmie was allowed to stay up, but she fell asleep in the chair about nine o'clock, so her grandad carried her up to bed.

'Can I write to you when you're back in Canada, James?' asked Marian. 'Just occasionally. As a sort of pen pal.'

'I'd like that,' he said warmly.

'I've always wanted a pen pal,' she said. 'So that will be really nice.'

'Oh really,' snorted Flo. 'When are you going to start acting your age, Marian? The idea of pen pals is for youngsters.'

'So I'll start a new fashion,' said Marian chirpily, but she looked hurt by Flo's criticism.

'I think you can have a pen pal at any age, can't you?' said Polly, defensive of her aunt. 'It's a way of finding out how people live in other countries and it's nice to get letters from abroad.'

'There's no harm in it, anyway,' added Wilf.

'I just thought it was a bit . . . well, juvenile,' said Flo, realising that hers was a lone voice.

'You know me,' said Marian. 'I'm just a big kid.'

'You keep us both young, don't you, love?' said Archie supportively.

'I try to.'

It was a very jolly gathering and Polly was enjoying herself, but all the talk of James returning to Canada cast a shadow. It had always been there at the back of her mind as something for the future, but now it could happen at any time. She'd never been used to seeing him every day but she'd always had his weekend passes and leaves to look forward to. Once he went back to Canada, she would never see him again, and that was hard.

It must have been on his mind too, because he mentioned it later when he and Polly were alone together.

'I shall miss England a lot,' he said. 'I've become very fond of the place. This little island of yours with its funny customs.'

'Such as?'

'Always talking about the weather and how long it takes to get places, and your queues . . .'

'There are a lot of us so of course we have to queue,' Polly said. 'Just because you've got miles and miles of emptiness and not enough people to fill it all.'

'Then there's your intelligence and sense of duty, and your bravery,' he continued.

'That's better.'

'Seriously, Polly, I love this country and I feel blessed to have been able to spend time here.'

'Ah, you'll have me in tears in a minute.'

'I'm feeling emotional too . . . it really is good to be back.'

'Not for long, though.'

'No.' He paused. 'Anyway, it's been a swell evening, so don't let's spoil it with talk of my leaving. We have better things to do.'

'Exactly,' she said, going into his arms.

Settled down on the sofa later on, staring into the dark and idly watching the pattern on the ceiling made by the lights outside through the net curtains, James was turning his dilemma over in his mind.

Seeing Polly again had been an emotional experience for him. He was in love with her and wanted to marry her. But how could he ask her to give up her life here in England with her strong family ties to go and live in a strange place where the only person she would know was him? She would make new friends eventually, of course, and his people would welcome her with open arms. But she was so close to her family, it would be a terrible wrench for her. It would be an entirely different sort of life for her in Canada too. She had only ever known town life; she was urban through and through. Where he lived in Ontario it was all farmland. They had towns, of course, but they weren't close at hand, and town people had a different way of living and thinking. Then there was Emmie. Polly wouldn't want to take her away from her aunt and grandparents and everything she knew.

On the other hand, he knew she loved him as he loved her and they needed to be together. What if he was to come here to live? No, that really wouldn't be possible. He had family responsibilities at home. Anyway, his parents would be devastated if he went away for good. They'd found it difficult enough these past years by all accounts.

So one day soon he'd have to go away and leave Polly behind forever. How could he do that? He sat up and held his head in his hands. He'd been too busy being a soldier and living from one leave to the next to think too much about the ultimate separation, which had always been in the distant future, after the war. Now the future was almost here.

He went to the window and looked out into the street with its small terraced houses and tiny front gardens, all lit by the amber glow of the lamp posts. There were no gates because the metal had been needed for the war. The road and the sidewalk – or pavement, as they called it here – were narrow, which meant that the houses on either side were much closer together than he was used to. Privacy here was closely guarded with net curtains and respect, and somehow people managed to live in close proximity.

Although it seemed strange to him, it was very dear to his heart. England, this family and most of all his beloved Polly meant the world to him. He would cherish every moment he got to spend with her. But they needed to talk about things instead of pretending that the parting wasn't going to happen.

Upstairs in her bedroom, Polly was also wakeful. She was surprised that James hadn't proposed to her and wondered if he might do so before he went back. They both knew she couldn't accept, but it would be nice to be asked.

It was lovely to have him around again, even if the whole thing had the dark cloud of parting hanging over it. Still, he had some leave, so he would be around for a while, and she intended to enjoy every second.

'So why didn't you ask your niece to enquire about your necklace, since she works here?' Mr Wood asked Marian, who had been let into the Cherry by one of the staff.

'I just happened to be passing, so I thought I might as well call in and find out about it myself,' she fibbed.

'Have you any idea where in the office you might have left it?' he asked.

'If it's anywhere, it will be in the top drawer of the desk.'

He opened the drawer wide to show paper clips, pencils

and other sundries. 'No sign of a necklace in there. See for yourself.'

She went through the motions. 'You're right. I must have mislaid it somewhere else. I'm very sorry to have bothered you.'

'I'd have seen it if it had been here, since I spend most of my life here,' he said edgily.

This was just the lead she needed. 'You're working long hours, then?'

'And some,' he said. 'But you know all about that because you used to do the job.'

'I didn't find the hours all that bad,' she said. 'They were unsocial but not particularly long.'

'Well, they're long for me,' he said gruffly. 'I just can't get everything done unless I work every hour God sends.'

'It is a very demanding position, I agree,' she said. 'Everything has to be in place so the show can go on, you might say. If one thing is wrong, it puts everything else out.'

'You're telling me. And you have to stick to the budget. That's the worst thing.'

She gave him a close look, noticing the dark shadows under his eyes. He appeared to have lost some weight since she'd last seen him. She decided to push her luck. 'Are you not enjoying the job, then?'

He seemed to crumple before her eyes. He struggled to compose himself, but his face contorted and tears poured down his cheeks. Pulling a handkerchief from his pocket, he hurriedly wiped his face and blew his nose.

'Nearly six years I did in the army, and saw my fair share of action, and that didn't break me, but this job has,' he said thickly.

'Not your sort of thing, then?'

'I hate it,' he said. 'I'm not cut out for it. I lie awake at night dreading the next day.'

'What exactly don't you like about it?' she asked.

'Everything, but mostly the responsibility. It's all on my shoulders and it weighs me down something awful. I know I'm doing it all wrong but I don't know how to do it right. Management isn't my game. I had no idea it would be so difficult when I took it on.'

'I thought you said you were in dance halls before the war,' she said.

'I was, but on the door,' he explained. 'That's where I like to be. Out there with the people. Not stuck in here struggling with stuff I don't understand. I don't want to be worrying about the job after hours. I like to knock off and forget work until I'm back on duty. No chance of that with this lot.'

'I suppose you changed the cleaning staff to save the firm money?' she asked.

'Yeah. That's why I got rid of Ted and the boys, too,' he said. 'I daren't lose money for the boss – who just happens to be my wife's brother. But now a lot of people have stopped coming, so the takings are down anyway.'

'Why don't you talk to your brother-in-law about the struggle you're having?' Marian asked. 'He could probably find you something more to your liking in one of his other businesses, or put you on the door here.'

'I don't want to upset my wife,' he said. 'The job pays well and she likes the idea of her husband being the manager of a well-known dance hall, though it won't be well known for much longer if I don't get to grips with it soon.' He paused and dabbed at his eyes with his handkerchief. 'Trouble is, I know I'll never be any good. I'm just not suited to it.' He pointed to his head. 'I don't have it up here.'

'I think it's more a question of us all being suited to different things,' she suggested. 'You're probably very good at being on the door because of your personality, whereas someone else might be hopeless. There are other, less responsible jobs than this that you could do, apart from the door.'

'Do you reckon?'

'Of course.'

'You did this job all right, didn't you?' he said.

'It was very demanding,' she said. 'As you say, there is a lot to think about and everything has to be properly in place for it to work. But I enjoyed it. I thrive on responsibility.'

'I suppose I'm just not clever enough,' he said.

'I don't think you should think about it in that way,' she suggested. 'We all shine at different things. I would never have got the job at all if it hadn't been for the war, and because of it I was able to show my true potential. Now I'm working on the counter in a shop and loathe every minute. So you're not the only one who hates going to work every day. But that's all I can get now that the men are back, so there's nothing I can do about it. But you . . . you're young. You can't spend the rest of your life doing something you hate, something that keeps you awake at night.'

'Plenty of people do.'

'But you don't have to be one of them; you'll make your-self ill if you carry on as you are, not to mention the damage you'll do to the Cherry. As you say, its popularity is waning fast. If it carries on, it'll have to close, so you need to do something before that happens. Once your brother-in-law realises what's going on, he'll have you out anyway.'

'What will I tell the wife?'

'The truth is your best bet,' she said.

'She won't like it.'

'She won't want you to make yourself ill either.'

'No, I suppose not,' he said. 'She's a good sort, my missus.'

Marian gave him a close look. 'By the way, I have no ulterior motive in advising you about this. Your brother-in-law wouldn't ask me to come back. He's all for jobs for the boys now that they're coming home. I accept that as being right, even though I don't like the idea from a personal point of view.'

He nodded.

'Anyway, I'd better be off,' she said. 'Unless there's anything you want me to do for you. If I can help in any way, I'll be glad to.'

'You've done enough,' he said, without rancour. 'Our talk has cleared my mind and I know what I have to do. Just the thought of not having to struggle with this job every day has made me feel better, and it will be worth a bit of bother with the wife to get out of this office for good.'

'Talk to your wife about it before you do anything else,' she advised, and left.

'I felt really sorry for him,' Marian told Archie when she got home. 'The poor bloke is in pieces. I hope his wife is the sympathetic type. She likes the idea of being married to a dance hall manager apparently. Likes the wages, too.'

'When she realises it's making him ill, she'll understand, I should think,' he said.

'I hope so, because I know what it's like to hate your job, though I don't dread going to work like he does. I'm just

141

bored witless and irritated by Miss Harris. It certainly doesn't keep me awake at night. It must be awful for him.'

'So you did right in going to the Cherry,' he said. 'I must admit I had my doubts.'

'I couldn't sit back and do nothing while the place went downhill,' she said. 'With a bit of luck, things might get put right now.'

'Well done,' said Archie.

'Thanks, love,' she said.

When Marian got a message the next day via Polly from the owner of the Cherry, Mr Banks, asking her to call in and see him as soon as possible, she thought she was in for a trouncing for upsetting his staff. She asked Miss Harris for a late lunch break and hurried to the ballroom ready to defend herself.

'I need you back here right away,' said Mr Banks, surprising her. 'I need someone to pull this place back from the brink of disaster, and you're the only one who can do that.'

'Your brother-in-law has spoken to you, then?'

'Yeah. I had no idea he was in such a state, though of course I knew the Cherry was in trouble and that I was going to have to deal with it sometime soon.'

'What's happened to him?'

'I've moved him to security in one of my clubs. I've made sure he won't lose out financially, so his wife is happy about it. She didn't realise he was having such a bad time and doesn't want him to be miserable. I pay my security people well because of the risk involved. Thank goodness it's all out in the open. I'm really grateful to you, Marian.'

'And there I was wondering if I should interfere,' she said.

'You always were a cheeky cow,' he said. 'But in this instance you did the right thing.'

'Good, but I can't just drop everything and come back,' she said. 'I have a job and I have to give a week's notice. Anyway, once I've put things right, you'll want me out again in favour of a man, won't you?'

'Your job here will be safe for as long as you want it, I promise,' he said. 'Yes, I do want the troops to have jobs to come home to, and wherever possible I will place them in my organisation, but you are the best person to manage the Cherry. Please say you will, Marian. I need you back right away.'

'I'll have to work my notice, but I could come here as soon as I finish at the store every day and start to put things right in the evening until I come back properly.'

'If you could do that I'd be very grateful, and I'll see you right financially.'

'The first thing we need to do is try and get Ted and the boys back and get some decent music into the place again,' she said. 'You could start the ball rolling with that while I go back to work. His number is in the office phone book. He might take some persuading, though.'

'I'll offer more money,' Mr Banks said. 'If that doesn't work, I'll have to rely on you to get cracking with your charm.'

Marian went back to work to give in her notice with a spring in her step.

Chapter Eight

The long-awaited first peacetime Christmas turned out to be like wartime without the war. The continued austerity and the bomb-damaged landscape were not much of a reward for the punishing war years, but nothing could diminish the joy of peace for the Pritchard family and friends.

Marian was on good form now that she'd got her job back, though she admitted it would take time and hard work before the Cherry was returned completely to its former glory. She enjoyed a challenge, though, and was in her element. Between them she and Mr Banks had managed to persuade Ted and the band to return, which was an enormous step forward. With her aunt back at the helm, Polly's joy in the job revived and she was keen to help put the Cherry back on top.

'At least you don't have to do the evening classes now that you've got your job back,' said Flo when they were talking about it over Christmas dinner, another culinary triumph for her with the usual scant ingredients.

'I don't have to do them but I'm going to finish the course,' Marian told her.

'What on earth for?'

'Because I like to finish what I start; because it will be useful if the bookkeeper is off sick, or if I ever need to find another job; and to improve my mind,' she said. 'All of those things. Anyway, it puts my night off to good use, and it isn't forever.'

'A waste of time, if you ask me.'

'Which she didn't,' Archie interjected. 'Personally I'm very proud of her.'

'It seems a bit strange to me, but to each their own, I suppose,' said Flo, and Wilf complimented his wife on her expertise in the kitchen to gloss over any lingering tension.

James had managed to get a forty-eight-hour pass for the Christmas period, which was lovely for Polly. He seemed quieter than usual, but insisted that he was fine. It wasn't until the evening of Boxing Day that he told her what was bothering him.

'I'm going back to Canada in mid-January,' he said. 'We were told just before the holiday.'

For Polly, the pain was hardly bearable. 'I know I should be pleased because you've been away from home for so long and you must be keen to see your folks again, and I've always known you would be going back, but, oh, James, I shall miss you so much.'

'Likewise,' he said, holding her close.

'I should be prepared,' she said. 'Yet I feel as though my world has just fallen apart. But I will be strong when the time comes, James, I promise.'

Then James did something he had promised himself he wouldn't do.

'Polly,' he blurted out. 'I love you and I want to marry you.

145

I want you to come to Canada with me as my wife. You and Emmie, as a family.'

Tears were falling now. 'Oh, James, I love you too and I would love to marry you and come to Canada more than anything. I want to spend the rest of my life with you.'

'Really?' His eyes were bright with hope.

'Yes, really, but how can I leave Mum and Dad when they've already lost their son?'

'Oh.' His expression darkened. 'I know I shouldn't have asked you, but it just came pouring out. Anyway, I want you to know how I feel. Is there any chance you could think about it? It wouldn't be for a little while. I'll go back with the army and would arrange for you and Emmie to come afterwards. It's a huge thing to ask of you, I realise that.'

'I'm honoured that you have asked me, I really am, but I can't do it. I'm so sorry, James,' she said. 'Oh, why do things have to be so hard?'

'It's the nature of life, I suppose, though I do think things have been particularly difficult for you, losing your husband and then your brother. Now I've added to it by asking you to leave your family when I know that you can't.'

'Please don't be sorry you asked me,' she said. 'I shall cherish the memory of it.'

'I keep thinking that there must be a way we can be together, but I haven't come up with anything. I'm needed at home on the farm, otherwise I'd look into the idea of moving to England to be with you.'

'We can write to each other,' she suggested.

He nodded, thinking it would be small compensation. 'Anyway, there's a bit of time left before I go, though I don't know if I'll get another weekend pass. If I don't manage to work it, then I'll come to the Cherry to see you and go back to camp the same night.'

Polly nodded speechlessly, then held him as though she never wanted to let him go.

There was an air of gloom in the house the next day after James had left, having told Polly's parents his situation. Flo and Wilf had grown fond of him and Emmie adored him, though she was too young to realise the significance of his leaving. Living in the moment, as young children do, she would soon forget him, Polly knew.

'We wouldn't stand in your way if you really wanted to go to Canada to be with him, would we, Wilf?' her mother told her not very convincingly.

'I suppose not,' he said without enthusiasm.

'Don't worry,' Polly said. 'I've made my decision. I won't be going. My place is here.'

Flo couldn't hide her relief, but she seemed genuinely sorry that James was leaving. 'His mother will be pleased to have him back anyway,' she said. 'The poor woman must have missed him something awful.'

Although she didn't actually say the words, Polly knew that Flo was wishing she had been able to welcome her own son home. If Polly had ever considered a new life in Canada for herself and Emmie, she knew in that moment that she could never have it.

She was an adult and as such it was natural to fly the nest. But she couldn't do it to her mother; not go to the other side of the world and never see her parents again.

★   ★   ★

Although Polly didn't feel able to tell her mother about James's marriage proposal because she didn't want to make her feel guilty, she did tell her aunt.

'I thought he would probably propose because it's obvious he's mad about you,' Marian said when Polly spoke to her about it one evening at work. 'But I guessed you'd turn him down because of your parents. Plenty of women aren't so loyal to family ties. There are a great many GI brides and women going abroad to other places to be with men they fell in love with during the war.'

'I know, but I just couldn't do it to Mum and Dad, especially as they've lost Ray.' Polly paused. 'Anyway, I'd miss them and you and Archie too much.'

'Being purely selfish, I'm glad you're not going, but it's a shame that you and James can't be together.'

'At least I have the proposal to look back on,' Polly said. 'It was very romantic and I shall never forget it.'

Marian hugged her, feeling emotional and a little sad for her niece. 'When is he leaving?' she asked.

'Mid-January.'

'Not long then. Will you see him before he goes?'

'He said he'll do his best.'

'Anyway, kid,' Marian said, changing the subject because Polly looked so sad, 'you'll have plenty to take your mind off it. We've a massive challenge on our hands in the New Year as far as the Cherry is concerned.'

'I notice you've got an UNDER NEW MANAGEMENT sign outside,' Polly said.

'I thought it was important that people know that, as the last manager did such a bad job. I made it myself, with Archie's help.' She pulled something from under the desk and held it up. 'And this one too.' It was a poster saying: DON'T MISS NEW YEAR'S EVE AT THE CHERRY BALLROOM, with drawings of people dancing and HAPPY NEW YEAR written at the bottom.

'Well done,' said Polly.

'Thanks, kid,' Marian said. 'We've got to put this place back on the map.'

'We're on our way,' said Polly. 'Ticket sales were up on Christmas Eve.'

Her aunt nodded, smiling. 'Ted and the band make a lot of difference, and word will soon get around that things are better here. It might take a while to get completely back to normal. When a place is going downhill, people find some-where else and then get used to it so stay with it. We have to lure them back by making the Cherry irresistible. New Year's Eve will be a good chance for us to show what we have to offer. People like to go out and have fun that night, and we're going to guide them in our direction.'

Polly tried not to show how much she was dreading the new year and the thought of losing James soon after.

They turned up in droves for the New Year's Eve dance; all dressed up and ready for fun.

'I won't stay to see the new year in if you don't mind, Auntie,' Polly told Marian when she came into the ticket office to find out how sales were going. 'I'll get off home as soon as I've finished in here.'

Marian was disappointed. Archie was coming along later, and she would have loved Polly to be there too, but she could understand her wanting to miss out on that particular ritual.

'Auld Lang Syne' without a special partner could be very depressing.

'As you wish, love,' she said. 'Come and see me before you go, though.'

'Will do.'

Polly had done the cashing-up and was getting her coat on when there was a knocking on the window. There's always one latecomer, she said to herself, then turned to see James on the other side of the glass.

'What a wonderful surprise,' she said, letting him into the office and hugging him. 'And there I was feeling all miserable about New Year's Eve on my own. Oh, James, it's so good to see you.'

'Likewise.'

Something about the tone of his voice made her say, 'There's something wrong, isn't there?'

He looked at her sadly. 'We're moving to the coast tomorrow ready to get on the ship. I won't be able to get away again.'

'So this is the last time . . .'

'Yeah,' he said. 'They sprung it on us. I had to come and see you. I won't be able to stay the night, though. After the New Year celebrations, I'll head back to the station and wait for the early train. I won't be the only one. A few of my buddies wanted to come to London one last time.'

'Well,' said Polly, struggling to compose herself. 'As you've come all this way, we'd better get out there dancing, hadn't we? Tickets are sold out, so you'll be my special guest.'

'Lead the way,' he said, holding her hand tightly.

★　　★　　★

The atmosphere in the ballroom was a riot of gaiety and excitement as the evening moved inexorably towards midnight. Marian hadn't been able to get any balloons or streamers, but she'd decorated the place with flags and bunting and put a huge home-made poster on the stage proclaiming: PEACE AND JOY FOR THE NEW YEAR OF 1946.

All Polly wanted was to spend this last morsel of time alone with James, but she guessed they would both just sink into a pit of despair. Better they had happy memories to look back on. So she sparkled as they danced the foxtrot and tango and really let their hair down in the jive. When the band played 'We'll Meet Again' in the run-up to midnight, they moved around the dance floor, lost in each other.

Then it was midnight, and the chimes of Big Ben sounded from a wireless they had fixed up on the stage near the microphone. As soon as 'Auld Lang Syne' had finished, Polly and James slipped away.

'I'll walk you home but I won't come in,' he said.

'I'd rather we said goodbye here,' she said. 'Where we met, so we shall part.'

'I don't like the idea of you walking home alone,' he said. 'There'll be a few drunks about tonight.'

'I'll be fine; it isn't far.'

'If you're sure?'

'Absolutely.'

'There's no point in prolonging the agony, so I'll be on my way then,' he said gruffly.

'This is really it, then,' she said.

'Afraid so.'

'James, when you get home to Canada, you must live your

life to the full. Find a girl. Get married. You and I can't be together, so move on and let things take their course.'

'I don't even want to think about that now.'

'Neither do I, but I want us both to be realistic. Life will take us with it, so embrace it. Don't waste it in thoughts of what might have been.'

'I'll try not to, and you must do the same,' he said. 'But I'll write. Is that allowed?'

'Only until you meet someone else,' she said.

'I have to go back inside,' he said suddenly. 'I didn't say goodbye to Marian and Archie.'

'I have to get my coat, too,' she said, following him in.

When they re-emerged a few minutes later, they embraced for the last time and she watched him walk away, oblivious to the sounds of merrymaking blaring from the dance hall. When he had disappeared, she set off down the familiar streets alone, at last feeling able to let the tears fall. There was nothing else to do but keep going, she told herself, but she knew only too well that the pain was just beginning.

'We need to do something to cheer Polly up,' Marian said to Flo one morning a few weeks later when she visited while Polly was at her typing job, the factory having gone back to making machine parts now that the war was over. 'The poor girl is in despair, even though she tries to hide it.'

'Nothing we do will cheer her up,' said Flo. 'Nothing short of James turning up on the doorstep and saying he's going to stay will do that.'

'I know, but we can at least try to take her mind off it.'

'She's a strong girl,' said Flo. 'She showed that when George died. It will take time, but she'll be all right.'

'We're lucky she didn't decide to go to Canada; plenty of women have chosen to go abroad with their men.'

'Yeah, I saw something in the paper about the GI brides getting very well looked after by the American army,' said Flo. 'They're staying in a transit camp in Hampshire before sailing to New York. Fifty thousand of them apparently, some married to their Yank with a kid already. They reckon it will take until the summer to get them all away.'

'Well blow me,' said Marian. 'I didn't realise there were that many.'

'It's hard to imagine how they can cut their family ties and go,' Flo said.

'I expect some of them struggled with the decision,' said Marian. 'But a new life in America is very appealing to a lot of young women. Excitement, adventure, that sort of thing. We've all seen it at the pictures and we like what we see.'

'Real life won't be like the films,' snorted Flo. 'They'll soon find that out.'

'Of course it won't be like the films, but they have a good standard of living there, certainly better than here. Not that that's saying much.'

'Things will get better here eventually.'

'I bloomin' well hope so.' Marian was thoughtful. 'I reckon if I'd had the chance of a new life in America when I was young, I would have gone.'

'You always were headstrong.'

'I've always had a sense of adventure,' Marian corrected. 'There is a difference, Flo.'

'Well, anyway, James is from Canada, not America,' Flo reminded her.

'Yeah, and he was at pains to point that out to us, wasn't he?' Marian said.

'Indeed.' Flo looked at her sister with a serious expression. 'I didn't stop Polly from going, you know. I told her several times that if it was what she wanted, she must go ahead and do it.'

'I'm sure you did,' said Marian, guessing that her sister's approval would have been half-hearted. She didn't blame her. None of them wanted to lose Polly. 'But I'm very glad she didn't go.'

'Me too.'

'Anyway,' began Marian, 'I want to give her a treat, so I've decided to take her to the Savoy for tea one Sunday afternoon; her and Emmie.' She thought for a moment. 'In fact why don't we all go? My treat. A family outing.'

'The Savoy,' said Flo, appalled. 'People like us don't go to the Savoy.'

'They do if they can afford it,' Marian said. 'Times have changed, Flo. The war evened things up a little because ordinary people have been doing extraordinary things and it's given us confidence. We still have the class thing, of course, but I don't think people are so keen to bow and scrape now.'

'But why should you pay for us all?'

Marian shrugged. 'Because I suggested it and I'd like to do it. I earn decent money and I have Archie to help with expenses now. Anyway, it's only tea. I'm not suggesting a five-course dinner for us all.'

'I don't usually go on outings,' said Flo.

'Then it's high time you did.'

'I don't know if Wilf—'

'It will be a nice change for him to go out on a Sunday afternoon instead of sleeping off his lunchtime beer in the chair,' Marian cut in. 'I won't take no for an answer, Flo.'

'Really?'

'Yes, really. But there's one condition.'

'Which is?'

'You take off that bloody hairnet.'

'What's the matter with wearing a hairnet? It keeps my hair tidy.'

'It puts years on you.'

'You know I don't bother about that sort of thing.'

'I am *not* going to the Savoy with you in a hairnet, so if you want to come, get rid of it.'

'I'll see what Wilf says,' Flo told her.

Wilf wouldn't notice if she had a nest of robins on her head, Marian thought, but said, 'You do that, but the hairnet isn't coming and it isn't negotiable.'

This was such a delight, and it was so kind of Auntie to treat them all, thought Polly, when they were seated around the table in the Thames Foyer at the heart of the famous Savoy Hotel. She gazed with pleasure at the beautifully laundered tablecloths, elegant tableware, and dainty sandwiches, scones and little cakes arranged on tiered stands.

'A bit different to your doorsteps, eh, Flo?' said Wilf, helping himself to a sandwich.

'If I gave you sandwiches like this to take to work, you'd throw them back at me.'

'I would and all,' he agreed. 'They're not the thing to sustain a hard-working man, but I'm a man of leisure today so I can be a bit classy.'

'We're all posh today, mate,' said Archie.

It was elegant to the point of breathtaking, thought Polly, who had never been to the Savoy before. Natural light flooded in from the glass dome in the ceiling; there were beautifully arranged flowers, highly polished furniture, chandeliers and the sound of a piano playing in the background. Despite the splendour, there was a cosiness about it somehow.

She guessed that her aunt had arranged this in an attempt to cheer her up after James's departure. It was typical of her to be so thoughtful. Only time would heal, and as a mother with a child to care for, Polly couldn't dwell on personal sadness, except perhaps when alone in bed at night, but she was touched by Auntie's generosity. There was something very warming about being out together as a family, away from the humdrum familiarity of home. Everyone had made an effort, the men in suits, the women in their best coats. Even Mum, who looked so much nicer without her hairnet, seemed to be enjoying herself.

'So is everybody happy?' asked Marian.

'I'll say,' said Polly.

'It's lovely here, Auntie,' said Emmie politely. 'Please may I have a cake?'

'Course you can, darlin',' said Marian.

Polly was proud of her daughter's good manners and managed not to insist that she had a sandwich first. What did it matter in which order she ate? After six years of shortages, no one had to be persuaded to tuck in. The spread here probably wasn't as lavish as in less austere times, but it was still a banquet compared to their normal diet.

The ambience was somehow exciting and relaxing simultaneously and Polly felt quite sad when the meal came to an end. When her aunt had paid the bill with great aplomb, as though she was a regular customer, Polly said, 'Thank you, Auntie. It's been lovely.'

The others added their agreement, and they left feeling like proper toffs.

It was almost dark as they walked from the Savoy to Piccadilly so that Emmie could see the lights. Polly couldn't remember ever going to the West End when it hadn't been crowded, and today was no exception. It was like being at a huge party, with people milling about everywhere, not seeming bothered by the seasonally cold weather.

'Have you enjoyed yourself, Dad?' she asked Wilf when they were sitting together on the homeward train.

'Not 'alf,' he said.

'That's good, because a posh tea out isn't really your sort of thing, is it?'

'Not really, no. I'm more of a pie and a pint sort of man,' he said. 'But it's good to see how the other half live now and again. And it was nice, all the family being together.'

'Auntie is very generous, isn't she?'

'Mm. She's a good sort.'

'Very confident, too,' said Polly. 'She behaves as though she's used to posh places.'

'She's done well for herself, considering . . .'

'Considering what, Dad?' asked Polly.

'Oh, nothing.'

'You must have meant something.'

157

'Well . . . just that she's from a humble background and she's got a good job, I suppose,' he said.

Polly wasn't convinced. There was more to it than that. But she knew there was no point in pursuing it, because she'd encountered this wall of silence before when her aunt's early life had come up. Whatever it was, it wasn't for her to know, so she changed the subject.

When they came out of the station, they parted company with Marian and Archie, who wanted to go straight home.

'Well, what a lovely afternoon we've had,' Polly said. 'Did you enjoy it, Mum, even without your hairnet?'

'Don't be saucy,' said Flo, but she was smiling.

They were all feeling happy as they turned the corner into their street, Emmie skipping beside them.

'That's funny,' said Wilf as they approached the house. 'There's a light on. Did you leave it on for us to come home to, Flo?'

'Of course not,' she replied. 'I would never waste electricity in that way.'

'Must be in the living room at the back,' said Wilf. 'It's shining into the hall and through the glass at the top of the front door.'

'Probably one of the neighbours called in for some reason,' suggested Flo, unworried by the development; they'd known their neighbours for years. 'They all know there's a key on a string behind the letter box.'

'They wouldn't come in when we were out,' said Wilf, marching up the front path with the others following.

'No, I suppose not,' his wife agreed. 'We must have accidentally left the light on.'

'Is it a burglar, Mummy?' asked Emmie.

'Of course not, darling,' said Polly with confidence. This

wasn't the sort of area that was popular with burglars, because no one had anything of value to steal.

'That's a shame. None of my friends have ever had a burglar,' said Emmie, sounding keen on the idea. 'So I'd be the first kid to have one.'

Honestly, children could be really brutal at times, thought Polly, smiling.

'I think everyone enjoyed it, don't you, Archie?' said Marian as they walked home.

'Absolutely!' he said. 'There would be something wrong with them if they didn't. Being taken out to tea in the West End with all expenses paid. Not many people would be as generous as you are, Marian.'

'They're my family and they mean the world to me,' she said. 'Polly seemed to enjoy herself, and that was the object of the exercise.'

'She had a lovely time, you could tell. She isn't the type to moon about, however she's feeling. Not while she has Emmie to think of.'

'You're right about that,' said Marian. 'It's a damned shame about her and James. They seemed so right together.'

'Yeah, they did, and he was a nice bloke.'

'The poor girl has already been through the mill when her husband died.'

'That must have been awful for her,' Archie said. 'What was he like, her husband?'

'Very likeable, but a bit of a wide boy,' Marian said, thinking back. 'We were never quite sure if he stayed on the right side of the law with his wheeler-dealing. He was a plumber by trade but ran a little sideline in his spare time. You know the sort of thing. No paperwork and no questions asked.'

'Flo wouldn't have approved of that,' Archie said.

'No, she didn't, but she turned a blind eye for Polly's sake. It was only a small-time earner anyway, and he kept it quiet.'

'Still sounds a bit dodgy.'

'He was a bit, I think, but only in a very small way. He had a warm heart and an entertaining personality. Always ready for a laugh and a joke was George; you know the type. Never lost for words. He could make the smallest incident into a funny story, so he was very popular.'

'Did he treat Polly right?'

'Oh yeah. He thought the world of her,' Marian said. 'He was a handsome devil too. It's no wonder Polly fell for him.'

'Sounds as though you fancied him yourself,' Archie said with a laugh.

'If I'd been a good bit younger I probably would have,' she said, smiling.

'But you settled for me instead.'

'After a very long wait.'

'For both of us. All those years together we lost, I can hardly bear to think about it.'

'Yeah, it is a shame,' she sighed. 'But there's no point in regrets, Arch. We might have drifted apart anyway, as young people do. There are so many temptations when you're just starting out. By the time we did get back together, we were fully mature and knew our own minds.'

'That's true, but I still regret the lost years.'

'Stop looking back, Archie,' she admonished. 'We're together now. That's the important thing.'

'I suppose you're right, as usual,' he said, slipping his arm around her.

'Get a move on, Dad,' said Polly as her father fumbled with the key. 'It's freezing out here.'

'I'm going as fast as I can,' he said, pulling the key through the letter box and turning it in the lock. 'You lot wait here while I find out what's going on.'

'Blow that,' said Flo, following him in. 'We want to get inside in the warm.'

After a short while, Wilf reappeared, looking shaken. 'You need to prepare yourself, Polly,' he said quietly.

'What for?'

'There's someone in there . . . it will be a shock for you. I'm still trembling.'

'Who is it?' she asked, puzzled.

'I can't believe it myself.'

'Oh for goodness' sake, Dad,' she said, and walked past him into the living room.

When she saw who was standing there, she stopped in her tracks, staring in amazement.

'Hello, darlin',' he said.

'George?' Her voice was almost a whisper.

'There's no need to sound so surprised,' he said, coming over to her. 'You must have known I'd turn up sometime.'

'We thought you were dead,' she told him through dry lips, her heart racing. 'We had formal notification from the army to that effect.'

'You never did.'

'We did. The dreaded telegram.'

'Oh no. What an awful thing to happen. I shall have to have a few strong words with them about that. Upsetting people for no reason.' He sounded annoyed. 'I was captured at Dunkirk and was in a prison camp for the rest of the war.'

'Oh, George,' said Polly. 'How awful for you.'

'It wasn't good, but it's all in the past and I won't waste any time thinking about it. I'm home now, so come on, give us a kiss,' he said, putting his arms around her while the rest of the family looked on in disbelieving silence.

Chapter Nine

Polly's emotions were in turmoil following the shock of seeing her husband again so unexpectedly, but the prevailing feeling was guilt. The man she had once adored was home safe, and while he had been suffering in some hellhole of a prison camp, she had been falling in love with someone else. Now here he was, much thinner, but as cheerful as ever despite his terrible ordeal, and thrilled with his daughter, whom he was seeing for the first time.

'I'm your daddy so it's my job to look after you,' he told Emmie after the situation had been explained to her and there had been welcome-home hugs all round.

'Mummy and Gran do that,' she said.

'I'll be looking after you as well now that I'm home,' he said.

Polly was holding her breath for fear that Emmie would mention James. She would tell George herself when the time was right, but that definitely wasn't at this precise moment.

Her hopes were dashed when the little girl said, 'Like James did, you mean?'

The silence was palpable.

'James?' said George after a while.

'A family friend,' Flo intervened quickly. 'But I think we should leave Polly and George alone for a while to catch up. Come on, Wilf, I'll get Emmie ready for bed.'

'Thanks, Mum,' said Polly gratefully.

'So here you are,' said Polly awkwardly. George seemed like a stranger. The handsome face she remembered was still perceptible but had been altered by time and emaciation, his dark eyes seeming to protrude above his hollow cheeks. 'I'd like to say you look well, but you're so skinny now.'

'None of us got much to eat at the camp,' he told her in a matter-of-fact manner. 'We've been well fed since we were liberated, but I suppose it will take a bit more time to get back to normal. It isn't wise to overeat after a period of very little food, even though you may feel like making a pig of yourself.'

She nodded in agreement. 'I dread to think what you were like before liberation, then.'

'Let's not talk about that,' he said. 'I'm fine now and more interested in the future. So who is James? I don't buy the family friend thing.'

'He's a Canadian soldier I met at the Cherry Ballroom.'

'You've been out dancing then,' he said, without sounding judgemental. 'I can't say I blame you.'

She shook her head. 'No, I haven't been out dancing. I work there . . . in the ticket office.'

'You're working?' he said, seeming far more worried about that than the idea that she might have been out having fun.

'Yeah, I have two jobs actually,' she said and went on to explain. 'How else did you think I would manage?'

'I did worry about you but I was powerless to do anything about it,' he said. 'Anyway, now that I'm back, you won't need to work, because I'll take care of everything.'

While she would be glad to see the back of the typing job, the thought of not working at the Cherry with her aunt filled her with dismay. 'I'll need to carry on until you get a job though, won't I?' she said, suddenly aware of how much she had changed while he'd been away.

'I have a lot of back pay to come,' he said. 'That will see us through until I'm working again. Anyway, you know me. I won't hang about. I'll soon be bringing home the dosh again.'

'I do actually enjoy having a job, George,' she informed him. 'Especially the one at the Cherry Ballroom. And Mum is more than happy to look after Emmie while I'm out, so you wouldn't have to do anything. There's no reason why I can't carry on.'

'I'm the reason. I'm back now, Polly, and I shall take my rightful place as the breadwinner. No need for you to worry. You've done your bit and kept things going while I've been away and I admire you for it, but it's my responsibility now.'

'Actually, things have changed a bit while you've been gone, George,' she began. 'Married women have been working during the war and it's become more acceptable.' She didn't add that many of them had returned to the home as soon as the war was over.

'No wife of mine is going out to work,' he stated categorically. 'It's my job to keep you and Emmie and that's what I intend to do. So you won't have to worry any more now that I'm back.'

'I'll have to work my notice.'

'Yeah, all right, as long as it will only be for a short time,' he said casually. 'But why are we talking about work on my first night back? How about a kiss for your old man before we go and be sociable with your folks?'

As she went into his arms, she realised that the life she had made for herself was about to disappear, but instead of being delighted at the thought of not having to go out to work, she suddenly felt trapped.

'You'll need to go and see your gran, George,' said Polly when they were finally alone in bed after a chatty evening with her parents, helped along by a few bottles from the off licence and Mum feeding George up with her own brand of doorstep sandwiches and Victoria sponge. 'It will be a shock for her to see you alive and kicking after I told her you were dead. I'll go with you in case it's too much for her.'

'Gran's a tough old bird; she'll be all right, but it will be nice if you come.'

'I've visited her with Emmie every now and again while you've been away,' she told him.

'Is she okay?'

'Seems to be. She'll be even better when she knows that you're alive after all.'

'It's good of you to go over to the East End to see her,' he said. 'The journey's a bit of a drag.'

'I don't mind. I like your gran, and I want Emmie to know her. Anyway, it doesn't take very long on the tube.'

'Right, so now that you've got me up to date about Gran, you can tell me more about this Canadian soldier.'

'James and I were close for a while,' she told him without

hesitation; he deserved the truth. 'I thought you were dead, George. It wouldn't have happened otherwise.'

'It's all right, Pol. I'm not a jealous man. I've been away a long time. It's only natural you would meet someone else. So what's the situation between you now?'

'There isn't one,' she explained. 'He went back to Canada when the war ended.'

'Right, that's all I need to know. I don't want to hear anything else about him, what you did or how you felt about him. That way lies trouble. It's over and I'm back, so we move on from here, getting our life together back on track and looking to the future for the three of us. What do you say?'

'What else would we do, George?'

'Exactly,' he agreed. 'And although I'm not a jealous man, I am a proud one. It means a lot to me to support my family, so the sooner you pack your jobs in, the better I will like it.'

'Surely you wouldn't mind if I were to do a couple of nights a week at the Cherry?' she said. 'I'm not out long and Mum would continue to look after Emmie. You like to go to the pub of an evening anyway, as I remember, so you wouldn't even notice I was out.'

'It has nothing to do with that,' he told her firmly. 'It's all about me looking after my own family. You can have all the freedom you like. If you want to go out to the pictures with your mates, you won't hear me objecting, but I really don't want you to go out to work.'

What could she do? He was a decent man who wanted to provide for his family. 'All right, I'll see to it,' she said, feeling imprisoned and hating herself for it.

★　　★　　★

George was lying awake thinking. Despite what he'd said to Polly, he did mind about the Canadian soldier. It hurt him to think about it. But he daren't allow it to fester. While his rational side could understand why it had happened, his heart made him want to scream with the pain of imagining her with him. But he'd been through too much to waste a single moment looking back at something that couldn't be changed. The liaison was over and the man was on the other side of the world so no longer a threat.

The future for Polly, Emmie and himself was what mattered. He needed to get to know his daughter and reacquaint himself with his wife, who felt like a stranger after such a long time apart. He needed to think about practicalities, too. Earning a living and finding them a place to live. He had no intention of staying with his in-laws indefinitely.

He'd trained as a plumber so would go back to that once he was demobbed, which he'd been told would happen soon. Plumbing would never make him rich, but a bit of business on the side would pay for a good few extras. He needed to get out and about to find out if any of his old contacts were still around, and make new ones if not. Everything was in short supply, which meant good business for traders like him who operated outside of the usual channels. Strictly cash and no questions asked. After a little rest, recuperation and family time, he'd find out what was doing.

Meanwhile, there was something more important that he'd been dreaming of for nearly six years but was feeling nervous about after all this time. He turned towards his wife and moved closer to her, reaching out and waiting for her response . . .

★　　★　　★

'I'm very disappointed to be losing you, I won't deny it,' said Marian the following evening when Polly told her she would be leaving. 'But it's such good news about George being back. The army really dropped a clanger telling you that he was dead.'

'It's all down to the chaos of war, I suppose; mistakes are bound to happen with so much disruption. But he's going to have words about it and set the record straight.'

Marian nodded. 'How about you, kid? How does it feel having him back after all this time?'

'I'm pleased to see him, of course, but it will take a while for us to get used to each other again. He knows about James; Emmie blurted it out.'

'Ooh blimey.'

'I was going to tell him anyway in due course, but she went and said something so I had to explain right away,' said Polly. 'He was very good about it and it couldn't have been easy for him.'

'I suppose not,' agreed Marian. 'So you've got some adjusting to do, then, love?'

'I certainly have. I only hope I can make George happy after all he's been through. But I suspect it isn't going to be easy, because I've got used to being without him.'

'Will he be all right if you stay on here until I get a replacement?'

'I should think so, as long as it isn't for too long,' Polly said. 'He's got a real thing about being the breadwinner. I'll be glad to get shot of the typing job, but the Cherry has never felt like work to me. Still, I suppose it will be nice not having to rush off and leave Emmie of an evening.'

'I'm sure it will.'

'A lot of men are dead set against their wives working, aren't they? Almost as though it threatens their manhood somehow,' Polly remarked. 'Archie isn't like that, is he?'

'He could be, I think,' Marian said. 'He would willingly support me if I let him, bless him, but he can't make a big thing about it because we aren't married.'

'No. I always forget that,' Polly said. 'Would you like to be?'

'I'm quite happy as we are. I don't feel any the less devoted to him because we don't have a piece of paper. I love him to bits. He'd like us to be married, though. I only have to say the word and he'll have me down the registry office.'

'It would be nice for you, Auntie.'

'Yeah, very probably, but I won't get married just to be respectable,' she said. 'If something works, why change it?'

'But if you love him . . .'

'I've promised him I will do it one day when I feel it's right,' she said. 'Meanwhile, we're happy as we are.'

There was an air of finality about her tone, so Polly said, 'I hope the two of you will come over to see George sometime soon. I think he'd welcome the company.'

'I'll pop around tomorrow morning,' Marian said. 'Archie will be at work, but he can see him at the weekend.'

'Okay,' said Polly.

'You're still a handsome devil then, George,' said Marian the next morning when she called at the house.

'It's nice of you to say so, but I'm sure it isn't true.'

'Don't fish for compliments,' she said, smiling, but she was actually still trying to get used to his changed appearance. It wasn't just the loss of weight, though that was bad enough;

his eyes, which had once been so bright and lively, seemed to have lost their sparkle. 'But yeah, I would still fancy you if I was twenty years younger.'

'Trust you to lower the tone,' admonished Flo.

'Rubbish,' said Marian. 'George and I enjoy a joke, don't we?'

'We always did,' George agreed.

'Seriously, love, how are you?' she asked.

'Not so dusty, thanks,' he said.

'Well it's lovely to have you back,' she said, feeling slightly tearful. He must have gone through hell these past few years, but here he was with that same old grin, as though nothing much had happened to him. 'I hope Flo and the family are going to give you some spoiling.'

'They don't need to,' he said. 'Just being home is enough for me.'

'Ah bless you,' she said. 'I'll bring Archie around to see you on Sunday.'

'Your husband?'

'No,' Flo cut in disapprovingly. 'She lives with him, though, and gives us all a bad name.'

'Don't listen to her,' said Marian. 'At least I've got the grace to live in a different neighbourhood.'

'I look forward to meeting him,' said George tactfully.

'He's a similar type to you,' said Marian. 'Down-to-earth and enjoys a joke. I think you'll like him.'

'I'm sure I will.'

'Have you got the kettle on, Flo?' asked Marian. 'I could murder a cuppa.'

'Honestly, she comes around here, barking her orders,' muttered Flo with mock annoyance. 'Of course I've got the kettle on. When have you ever been to this house and not been given refreshment?'

'That's my girl,' said Marian, winking at George, who smiled broadly. 'Welcome home, son!'

Emmie thought it was great fun to have a dad, which wasn't surprising because he spoiled her something awful.

'You mustn't let her have her own way about everything, George,' admonished Polly one day in early spring when he had said yes to his daughter when her mother had said no. 'And you certainly shouldn't go against me. We need to be a united front or she'll run rings around us.'

'Sorry, Pol, but I just can't resist her,' he said. 'I've missed so many years with her, I don't want to be telling her off all the time.'

'And you don't have to be. Just don't give in to her every single time. Kids are artful little things and they like their own way. It's a natural part of being a child. We have to make sure we give her a balanced upbringing, and part of that is discipline. We don't want a spoiled brat on our hands.'

'I want her to like me.'

'She adores you, and that won't change if you learn to put your foot down now and again.'

'I'll try,' he said. 'But it's hard to refuse her anything.'

'I know it is, but if you want to do your best for her, you'll have to stop spoiling her; at least for some of the time. She's got you wrapped around her little finger. She needs discipline from both of us, not just me.'

'Righto.'

He had been back for a couple of months and Polly had

got used to her new life as a stay-at-home mum. She certainly didn't miss the typing job, but she couldn't say the same about the Cherry. When she'd worked there she'd felt in touch with things outside the home, which had added interest to her life, and she missed it. Still, it was nice not having to leave Emmie. Anyway, it was her duty to do what George wanted after what he'd been through.

He'd gone back to his trade as a plumber but had decided to go self-employed. He already had a full set of tools, and with his army back pay he'd bought a van and had placed a card advertising his services on various notice boards and in shop windows, where they also took messages for him. So far he'd been kept busy, so there was money coming in.

Of an evening he put on his suit and went out around the pubs renewing old contacts and making new ones. Plumbing was his bread-and-butter, trading his passion. Polly was never encouraged to ask about that part of his life so she waited for him to tell her, but he never talked about it in detail. Having got used to having her own money, it was hard for her to have to ask for what she needed. He was generous enough but she was no longer in control, and that felt odd. But she wasn't about to complain.

She tried to encourage him to talk about his time in the prison camp because she thought it might be good for him, but he never would; he said he wanted to look forward, not back, which she supposed was understandable. She guessed he'd had a hard time and thought he deserved the best life she could give him now that he was home.

She'd known within a very short time of his being back that she didn't love him in the same way as before. James had changed all that. But she did still have feelings for him and wanted to be a good wife. So she made a determined effort to dispatch James to the past and concentrate on her husband. Maybe spoil him a little after his wartime ordeal.

'Do you fancy a day out sometime soon?' he was saying now. 'You, me and Emmie.'

'Yeah, that would be nice. It'll be Whitsun soon,' she said. 'We could go somewhere on Bank Holiday Monday. The weather should have warmed up a bit by then.'

'That's settled, then,' he said. 'I'll look forward to it.'

'Me too.'

With sandwiches, swimming costumes and towels packed in a shopping bag, the three of them set off for Runnymede on the train.

'I think you're being a bit optimistic, bringing swimming costumes,' said George when they were settled in the carriage. 'It isn't very warm and there are a few dodgy-looking clouds floating about up there.'

'Optimism is the key word when dealing with the British weather,' Polly said. 'Anyway, Emmie insisted.'

'Who's giving in to her now?' he said jokingly.

'I only agreed to bring the costumes,' she said. 'I didn't promise that anyone would be swimming in the river.'

'Now you're just being clever,' he said.

'Kids don't seem to feel the cold when it comes to stripping off and getting in the water.'

'Can she swim?'

'Not yet,' Polly said. 'She'll be having swimming lessons with the school later on. They take them to the baths.'

'I'll have a go at teaching her if you like,' George said. 'I'm not bad in the water if I do say it myself. Well, I used to be all right. I haven't done any swimming since before the war.'

'All the better if you can teach her,' she said. 'Especially as we live so near the Thames. The sooner she learns, the better for her own safety.'

'I used to go to Runnymede with my mates when I was a lad,' he said reflectively.

'All the way from east London?'

'They do have trains there, you know,' he said. 'Anyway, me and the lads used to swim across the river to the other side. We used to have races. It was a right laugh.'

'Don't get any ideas of teaching Emmie to swim across,' Polly said, laughing.

'It'll be a good few years before she can do that,' George said.

'I could try,' Emmie piped up.

'You certainly cannot,' said Polly firmly. 'Absolutely not! You are not to go far from the bank.'

'All right, Pol,' said George. 'Don't get your knickers in a twist. I'll look after her.'

'I can swim too, so between the two of us I reckon our darling daughter will be safe.'

'Not half,' grinned George.

They had all suffered hardship over the last few years, so that the simplest pleasure felt like an immense treat. All the more so for George, who had known real deprivation. Polly felt a strong sense of empathy towards him and hoped the sun shone for him.

The bank holiday crowds were out in force in Runnymede meadow. Families with picnics, courting couples, groups of flirty young girls and boys, most of the youngsters in swimming costumes, despite the chilly breeze. People swarmed around the café at the entrance where Polly and George would go later on for the luxury of the day, a cup of tea and a cake. This field on the banks of the Thames between Windsor and Staines had been a magnet for day trippers from London for as long as Polly could remember.

Having found a spot on the grass and left their things as a sort of claim on it, the three of them headed for the wooden changing rooms and emerged in plain navy-blue swimming costumes, like most of the people around them.

'Can we go in the water?' said Emmie, jumping up and down excitedly.

'You two go on,' said Polly. 'I'll take the clothes back to our spot.'

When she eventually got to the riverbank, George and Emmie were already in the water, the latter squealing with delight as she splashed about. Father and daughter were totally engrossed in each other. Polly felt a pang as she thought of the years they had lost.

The bank was lined with people and there were a lot in the water, some in the shallows, others further out. Swimming to the other bank had always been popular here, and there were plenty of people doing it today.

'Ooh!' squealed Polly as the cold water went past her waist. 'It's freezing.'

'Not when you get used to it, and the sooner the better,' said George with a wicked grin before splashing her all over.

'You rotten devil,' she said, catching her breath and treating him to some of his own medicine, while Emmie screeched with laughter.

Polly stayed close to the bank with her daughter while George swam to the far bank and back to make sure he still could after all these years, then she went to their picnic spot and left them to it. Watching them enjoying themselves together brought a lump to her throat. It was so right for Emmie to be with her dad, and her daughter's happiness meant everything to her.

It hardly seemed possible that she had had a love affair with another man. George hadn't mentioned it since she'd told him about James. It was as though they had both erased it from their lives, except that she would never be able to do that. Sometimes she wondered how hurt George must have been by it. But he just carried on as though nothing had happened, which was obviously his way of coping.

The alternative would have been endless arguments, and separation or even divorce, which would have been traumatic for Emmie. So he'd buried it. Pretended it hadn't happened. Sometimes she wished he hadn't been so good about it. Maybe if he'd given her a hard time she would be able to forget it, or at least get it into perspective. It had been a romance born of war and separation, when she had thought she was a widow. It had never had a future because of the geography of the whole thing. She had known it wasn't going to be forever.

But she couldn't do what George had done and pretend it had never happened, because it had. She would never forget James and their time together; he had meant so much to her and still did if she allowed him into her thoughts. She had written to tell him that her husband had returned so she wouldn't be in touch again.

Her thoughts were interrupted when George and Emmie appeared, laughing and breathless.

'We've had such fun, Mum,' Emmie said as Polly wrapped her in a towel and dried her. 'Dad is a really good swimmer and he said that I will be soon. He's going to take me to the swimming baths and give me some lessons.'

She beamed at them both. She was so lucky to have them; to have this after what she had done to George.

In the afternoon, they went to the café for refreshments, then Polly started packing up their things. But Emmie had other ideas.

'I want to go in the water again,' she said.

'Not now, love,' said her mother. 'You've had enough for one day.'

'Please can I go back in?' she persisted.

'No,' said Polly firmly. 'Everything is packed up now. We'll have a game with the ball and then go home.'

'I'm going back in,' Emmie said defiantly, becoming tearful. She turned to her father. 'Daddy will let me, won't you, Dad?'

Polly met his eyes, daring him to go against her. She could see him weakening.

'No, Emmie,' he said firmly. 'You've had enough time in the water today. We'll come back another day.'

Now came the tears and the fury because she couldn't get her own way. 'It isn't fair,' she wailed, sounding like a spoiled brat. 'I want to go in the water.'

'Stop making that silly noise,' said Polly sternly. 'You're not a baby, so stop behaving like one.'

The child sniffed and snuffled, then raised the volume. People were looking at them disapprovingly.

'Emmie,' said George commandingly. 'That's enough.'

She looked at him as though he had betrayed her and cried even harder.

'Stop it,' he said. 'You've had a good day and we've done everything we can to make it nice for you, so stop that noise *now.*'

There was a bit more sniffling before Emmie's sobs gradually petered out. Polly exchanged a look with George, then wiped her daughter's face with a handkerchief and said kindly, 'That's better. Now shall we go and have a game with the ball before we go home? Would you like that?'

The little girl nodded, her eyes red and face blotchy. Within a few minutes, she was playing catch as though nothing had happened.

'It actually made me feel quite ill, telling her off like that,' George confessed to Polly on the train when Emmie had fallen asleep. 'In fact I'm still feeling a bit shaky, though she seems to have forgotten all about it.'

'That's kids for you,' she said. 'They tear your nerves to shreds then carry on as if nothing much has happened.'

'Are they all like that, then?'

'I'm no authority, but judging by other mums I've spoken to, you do have to take a firm hand every now and again. It's part of the job. She's a good kid really, but they all have their moments. She should be past the age for that sort of screaming fit, so it was probably just a one-off. But it's still a battle of wits whatever form their temper takes. Once they get the upper hand, you've no chance.'

'You make her sound like some sort of hardened criminal instead of a lovely little girl.'

She laughed. 'That's the last thing I intended,' she said. 'I love her more than words can say, but you're new to the parenting game so I'm taking you by the hand – so to speak.' She glanced at Emmie fast asleep on the seat between them. 'Just look at her. Butter wouldn't melt . . .'

'But we know different, don't we?'

'We certainly do,' she agreed, suddenly feeling close to him and enjoying the moment. 'But we wouldn't want to be without her, would we?'

'Never in a million years,' he said, reaching for his wife's hand.

Chapter Ten

It was Saturday night and there was a full house at the Cherry. Hearing the music from her office and humming along with it, Marian decided to go into the ballroom to assess the atmosphere. She liked to do this every so often, just to see if it felt right. She slipped in and made her way towards the crowded dance floor, where a quickstep was in progress to the tune of 'Blue Skies' and a cluster of couples were jiving near the band. Although most people were dancing, there were a few hopefuls standing around trying not to look too despondent.

The mood was lively and exciting but the raw emotion and frantic enjoyment of the war years was no longer evident. People had lived every moment as if it was their last back then. Thank God they didn't have to do that now, thought Marian. The Cherry was still sold out most nights, and always on a Friday and Saturday. They also now did a tea dance one afternoon a week. This attracted a more mature clientele and they didn't sell as many tickets as for the evening sessions, but they sold enough to make it worth their while putting on the event.

Marian missed having Polly around. They had a shared affection for the place. There had been several ticket clerks since her departure but none had any interest in the job and didn't stay long. It was simply a means of earning some extra cash to them, whereas Polly had felt like a part of the place.

There was no chance of getting her back because George remained dead set against her going out to work, a common feeling amongst men. The minute the war was over, it was back to the kitchen for their wives. Still, it was nice that Polly could be around for Emmie of an evening, and George didn't keep her short of money. He was doing well, apparently, with his plumbing business, but she guessed that his earnings were substantially boosted by his little sideline.

Although many people outwardly disapproved of the black market, it continued to thrive because everybody had gone without for so long and wanted luxuries again. Those who did business with spivs, often through a friend of a friend, weren't likely to spoil their access to a few treats by telling the police.

Marian didn't know for sure if George was involved but suspected that he might be, which was worrying because she'd read in the paper recently that the police were coming down hard on anyone dealing illicitly. She got the impression, though, that they were mainly interested in the big operators, whereas George was just small fry, dealing in luxury items such as cigarettes and nylons that were sold mostly through pubs or by word of mouth. There had always been something of the spiv about George, even before the war when things hadn't been short. If Polly was worried about his nocturnal activities, she hadn't said anything, but then she probably wouldn't because she was fiercely loyal.

Anyway, George was a hard worker and a good husband as far as Marian could tell. He was certainly an excellent father to Emmie, and very easy to like even if you did suspect that he might be up to no good. He'd been a little subdued for a while after his return from the war but seemed to be back to his old self now, full of unaffected charm. He must have had a hard time, by the very nature of the circumstances, but he never mentioned it and behaved as though he'd never been away.

Naturally she was pleased that George had turned up and he and Polly were reunited, but she couldn't help but feel sad that it was all over with James, whom she was personally rather fond of. She'd always felt she could trust him implicitly with her niece's happiness. He'd come across as an honest man of the soil who wouldn't know how to do a deal or talk someone into buying something. He would probably be somewhere respectable of an evening, not in a back-street pub with an eye on making a few shillings.

Still, his love affair with Polly had been doomed from the start because of the distance between them. Polly had rarely mentioned him since the day George got back, which was only right and proper. Her husband had given a large slice of his life for his country and he deserved a devoted wife.

'It's about time that husband of yours had a night at home with his wife,' said Flo to Polly one summer evening. 'He spends far too much of his time out at the pub.'

'He isn't doing any harm, love,' said Wilf, who had been for a pint himself earlier. 'A man needs to unwind after a day's work.'

'He doesn't need to stay until they close every night,' she came back at him.

'He's probably got talking and forgotten the time,' said Wilf with male loyalty.

'I don't mind him going out of an evening, Mum,' Polly said. 'Surely that's the important thing.'

'As his wife, you should mind,' her mother rebuked. 'Going for a quick pint is one thing, staying till closing time quite another. And he doesn't even go to the local like your dad.'

'I think his mates go to pubs in other parts of London,' said Polly, irritated by her mother, who became critical every time George was out past ten o'clock. 'Anyway, he doesn't go out until late so he isn't gone all that long, and he never comes home the slightest bit drunk. It must be the male company he enjoys.'

'That's all very well, but he's a married man and his place is at home with his wife of an evening.'

To sit here all night watching her mother knitting and not being allowed to speak when the wireless was on, and Mum ready to criticise him for the slightest thing: it was enough to send any man heading for the pub.

'Give it a rest, Flo, for Gawd's sake,' said Wilf. 'It isn't any of our business. It's between Polly and George.'

'I just don't think it's right, that's all,' Flo said. 'Anyway, he's living under our roof, which makes it our business.'

This stung Polly. When it was just herself and Emmie, living here had worked well enough. With George in the picture, making them a separate family unit, it didn't, and there wasn't a damned thing they could do about it because they had nowhere else to go. 'I'll make some cocoa,' she said, glad to leave the room.

*　　*　　*

'Do you have to stay out late every night, George?' Polly asked in the privacy of their bedroom that same evening. She was in her nightdress at the dressing table, putting cold cream on her face. He was already in bed. 'Mum has been having a real go about it again.'

'Oh blimey, has she? Sorry about that, love. I know she tends to go on a bit,' he said.

'You know me, George, I really don't mind you going out, but I do wish you didn't stay out so late, because it gives Mum cause to criticise and she doesn't half go on.'

'We need our own place so that we can come and go as we please,' he said.

'Don't we just. But many other young couples are in the same position and there's nothing we can do.'

'I'm not so sure about that. In fact, I've been trying to sort something out for us,' he told her. 'When I'm out of an evening I'm not aimlessly drinking, you know.'

'I know you don't drink much, George,' she said. 'But I don't see how you can do anything about our accommodation problem. There's a terrible housing shortage in London, so there isn't anything you or anyone else can do about it. With only one child, we're right at the bottom of the council housing list.'

'Bugger the council list,' he said. 'There is something you can do if you're prepared to pay key money.'

'Oh,' she said, sounding wary. 'I don't want you to do anything iffy.'

'There's nothing iffy about key money,' he said. 'It's quite common outside of council housing. And available if you know the right people.'

She had heard of people paying to get access to rented

accommodation and thought it sounded a bit suspect, but she didn't see how it could be illegal, not for the people who handed over the money, anyway.

'Can you afford it, then?' Polly knew nothing about her husband's finances but guessed he was doing well because he was always busy. He gave her whatever money she wanted without question and regularly asked if she needed more. But he did his own books as a self-employed person and kept that side of things to himself.

'Yeah, I can afford it, and I've got feelers out as regards a place for us,' he said. 'Just waiting for something suitable to come up.'

'We can't move out of the area, George, because of Emmie's school.'

'They do have schools outside of Hammersmith, you know,' he laughed.

'No need to be sarky,' she said. 'I don't want her to have to change schools when she's settled and happy where she is. It wouldn't be fair.'

'All right, I'll bear that in mind,' he told her. 'Now are you coming to bed or are you going to spend the whole night putting cream on your face?'

She threw a book at him.

'Ooh, I love a bedroom fight,' he said, laughing as he dodged the missile. 'They always have such happy endings. Shall we do it with pillows, though? It might be safer.'

'Just for that, I might go and sleep next door with Emmie,' she said, but of course, she didn't.

True to his word, George did find them somewhere to live: a small Victorian terraced house a few streets away from her parents. It had two bedrooms, a good-sized living room and kitchen, and a small bathroom built on at the back. It wasn't a palace but it felt like one to Polly, as it was the first time she'd ever had a home of her own.

With the help of George's contacts, which he seemed to have in every line of business, they were able to furnish it quite cheaply. Mostly second-hand stuff, but at least they were comfortable. Polly adored looking after it and making it cosy. It was such a joy having privacy and not being in the firing line of her mother's disapproval of George.

As the autumn came in with its glorious colours and smoky scents, the little house began to look and feel like home. Emmie got to know the local children and played outside with them. Polly, who had never had a chance to cook because her mother had always done it, learned some culinary skills.

She cooked and cleaned, made cakes and pies, and became acquainted with the mothers of Emmie's friends. She became the perfect housewife whilst all the time pretending that this was all she had ever wanted.

'You've got it looking lovely, Polly,' said Marian one Sunday when the family were invited to tea. 'A proper little palace, isn't it, Archie?'

'Very nice,' he agreed.

'They're doing well,' said Flo, who might not agree with George's pub-going ways but who was pleased that her daughter had a nice home.

'She's got something to help her keep it shipshape now, haven't you, love?' said George.

'We've got a vacuum cleaner,' Emmie chipped in proudly.

Polly nodded, smiling. 'Come and have a look,' she said, and they all trooped into the kitchen.

Out came the shiny new appliance and a demonstration was given.

'Oh, isn't that smashing,' said Marian. 'It must save hours of cleaning time. I wish we had one.'

'I can get you one at a reasonable price,' said George.

She gave him a close look. 'I don't want anything dodgy.'

'Would I sell you anything dodgy?' he said with a sparkle in his eye.

'I don't know the answer to that, George.'

'I get them from a bloke who deals in bankrupt stock,' he said. 'All legit.'

'I'd be interested if the price was right,' she said.

'I'll bring one for you to have a look at if I can get hold of one. No obligation to buy.'

'All right,' she agreed.

'What about you, Flo?' he asked.

'I'm quite happy with my broom and brushes, thank you,' his mother-in-law said primly.

George gave her a sharp look, then shrugged. 'If you change your mind, just let me know.'

'If I do, I'll get one from a shop.'

'You'll pay a lot more.'

'At least I'd know it was above board.'

He gave her a studious look, then shrugged and said, 'Fair enough, Mrs P.'

Marian was examining the object closely. 'You're the only person I know who has one of these, Polly,' she said excitedly.

'Not many people have got one yet,' said Polly. 'But they soon will, I reckon.'

'That would embarrass me, being the only one in the street to have something,' said Flo prudishly. 'People will think you're showing off.'

'I don't walk up and down the street with it, Mum,' said Polly, laughing. 'Or drag people in to have a look. In fact, I don't usually mention it.'

'What about tea, Polly?' said her father, hoping to avoid further criticism from his outspoken wife.

'Yeah, of course, Dad,' she said, and they all went back into the living room for a tea of fish-paste sandwiches, an eggless sponge and an apple tart with margarine pastry, even though the war had been over for nearly a year and a half. But thanks to George, there was one treat: a tin of pineapple chunks. Oh the joy at that tea table!

George was enjoying the praise for their home and was proud of Polly, who had worked such wonders with it. All this didn't come easy, though. He had to put in long hours to get the dosh and he was tired most of the time. But he had a plan. As soon as he was sure he could make enough from his sideline, he was going to ditch the plumbing job. He didn't want to be crawling about under people's sinks and mending leaks for the rest of his life. He'd only done the training because his gran had said he needed to get a trade when he left school.

Business was his forte. Buying and selling gave him a thrill, and with things being so scarce, there was an extra buzz in finding something to offer. Contacts were the answer, and he had those: a few from before the war, others he'd found since he'd been back. Being in a suit and tie boosted his confidence, and he'd always been able to talk his way into people's confidence. There was no shortage of buyers, either.

He liked to think he was a fair man by his own standards. He would never knowingly cheat anyone. Obviously, to make a living you couldn't worry too much about the source of the goods. These were hard times, and people were hungry for luxuries. They deserved them, too, after years of austerity. So someone like him with a bit of nous and plenty of front could earn a reasonably good living.

There were a lot of wide boys in the game who fancied themselves as hard men, so he had to watch his back. But after what he'd been through in the camp, it would take more than a few spivs to scare him. He wanted the good life for himself and his family, so it was worth taking a few risks. This little house was just the beginning. One day he'd have a big house with a car on the drive and the best of everything inside. Oh yes, he could see it all as clear as day.

The downside of his current lifestyle was that, apart from Sundays, which he always tried to take off, he was hardly ever home to enjoy the comfortable life he was providing. Fortunately Polly was very understanding and didn't seem to mind him being out of an evening. Maybe she didn't want him around because she was still hankering after the Canadian. No, he mustn't think about that. He'd promised himself he wouldn't. The only way forward was to pretend it had never happened, and he could for most of the time. It was just that sometimes it slipped into his mind and he felt this little pain in his heart.

Polly and Emmie were everything to him. He'd been surprised at how much he enjoyed being a dad. It had seemed to come naturally even though he'd never had much to do with kids since he'd been one himself. But from the minute he'd set eyes on his daughter he'd been enslaved to her. So he had a lot to be thankful for and he certainly wasn't going to let thoughts of some wartime romance of his wife's spoil their golden future together.

James was in the farm truck, driving across the wide-open plains of Ontario on his way to get a part for his tractor. It was almost a hundred-mile round trip, though this was nothing in this part of the world, where they would drive for an hour just to borrow something from a neighbour. It was a beautiful landscape: mile upon mile of lush farmland and not a soul in sight; just cattle grazing in some of the fields.

His thoughts turned to Polly, as they so often did, and he thought how lost a town girl like her would be in a place like this. It had been unrealistic of him ever to have imagined bringing her home as his wife, and selfish too. Anyway, he'd had a letter from her to say her husband had come back from the war after all, so that really did demolish the dream.

He still wasn't going to forget about her, though, and his time in England was something he looked back on with great affection. He had loved London. Despite the bomb damage and the shabbiness of everything, he had felt the beating heart of the place. Of course, during his time there it had been full of servicemen from all over the world, which had made it an exciting place to be. Then there was the Cherry Ballroom, throbbing with life and fun and romance. He would never forget that last visit on New Year's Eve, when he'd said goodbye to Polly.

He would be forever grateful to Polly and her family for their hospitality. They'd had so little, what with everything being rationed, but what they'd had they'd shared with him. They were plain-speaking people who didn't go in for frilly speeches but were full of heart. He still corresponded with Marian, as they had planned, and he valued the contact enormously.

But now he was driving into civilisation, so he turned his mind to his business here. Polly didn't disappear from his thoughts altogether, though. He doubted if she ever would.

'Why aren't we going to Great-Grandma's in Daddy's van?' asked Emmie when she and her parents were on the tube on their way to visit George's grandmother. 'I like going out in that; it's good fun.'

'There isn't enough room when there are three of us,' explained George.

'I could have gone in the back,' suggested his daughter.

'You'd get dirty sitting among all my plumbing gear,' said George, though he was actually more concerned about her prying fingers discovering the other things he had in the van. He'd moved up a notch with his trading and knew that Polly wouldn't approve. 'Anyway, I don't have enough petrol coupons for pleasure trips.'

'I didn't think getting extra petrol coupons was a problem for you with all your contacts,' Polly said.

'I'm not a magician, you know,' he replied. 'I can't just produce things out of thin air.'

'It seems like you can sometimes,' she said with a wry grin. 'What with your tins of fruit and your nylons.'

'It takes a lot of hard graft to get that stuff,' he said. 'I don't just wave a magic wand.'

Emmie thought this was hilarious and giggled. 'It would

be good if you did, Dad,' she said. 'You could change me into a princess.'

'You're already a princess to me, darlin',' he said, smiling warmly. 'Which is just as well, because I'm not a magician and I can't produce petrol coupons at will, so you'll have to make do with the train.'

'All right, Dad,' she said.

When they emerged from the station, the contrast with the landscape where they had boarded the train was extreme. West London was shabby enough since the war, and had its share of damage and bomb sites, but here it was far worse. The houses that had survived the terrible bombing were old, close together and dingy. Washing was strung across the narrow streets, where children played happily, unconcerned about their surroundings.

'Nothing changes for the better around here,' said George as they walked to his grandmother's house.

'I don't think it's changed for the better anywhere since the war,' said Polly. 'It certainly hasn't where we live.'

'This place doesn't just need doing up,' he said. 'It needs knocking down and rebuilding.'

'Your gran wouldn't agree with you about that,' she said. George's grandmother loved where she lived and wouldn't move from the East End under any circumstances. George had been brought up around here after his parents had died of TB when he was little. He had left when he and Polly got married, but his gran wasn't keen to follow.

'You're right there,' he said.

'The place does have a certain feel about it, though,' Polly said. 'A kind of homeliness.'

'Oh yeah, there's bags of community spirit. Gran knows

everybody and is never lonely. I've told her that it's still London where we live and people are just as friendly, but she reckons there's nothing to match the East End and says she's too old to move now.'

'That's understandable,' said Polly thoughtfully. 'Isn't it amazing what a difference a ride on the tube can make?'

There was a strong family likeness between George and his grandmother, Bess. She had the same dark eyes and olive skin; a handsome woman even though her hair was now streaked with grey and her face feathered with lines.

She gave them all a warm welcome, then George presented her with a couple of tins of salmon and a large parcel containing several packs of cigarettes. 'A present for you,' he said.

'Oh lovely! What a treat. Ta very much, George.' She gave him a sharp look. 'I hope you're not mixing with dodgy types to get this sort of thing.'

'Course not, Gran,' he lied.

'You be careful,' she said. 'I know you didn't get it from the Co-op, and there are some wicked types selling stuff through the back door. You concentrate on your plumbing business. It's a good honest trade.'

'Shall I take it back then?' he said.

'No, don't do that,' she said quickly. 'I just want you to be careful.'

'I am, Gran,' he assured her.

Bess turned to Polly. 'I'd never smoked a fag in my life until the Blitz. Now I can't stop. Totally dependent on them.'

'You won't be the only one,' said Polly. 'Lots of people turned to cigarettes to help their nerves during the bombing.'

'Thank God it's all over, eh?'

'I'll say.'

'Shall we have some tea?'

'Yes please, Great-Grandma,' said Emmie sweetly.

'Ah, hasn't she got lovely manners?' said Bess, smiling at the little girl. 'Remind me to give your mum my sweet coupons for you.'

'You mustn't do that,' said Polly. 'You'll have none left for yourself.'

'That won't worry me, love,' she said. 'As long as I can have a smoke, I've no need for humbugs.' She turned to George. 'Now promise me you won't get too involved with whoever you get the fags from. We all know that stuff goes on and people are only too eager to buy from people like you, but you need to be careful.'

'It's just a few bits and pieces, Gran,' he assured her.

'He's promised me that's all it is,' said Polly.

'I'm glad to hear you're keeping him on the straight and narrow, dear,' Bess said.

'George is his own man; he does what he wants, no matter what I say,' Polly pointed out.

'Yeah, he knew his own mind from a very early age,' said Bess thoughtfully. 'Anyway, let's have that tea, shall we? It's all ready.'

'Have we got seed cake, Great-Grandma?' asked Emmie.

'Yeah. I made one specially because I know you like it,' Bess said fondly.

'Thank you, Great-Grandma,' said Emmie.

The visit was so enjoyable, it was dusk when they left.

'Straight to bed for you when we get in, young lady,' Polly

said to Emmie on the train. 'Or we'll never get you up for school in the morning.'

'We should have left earlier,' said George.

'I intended to,' said Polly. 'But your gran is so nice, the time just flew by.'

'Yeah, she's a dear lady and means the world to me. She's so cheerful.'

'Must have been fun having her bring you up.'

'She was very good to me and we had plenty of laughs, but she was strict when she needed to be,' he said. 'I had to do what I was told.'

'Mm, I'm sure,' said Polly. 'She still tells you what to do even now, but I agree with her about the stuff you bring home. You do need to be careful.'

'Yeah, yeah,' he said in a tone that indicated he wouldn't take the slightest bit of notice.

While Polly had made several friends in her street and at the school gate, there was no one she felt she could talk to without having it repeated around the neighbourhood. Sometimes she felt she needed someone to confide in, and she found herself in that position one late afternoon a few weeks after the visit to George's gran. She'd been doing some shopping and happened to be passing the Cherry on her way home when she stopped, thought for a moment, then headed for the staff entrance.

'Hello, Polly.' Her aunt greeted her warmly in her office. 'What are you doing here?'

'I fancied a chat and I know you always come in to work a few hours before opening,' Polly explained.

'I like to get up to date with the admin before we open, while it's quiet,' Marian said.

'It was thoughtless of me to just barge in when you have work to do.'

'In case you've forgotten, I'm the manager here. So there's no one standing over me with a big stick.'

'You still need to get on, though,' Polly said. 'I know, because I used to work here, remember?'

'As if I would ever forget,' Marian said. 'I wish you still did, but I know that isn't going to happen.'

'Afraid not,' Polly confirmed. 'George is adamant about it. I do miss it, I must admit, but I concentrate all my energy into making a nice home instead.'

'I suppose I might feel differently about working if I didn't enjoy the job so much, though sometimes I think it would be nice to be at home of an evening with Archie. I might try and get another night off during the week. I don't want to push my luck, though. They already put a relief manager in one evening so I don't have to come in.'

Polly nodded, but she was clearly distracted.

'What's on your mind, love?' Marian asked. 'I know there's something.'

'How can you tell?'

Marian grinned. 'I just can,' she said. 'So get it off your chest, kid, before I have to get back to work.'

'It's George.'

'I hope he's treating you right.' Marian looked concerned. 'I shall have something to say to him if he isn't.'

'He's very good to Emmie and me,' Polly said. 'But I think he might be involved with the wrong people and he'll end up in trouble.'

'The stuff he brings home?'

She nodded. 'And the way he lives his life. He's permanently shattered. He's up early and working all day in a physically demanding job. As if that isn't enough, he's out nearly every night and home late. He'll ruin his health if he carries on like this.'

'You don't think it might be another woman keeping him out at night?'

'Oh no, nothing like that,' Polly said with confidence. 'It's definitely work.'

'I didn't really think he'd do anything like that,' Marian said. 'I was just making sure.'

'That would be easier to cope with than thinking of him mixing with all these dodgy types.'

'How do you know they're dodgy?'

'Well you don't get respectable types hanging around pubs every night, selling stuff, do you?'

'I'm not so sure about that,' said Marian. 'Many a respectable type has turned out to be a rogue. You only have to read the papers to know that. Anyway, George does it and we don't think of him as a villain, do we? He's a small-time trader who enjoys the buzz of business, that's all. The other blokes he mixes with are probably just the same.'

'I suppose they might be.'

'Why don't you just tell him that you don't like him being out all the time so he needs to change his ways?' she suggested. 'Perhaps he can go out a bit less often of an evening. Maybe get a few more early nights so that he doesn't feel so tired all the time.'

'Yeah, I'd like that,' said Polly. 'It isn't that I mind him being out. Just that I'm worried he's going to get into trouble or make himself ill.'

'Tell him, love.'

'I hate to nag him, Auntie,' she confessed. 'He came home from the war to find out that I'd had a love affair with another man, and he accepted it and has never once given me a hard time about it.'

'He realises that you didn't know he was still alive, though, doesn't he?'

'Of course he does. Even so, it must have hurt him dreadfully, but he's never shown any sort of resentment whatsoever. I think that takes some doing.'

'I agree with you. But that doesn't mean you have to be forever beholden to him,' said Marian. 'He wouldn't want that.'

'Mm. You're right,' said Polly. 'I really must tell him what's on my mind, but I'll have to choose my time. He's usually dead tired when he gets home.'

'It needs doing, though, and the sooner the better,' said Marian. 'Now on your way and let me get on with my work.'

'Thanks for the chat, Auntie. You've helped me to clear my mind.' She paused. 'Oh, and not a word to Mum about it. I don't want to give her an excuse to have a go at George. She doesn't need any encouragement.'

'I can imagine,' said Marian. 'But don't worry, she won't hear it from me.'

Polly believed her. Her aunt was the person she trusted most in the world. She knew she would never let her down.

On impulse on her way out, Polly poked her head into the ballroom. She was shocked at how different it was without all the elements that created the magic: the coloured lights, the music, the noise and excitement of the people. Without those things it was simply a large hall with a sprung floor and a stage. It really was rather eerie. She closed the door and hurried on her way.

Chapter Eleven

As it happened, Polly was forced to speak her mind to George a few nights later, when he came home late with his face showing evidence of a beating.

'Right, that's it,' she said sternly as she dabbed his cuts with iodine. 'It's time for you to give up this dodgy business you're involved in. It's getting dangerous now.'

'Don't be so dramatic, Pol,' he said. 'I tripped on an uneven paving stone and fell flat on my face, that's all. It's about time the council did something about the state of the streets.'

'Do you really think I'm stupid enough to believe that?' she came back at him fiercely. 'Someone has given you a pasting. I want you out of that world. Go out for a pint at the local of an evening or stay at home like any other married man. Keep away from the thugs you're mixing with.'

'I told you, I fell over,' he insisted. 'That's what comes of having one too many.'

'One too many, my foot. You're stone-cold sober, so stop taking me for a fool. You've upset someone in that seedy crowd you hang out with and they've retaliated with violence. Keep away from them, George, please.'

'All right, so I didn't fall over, but I'm not giving it up, not when it's all going so well,' he said stubbornly. 'It's only a few bruises. Nothing I can't handle.'

'But what will it be next time?' she asked. 'Broken legs, or worse? No, George, I'm not having it. I'm an undemanding sort of wife, but I can't put up with this.'

'You'd miss the treats I bring home if I were to give it up.'

'I won't deny it,' she said, washing her hands. 'But we can manage perfectly well without them. You have a good little plumbing business. All the rest is just greed.'

If only she knew how much he loathed the plumbing job. The thought of doing deals at night got him through the day as he worked with his tools under someone's sink. She was right: there was an element of danger attached to his sideline, but that didn't frighten him enough to make him want to give it up. If anything, it gave the whole process an added edge.

'It isn't just greed, Pol,' he said. 'Not at all. I really enjoy it. I've always liked a spot of trading; even as a schoolboy I used to double my pocket money by selling my sweets for a profit.'

'So you enjoy getting beaten up, do you?'

'Of course not, but it doesn't scare me.'

'Then it damn well should,' she said. 'You're a married man with a child. You shouldn't be putting yourself in danger.'

'There's no need to make such a big drama of it, Polly,' he said, peeved. 'They're not gangsters; just blokes with a bit of savvy making a few bob on the side.'

'Why did it happen?' she demanded.

'There are people out there who want all the business for themselves, so they send their hired help out to warn off newcomers like me,' he told her.

'So take heed of the warning and keep well away,' she advised. 'In fact, I've been meaning to speak to you about this for a while. Even apart from the danger, doing the two jobs is ruining your health. Your body was given enough of a hard time in the prison camp. Show it some respect now instead of abusing it.'

'I'm not prepared to give up my sideline, Pol,' he stated categorically. 'In fact I've been thinking of getting rid of the plumbing to spend more time on the other business.'

'Oh, George,' she cried, horrified. 'How can you even consider such a thing? You've been trained in a proper trade. You're providing a service. People will always need plumbers.'

'I hate it, Pol. I only became a plumber because Gran wanted me to learn a trade when I left school. I've had enough of crawling about unblocking sinks and mending pipes.'

'There must more to it than just fixing leaks.'

'Well yeah, there is, of course, but I still find it boring.'

Polly had had experience of work she didn't enjoy when she'd been in the typing pool, so she knew the feeing. 'Surely there must be some sort of job satisfaction when you mend something that only someone with your training can do.'

'Not for me,' George said.

'But tradesmen are usually so proud of their skills.'

'I know that, but I'm not. I'd rather be out of overalls altogether, and that's what I intend to do in the not-too-distant future.'

'You can't really be serious.'

'That's the plan,' he confirmed. 'Business is what I'm good at. I have to keep my wits about me and I enjoy that.'

'But you must be good at plumbing too, or else people wouldn't recommend you.'

'That's true, I suppose, but my heart isn't in it,' he said. 'I get no enjoyment from working with my hands all day. I suppose I can't be a true tradesman or I'd be proud of my work. I know some who are and I admire them for it, but it isn't for me.'

'So I don't have a say in this, then?'

'When it comes to earning a living, I think I'm the best judge, don't you?'

'But it affects all our lives, George.'

'When I give up the plumbing I'll be around more during the day, which will be better for us all,' he pointed out. 'I'll be home when Emmie gets in from school. I'll have more time to spend with you both.'

'I'm not concerned about you being at home more,' she tried to explain. 'I want you to be out of danger.'

'You don't half exaggerate, Pol,' he said with a wry grin. 'A sore lip and a couple of bruises, that's all it is. There isn't any serious danger. These people aren't gangsters. Just blokes who think they're tough.'

'So you're not going to give it up, even though it really upsets me?'

He looked at her shining blue eyes and blond hair and was reminded that he was a lucky man to have her as his wife, especially as he might have lost her to the Canadian. She and Emmie meant absolutely everything to him, but he just couldn't resign himself to plumbing for the rest of his life. It would make him miserable and that would affect them all.

'Sorry, Pol,' he said. 'You know I'd do almost anything for you. But not this.'

'Right,' she said angrily. 'In that case, I want nothing more to do with it. I want no more treats coming into this house. No chocolate, tinned fruit, nylons or cigarettes. Nothing that isn't bought from a shop. From now on, what you do is your business, but keep it away from this family. I should never have gone along with it in the first place.'

'Now you're just being daft.'

'No. I've come to my senses, that's all.'

'You'll be the loser without those little extras.'

'I'm willing to put up with that,' she told him. 'And I don't want to hear any more about it. Not a single word. Ever! Not unless it's to tell me that you've given it up.'

He shrugged.

'But come here and let me do something about that cut above your eye,' she ordered. 'It needs a bit more attention.'

She was an awesome woman in this mood and he had no plans to challenge her, not about the first aid anyway.

Polly was shaking inwardly after the argument with George and absolutely furious that he wouldn't give up his nasty little business. Of course she enjoyed the extras but she'd had to take a stand. The truth was, she was frightened by it. At first it had been all right, when he had just been bringing home the odd bar of chocolate or tin of fruit. She supposed she had begun to worry when the vacuum cleaner had appeared because it had indicated that he was moving into bigger things. He claimed that he wasn't breaking the law, that it was all just bankrupt stock, but she wasn't sure if he was being truthful about that.

She felt so helpless. He wouldn't stop his dodgy dealing, and there wasn't a damned thing she could do about it except refuse to have the stuff in the house.

He appeared by her side on the sofa. 'There's nothing for you to worry about, love,' he said. 'I'll be absolutely fine, I promise.'

'I won't change my mind,' she stated. 'None of it comes into this house, so there's no point in your trying to soft-soap me.'

'I wouldn't dream of it,' he said. 'But I don't want you to stay up half the night fretting.'

'In that case you should stop dealing in questionable goods.'

'Look,' he began, artfully steering the conversation on to safer ground, 'why don't you and me have a night out sometime soon; let's go out dancing like we used to. I'll ask your mum to sit with Emmie.'

'You think a night out will make everything all right?'

'Of course not,' he said. 'But I do think it will do us both good. It'll be a laugh, Pol.'

'But you're working every night.'

'So I'll take a night off and we'll go to the Cherry if you fancy it,' he suggested.

She wasn't in the mood to be enthusiastic about anything, but she thought perhaps a night out dancing might remind her that she was still a young woman and not just a nagging wife who apparently had no influence over her husband.

'All right,' she said. 'We'll get it organised.'

'I think you've been hard on yourself rather than him, banning all the extras from the house,' said Marian a day or two later. She had called in on her way to work for a quick chat and Polly had told her all about George's injuries and the ensuing argument.

'I had to make some sort of a stand, didn't I?' she said.

'Maybe, but I can't see what it will achieve.'

'It will show him that I seriously disapprove of what he's doing and I'm not just going on at him to be awkward.'

'Mm, I realise that,' Marian said. 'But George is a wide boy, not a criminal.'

'What's the difference?' Polly said.

'He doesn't go out stealing or beating people up. He just buys and sells.'

'The goods he deals in might be nicked.'

'All right, so the stuff doesn't come from Harrods with a sales receipt,' Marian said. 'We don't know for sure where it does come from, so we don't ask questions. Everybody knows it goes on and quite a few law-abiding people wouldn't say no to something nice for Sunday tea. It's the world we live in, Polly. Luxuries are scarce and people are fed up with it.'

'But he got beaten up, Auntie,' Polly pointed out. 'That's the sort of people he's mixing with.'

'I know it's worrying for you, love, but it was just a cut lip and a black eye, you said.'

'Isn't that bad enough?' Polly said, her voice rising. 'Anyway, what will it be the next time? They want him out and he won't go, so there's bound to be one.'

'You can't live your life worrying about what might happen,' advised Marian kindly. 'We had enough of living in fear during the war. George is a tough bloke. He can look after himself.'

'Why are you taking George's side?' asked Polly. 'I had the impression that you thought I should somehow find a way to be with James.'

'To be perfectly honest, I think James was right for you, but he's on the other side of the world. For all his faults, you are married to George, so your loyalties lie with him,' said Marian. 'George is what he is. A chancer with big ideas. He isn't a bad man but he's never going to settle for being a plumber. He likes the thrill of making a few bob too much. I think you'll save yourself a whole lot of heartache if you accept him as he is.'

'He wasn't like this when I first met him,' Polly said. 'He was quite happy as a plumber then. He always had an eye to make a few coppers on the side, but nothing like he does now. His day job was important to him then.'

'It's a different world,' said Marian. 'We can only guess what horrors he went through during the war. Now he has come home and seen a chance to make a few shillings, and has grabbed it with both hands. He's tasted success, or his idea of it, and there's no going back from that for him. I think it will be better for all three of you if you accept that. You don't have to like it, but you can't spend your life arguing with him over it.'

'I suppose you're right,' Polly agreed with reluctance. 'Anyway, he's suggested that we have a night out on our own, so we're going to the Cherry.'

'That's the best news I've heard in ages,' Marian said. 'Dress up and enjoy yourself and forget all about George's line of work.'

'I'll try,' Polly said.

'I'm a bit rusty at this dancing lark,' said George as they quickstepped rather clumsily around the floor to the popular song 'Five Minutes More'.

'I don't suppose they had many dances in the prison camp, did they?' Polly said with irony.

He laughed. 'Not too many, no,' he replied in the light-hearted way in which he reacted to any mention of his time away. Polly had accepted that they would never know much about it.

'You're doing quite well, anyway,' she said.

'The old place hasn't changed,' he observed. 'Except for all the jiving they do now up near the band. Inherited from the Americans, I presume.'

'That's right, and hooray to them I say.'

'Can you do it, then?'

'I've got a bit of an idea.'

The Canadian probably taught her, he thought, but he didn't ask. 'This place could do with a lick of paint,' he said instead.

'Like every other building in London.'

'Still, you don't notice it with the lights and the music, do you?' he said. 'At least we didn't used to when we came before the war. I can still remember the night you and I met, Polly. You stood out from all the other girls.'

'Flatterer,' she said.

'They were good times, weren't they, love?'

'Oh yeah, we had a high old time,' she said with honesty. At the time it had been wonderful. Back then she had thought George was the only man for her.

'We can again,' he said, moving away from her slightly to look at her. 'We should go out more often.'

Not here, she thought. All she could think of here was James and the last time she had seen him, but she said, 'Yeah, why not. We could go to the pictures sometimes. Or even to the West End for a meal out.'

'Yeah, I'd like that. I'll take time off and be at home more often of an evening.' He smiled at her. 'We're going to be all right, you and me, Pol.'

'Of course we are,' she said. He was making an effort, so she would too.

★   ★   ★

208

'Hello, you two lovebirds,' said Marian, approaching them as they came off the floor. 'Enjoying yourselves, I hope.'

'Not half,' said George. 'I'd forgotten how much I like a turn around the floor.'

'Well now that you've remembered, you must come again, and don't leave it too long.'

'We certainly won't,' he said. 'This place is full of memories for us, isn't it, Pol?'

'I'm sure it is,' said Marian, but she couldn't help but think, rather sadly, that he probably didn't feature in all of Polly's reminiscences.

When Polly, George and Emmie arrived for Sunday tea at Polly's parents the next day, Flo looked at George expectantly, surprised that he appeared to have come empty handed.

'No treat for us today, George?' she said.

George looked at his wife rather sheepishly, then said to Flo, 'You'd better ask your daughter.'

Flo looked questioningly from one to the other.

'His dubious stuff is banned from our house, but it's up to you what you do,' Polly explained.

'She wants me to give it up and just be a plumber.'

'Well that's between you two,' said Flo. 'The extras are certainly not banned from this house. So what have you got in that van of yours, George?'

'A tin of peaches?'

'Lovely,' beamed Flo. 'I've got some evaporated milk.' She looked at her daughter. 'You don't have to have any if you disapprove. But you didn't turn your nose up at the vacuum cleaner, as I remember.'

'I hadn't thought about it properly then,' Polly said. 'Anyway, you were very sniffy about it at the time. You turned your back on a vacuum cleaner but now you're asking him for stuff.'

'Only food,' Flo said. 'That we all share.'

'A principle is a principle, Mum.'

'So I bend the rules a little.' She turned to George. 'Go and get the goodies, then.'

He looked at his wife. 'I wouldn't dare to disobey my mother-in-law,' he said, making light of it to avoid a scene developing.

'You'd better get on with it then, hadn't you?' said Polly.

'Honestly, all this fuss over a flaming tin of peaches,' said Flo. 'Anyone would think he'd broken into the Co-op and stolen the damned things.'

'He hasn't sunk that low yet,' said Polly.

'You'd think I was Al Capone the way she carries on,' George said as a parting shot, then went outside to his van.

'You shouldn't be so hard on him, Polly,' admonished Flo. 'Not over these small items he gets hold of anyway. A tin of fruit or a packet of ciggies cheers people up. Not many would say no to either.'

'He's mixing in bad company to get the stuff and I'm afraid he might get hurt,' Polly said. She didn't mention that he already had been because she didn't want to worry her mother.

'Oh, I see.' Flo thought for a moment. 'George is a strong bloke. He can look after himself, love.'

'Yeah, I'm sure he can,' Polly said, not wishing to pursue the subject. 'I'm probably worrying over nothing.'

'I think you probably are,' agreed Flo.

★   ★   ★

Things were better between Polly and George. He was at home more often in the evenings so Polly felt as though they were closer to being a normal family. He still went out some nights and she knew he was doing business, but he was making an effort for the sake of their marriage and she didn't want to make more demands on him after what he'd been through. On top of that, her conscience still bothered her about James from time to time.

'Have you brought me any sweeties, Daddy?' asked Emmie one evening when he came in.

George looked at his wife.

'There are some coupons here,' said Polly quickly. 'Daddy will take you to the sweet shop and you can choose what you want.'

'Goody!' whooped Emmie. 'I love looking at all the jars and choosing what to have.'

'Come on then, sweetheart,' said George cheerfully. 'Let's go and see what they've got.'

Polly hated to deprive her daughter of anything but felt she would be guilty of double standards if she accepted George's stock into the house. So she used her own sweet coupons for Emmie and queued for ages at the shops for any treat she heard about. She was confident that their little family could survive without questionable extras. With plenty of effort from both herself and George they would be all right.

One evening in November, George was sitting at a table in the corner of a pub in Paddington, drinking his beer and reflecting. He'd just completed a nice bit of business and the gear was in the van, so he would finish his drink and then leave.

His dream of being able to give up the day job had been

put to one side for the moment, which was a huge disappointment to him. He couldn't yet make quite enough from his sideline to put his tools away. You had to be out there and in the know, not playing happy families at home. But his marriage had to come first; for the moment, anyway. As much as he loved Polly and Emmie, he couldn't cancel his plans permanently. The prospect of being a plumber for the rest of his life was too dismal to contemplate.

With all due respect to Polly, she accepted the fact that he wasn't at home every night, and so long as he kept his other life away from her and Emmie, she didn't make a fuss. She was a lovely woman and he enjoyed being at home, but he knew he wouldn't be able to keep it up forever. He got restless indoors of an evening, just listening to the wireless. Anyway, he had his fortune to make.

'Mind if I join you?' said a voice, and looking up he saw a smart but flashily dressed man of middle age wearing a navy pinstriped suit with a brightly coloured tie and a trilby hat.

'Not at all, mate. You carry on,' said George. 'I'm going when I've finished this one anyway.'

'That's a real shame, because I wanted to have a few words with you.'

George observed the man more closely, noticing his thin clean-shaven face and dark, deep-set eyes that had not a smidgen of warmth in them, and he knew that this meeting was not going to be a friendly one.

'I'm listening,' he said.

'The fact is, son, you're an amateur moving among professionals and I want you out,' the man explained. 'My boys gave you a friendly warning but you're still hanging around. That isn't very sensible.'

'There was nothing in the least friendly about that warning,' said George.

'Exactly,' said the man. 'If I have to send them to see you again, it will be even less friendly.'

'Is that right?' said George, meeting the man's eyes in a challenge. 'So you don't get involved in anything physical yourself then?'

'At my age, don't make me laugh,' said the man. 'That's a mug's game.'

George took a gulp of beer. Some of the men who'd been in the prison camp with him had had their nerves shattered irrevocably by the things that had happened to them. For George, the cruelty and fear had had the opposite effect and he wasn't afraid of anything now. If he could endure that, he thought, he could get through whatever was thrown at him in peacetime. He certainly wasn't scared of some spiv who was here to warn him off.

'So you'll be sending them after me again?' he said. 'That's the plan, is it?'

'If you don't disappear sharpish, yeah, that's the general idea,' the man told him. 'The fact is, there's only so much business to be had, and what there is belongs to us. We don't tolerate interlopers. You've had a good run. But it's over now, so get out before you really get hurt.'

George emptied his glass slowly. 'Who the hell do you think you are?' he asked. 'I don't know if you've heard, but we won the war. This is a free country and I don't have to answer to the likes of you. You can send your thugs after me as often as you like. I will do as I please.'

Leaving the man beside himself with fury, George got up and left.

*   *   *

George sat in his van for a while to let the anger subside before driving away. The man and his thugs were just a joke to him, but being threatened was annoying. Why did people always have to get greedy? They found a good thing and wanted it all to themselves. Well they'd picked the wrong enemy in him. He refused to be intimidated.

As soon as he was feeling calmer, he turned on the engine and headed home, thinking about his wife and daughter and how lucky he was to have them.

'Is something wrong, George?' asked Polly when he came into the living room, where she was listening to the wireless and knitting a jumper for Emmie.

'No, not at all,' he said.

'Good. That's all right then.' She didn't believe him but knew he wouldn't tell her. When things were going well, he liked to talk about it. When he was upset about something, he kept it to himself. 'Would you like a cup of cocoa? I'm going to have one.'

'Not on top of all that best bitter,' he said. 'But I'll get yours to save you getting up.'

'That's nice of you, thanks.'

He brought the cocoa in and sat on the couch beside her. 'Everything all right here?'

'Of course it is. You've only been out a couple of hours,' she reminded him.

'I know, but I can still ask, can't I?'

'Yeah. Sure.' Feeling a sudden rush of affection for him, she turned and smiled. 'You're a very nice man, you know, George.'

'Am I really?' he said, sounding surprised. 'I thought you thoroughly disapproved of me.'

'I do,' she said. 'But I still like you. I think you're a lovely bloke. I don't know if it's usual to disapprove of someone and like them at the same time, but it works for me.' She realised that it was true. He was no longer the love of her life and she found some of his values questionable, but she did care for him. She'd had to work at it, but the harder she tried, the easier it became.

Polly could have no idea of the effect her flattering remarks had had on George. They had destroyed his gloomy mood in an instant and reminded him that the spiv in the pub wasn't worth a second thought. He had everything he cared for here in this house. And if he wanted better things for them, it would take more than some small-time crook to stop him.

Sensing that he needed affection, Polly put her cocoa cup down on the coffee table and said with a smile, 'Come here and let me give you a cuddle.'

He didn't need to be asked twice, and they sat there in the firelight, snuggled up together.

George came home from work one day in December to find his daughter behaving as if she had the worries of the world on her shoulders.

'What's the matter, Em?' he asked.

'Father Christmas won't be able to find me, so I won't get any presents,' she said.

'Of course he'll be able to find you,' he assured her. 'Why wouldn't he?'

'Because we live in a different house now,' she reminded him. 'He's used to bringing my presents to Granny's.'

'Oh yeah. I'd forgotten about that,' he said, frowning.

'What can I do about it, Dad?' she asked, on the verge of tears.

'We'll have to write him a letter to let him know where you are now,' he suggested.

'Ooh, can we?'

'Course we can,' he said. 'I expect we'll be going to Granny's for the day anyway, so you could collect your presents then, but we need them to be delivered here, don't we, so that they're at the bottom of your bed when you wake up.'

'Yeah,' she said, breathless at the thought.

'Actually, I was going to talk to you about Christmas Day, George,' said Polly, entering the room.

'What about it?'

'I don't want us to go to my parents this year. I think it's time for a change.'

'What do you have in mind?'

'I'd like us to do Christmas dinner here,' she explained. 'It's our first Christmas in our own place. It will give Mum a break and it will be nice for Emmie to be at home with her presents.'

'Good idea.' He thought for a moment. 'Will your mother be happy with it, though? I think she probably likes to be in charge of the catering, especially at Christmas.'

'I thought about that too,' she said. 'But things move on, don't they? She's always done it; now it's my turn to do the honours. Anyway, I shall need her help in the kitchen and she'll probably end up taking over, so that should keep her happy. But I'd like us to host it.'

'Me too,' he approved. 'It'll be good.'

'There'll be a few of us. Mum and Dad, Auntie Marian and Archie, and I'd love it if your gran would join us if we're able to prise her away from her beloved East End.'

'That might not be easy.'

'Don't push her into it if she'd really rather not,' said Polly. 'But she's the only family you have, so it would be lovely to have her with us. You'll have to work your charm on her.'

'I'll do my best,' he promised.

'You can collect her in the van if you have enough petrol,' Polly suggested. 'I'm sure she isn't too proud to travel in a plumber's van.'

'I'll go over and see her and find out what she thinks of the idea,' George said. 'I feel quite excited,' he added. 'Our first Christmas in our own home and all the people we love to share it with us.'

'Not quite all,' she said.

'Your brother, of course,' he said sadly. 'I'm sorry, love, I really am.'

'It is very sad, but we won't be the only family with an empty chair. We'll just have to make the best of it and drink a special toast to him.'

'But what about my letter to Father Christmas?' Emmie reminded them.

'Go and get a piece of paper and we'll help you to write him a note with your new address, and Mum and I will see that he gets it,' said George.

He and Polly exchanged glances as Emmie scuttled off to find pencil and paper.

Chapter Twelve

'Would you like some more Christmas pudding, Gran?' Polly asked Bess.

The older woman smiled, looking tempted. 'It is delicious,' she said. 'But what about everyone else?'

'There's enough for small seconds for those who want them,' Polly assured her. 'Thanks to my clever mum. She can work miracles in the kitchen.'

'Yeah, she really can,' agreed Bess. Turning to Flo, she added, 'How did you manage to make something so good with such a shortage of ingredients and still make it taste like Christmas pudding?'

'I think they call it creativity,' Flo said, grinning. 'But I don't reckon it tastes the same as real Christmas pudding, no matter how hard I try.'

'Maybe by next Christmas food will be plentiful again and we'll be able to get the proper stuff to cook with,' said Bess hopefully.

'We said that last year and it didn't happen, so don't bank on it,' said Wilf.

'Don't be such a pessimist,' admonished his wife.

'Mum made the Christmas cake too,' Polly told Bess. The younger woman was flushed with pleasure because the day was going so well. 'You can give her your verdict on that later.'

As Polly had predicted, her mother had taken over in the kitchen with the confidence of a Savoy chef, but Polly didn't mind being the minion. She was glad that everyone seemed to be enjoying themselves.

'Please may I get down?' asked Emmie. 'I've finished and I want to look at my presents again.'

'Go on then,' Polly agreed.

The adults lingered at the table, talking.

'They managed to get you to leave West Ham for a few hours then, Bess,' Marian mentioned in a friendly manner. 'I've heard you're very attached to the place.'

'Yeah. I've always lived there so it's home to me. I don't usually go far, but George can be very persuasive when he wants something. Always could, even when he was a nipper,' she said. 'But I'm very glad he did persuade me to come today, because I'm having a lovely time.'

'Good. You should come and see us again now that you've tried it and found we don't bite in the west of London,' said Polly. 'You'll be welcome any time.'

'Thank you, dear,' Bess said. 'I might take you up on that.'

'I'll remind you that you said that,' George put in lightly.

'I think it's time for the toasts,' suggested Flo.

They raised their glasses to Ray and others who were no longer with them.

'We've one less dear departed to toast this year,' said Flo.

'Who's that?' asked Wilf.

'George, of course,' she said, smiling and looking at her

son-in-law. 'All this time we thought he was dead and have been raising our glasses to him.'

There was a ripple of laughter. The slightest joke caused a giggle in this warm and festive atmosphere with a little booze to help things along.

'Trust George to cause a drama and then come strolling in as if nothing's happened,' said Polly.

'It wasn't his fault, though,' said Bess.

'Of course not, and we're all very glad he isn't with our lost ones,' said Polly.

'I'm quite happy about it too,' said George with a wry grin.

'Anyway, if we've finished with the toasts,' began Marian, 'Archie and I have some news.'

They all waited expectantly.

'I've decided to make an honest man of him,' she said. 'We're getting married next year, in the spring.'

There was an outpouring of delight.

'About bloody time too,' said Wilf, laughing.

'You're telling me,' Archie agreed. 'She's kept me waiting for so long, I was beginning to wonder if I'd be too old to bother.'

'Congratulations,' said Polly, beaming.

'Hear, hear,' added George. 'We're really pleased for you both.'

'It won't be a fancy do, very low key,' said Marian. 'It'll be at the registry office, with a meal at a local restaurant afterwards, so there's no need for anyone to worry about clothing coupons to buy new stuff to wear.'

'And there was me thinking it was the perfect excuse for something a bit special.' Polly turned to her mother, who hadn't commented. 'What about you, Mum? Is a new outfit on the cards for you, as sister of the bride?'

'I've got plenty of things in the wardrobe I can wear.'

'Show a little enthusiasm, love,' said Wilf. 'We've waited a long time for this wedding, so we need to celebrate in style.'

'I'm very pleased for you both,' Flo said rather formally. 'And yes, it has been a long time coming, so I might have a look to see what I've got in the way of clothing coupons.'

'That's the spirit,' approved Wilf. 'So now let's drink a toast to the forthcoming nuptials of two of my favourite people.'

Glasses were raised again, Bess was invited to the wedding and Polly gave a silent toast of her own to someone many miles away. She did hope James was having as good a Christmas as she was. Even now, with her loved ones around her, she still missed him and thought about him.

The day continued in jovial mood, with games, songs and a fancy tea. George was the perfect host, attentive to the guests and keeping everyone amused with his easy-going ways and sense of humour. Today Polly felt that they were a team, and it was a good feeling.

Despite everyone claiming to be too full to manage anything else, they all tucked into Polly's savoury supper of sausage rolls and cheese straws. Portions were smaller than in pre-war times, which was probably why everyone always had space for something more, decided Polly.

After the rest of them had left and George had got back from taking his grandmother home, he and Polly sat by the fire together for a nightcap.

'This is the one night of the year you can't escape to the pub,' she said.

'There'll be one or two open for a couple of hours,'

he said. 'But even I draw the line at going out on Christmas night.'

'That's nice, but I'm not sure I quite believe you,' she said. 'If you thought you could get away with it, you'd be gone. It's a wonder Dad didn't drag you off to the nearest one, but he seemed content to stay in for a change. That's a miracle in itself.'

'It's been a really good day, hasn't it?' he said, sounding serious.

'It really has,' she agreed wholeheartedly. 'I enjoyed every moment and I think the others did too.'

'No doubt about that,' he said. 'Hard work for you in the kitchen, though.'

'Mum took over, so I was just the assistant,' she said. 'But you won't hear me complaining about that.'

'Thanks, Pol.'

'What for?'

'For making my first Christmas home so nice.'

'You did your share too,' she reminded him.

'But you were at the helm,' he said. 'You always are, in everything we do.'

'It's my job. You earn the money and I look after everything at home.'

'It works, doesn't it?'

She nodded. 'So long as you keep the sleazy part of your life away from me, yes, it does.'

'It isn't sleazy, Pol,' he said. 'It's just business.'

'We've had a lovely day; don't let's spoil it with talk of work,' she said.

'Okay, love.'

When George had first reappeared after such a long absence,

she had wondered how she would ever make it work. But somehow, together, they had done it. She guessed it hadn't been easy for him either, having been away for so long and knowing about James. But he had never once mentioned it and had proved to be a wonderful father to Emmie.

The future boded well for them and she was happy. Nothing was perfect for anyone, so you valued what you had. She and George were from the same roots; they understood the people and the culture of their London neighbourhood. They had a nice home, a beautiful daughter and a lot to be thankful for. Roll on 1947, thought Polly.

Many miles away, James was standing at the sitting-room window, sipping a glass of whiskey and staring out at the light shining on the snow, a sight that always pleased him. He'd never known a Christmas Day here without snow. He'd had a good day with the family; his brothers and sister with their other halves, along with Mom and Dad.

He'd taken quite a lot of kidding about his own single status; it was generally thought that it was about time he married and settled down. He had no plans in that direction, though. The only time he'd ever begun to think along those lines was with Polly. A feeling of affection spread through him at the memory of her, and he thought how horrified she would be at the idea of snow for most of the winter. He recalled the odd snowfall in Britain, and how the whole country had gone into panic mode as soon as the first flakes appeared, with everything grinding to a halt. Here they were well equipped for sub-zero temperatures and life went on as normal during the winter.

He remembered Christmas with Polly and her family in the house in London, which seemed very small to him now that he was back in the large family farmhouse. Oddly, though, he'd never felt cramped or restricted in the Pritchards' little house. His overwhelming memories were of being in love with Polly, the kindness and generosity of the family and the laughs they'd all had together.

He was recalled to the present when one of his brothers said in a jovial manner, 'What are you looking out of the window for? A second visit from Santa?'

'Just looking at the light reflecting on the snow and thinking how pretty it is,' said James.

'You'll be writing poetry next,' joshed his brother.

Everyone laughed, and James turned back into the room and rejoined the conversation.

Polly and the family went to the pantomime on Boxing Day and had tea at Marian and Archie's afterwards. Then it was back to normal until New Year's Eve.

'We'll go out somewhere tonight and join the celebrations if you fancy it, Pol,' suggested George that morning. 'I'm sure your mum will sit with Emmie if you'd like to go out.'

'I'd rather stay in if you don't mind,' said Polly. 'We haven't booked anything and all the pubs will be packed and everybody will be drunk. I hate it when some complete stranger slobbers over me after "Auld Lang Syne".'

'All right, love,' he said amiably. 'We'll see the new year in here together.'

'You won't want to stay in, though, will you, not on New Year's Eve,' she said, knowing what a sociable person he was.

'I'll go out for one early on to get the atmosphere, then I'll come back and we'll have a drink together here.'

'I'll believe that when I see it,' she said jokingly. 'You'll get caught up in things and forget to come home until they chuck you out.'

'This is my first new year at home since before the war and I am definitely going to spend it with my wife,' he assured her.

'Okay, I'll put some snacks out for us then. We've some booze left over from Christmas.'

'I'll look forward to it,' he said. 'I'll be back indoors by ten, so we'll have plenty of time to relax before the chimes of Big Ben come on the wireless.'

'That will be lovely,' she said happily.

It was no great shock to Polly when ten o'clock passed with no sign of George. Eleven and he still wasn't home; a quarter to twelve the same. She wasn't surprised but she was hurt and a little angry. Surely he could have made an effort just this once.

Oh well, that was just the way he was, so she would drink a toast to the new year on her own, she thought, pouring herself a glass of sherry. It wasn't quite the same, but she couldn't let the occasion pass without any recognition. A knock at the front door broke into her thoughts. So he's made it with just minutes to spare, she thought, wondering vaguely why he hadn't used his key.

Faced with two policemen on the doorstep, she froze but did as they asked and ushered them inside. The first policeman spoke quietly, but his words registered with horror.

'Found unconscious outside a pub in Paddington . . . seriously hurt . . . in hospital. You need to get there as soon as possible.'

The police took care of everything: they collected Flo to stay with Emmie and arranged for transport to take Polly to the hospital. So here she was, sitting by the bed of a man she barely recognised because his face was so bruised and swollen.

'Even on New Year's Eve you have to be mixing with thugs,' she said, tears streaming down her face, her concern for him manifesting itself in anger. 'I really believed you'd just gone out for a social drink at the local.'

There was no reply; George was unconscious.

'I was waiting for you at home with the drinks ready for a toast,' she went on. 'And all the time you were getting up to no good. Now look at the state of you. You'll take a long time to heal from this one, George.'

The nurse appeared to tell Polly that the doctor wanted to see her. She sat in his office while he gave her George's prognosis and told her she must prepare herself for the worst.

'But he's a young, fit man,' she said. 'He's been in a fight, that's all. He's been in plenty of those.'

'Your husband isn't actually that fit,' said the doctor.

Polly looked at him in surprise. 'He's never had a day off sick. He doesn't even get colds.'

'Maybe so, but his heart isn't in good shape.'

'A bad heart?' she said, astounded. 'No, he's never had any trouble like that.'

'Did he see action in the war?'

'He was in a prison camp for most of it.'

'The strain that will have put on his body, the close-to-starvation diet and harsh conditions, has taken its toll. With care, he could have had a normal life span, but a beating like the one he's taken today has had very serious consequences.'

'What are you actually saying?' she asked shakily.

'I'm saying that it's very unlikely he will regain consciousness, and if he does, he will be severely disabled. He's suffered several very serious blows to the head and we suspect that he has brain damage, though we don't know for sure at the moment.' He cleared his throat. 'His heart is extremely weak. Your husband is a very sick man. I am so sorry.'

'Poor George,' she said, her voice thick with tears. 'I must go to him.'

'Yes, I think that would be best,' said the doctor.

Marian and Archie made a point of seeing in the new year together, even though she was working. They were in the Cherry Ballroom with all the other revellers when Big Ben struck midnight. The place erupted after the last chime and the two of them slipped away to her office as 'Auld Lang Syne' rang out.

'Another year gone,' said Archie, pouring them both a drink. 'They don't half fly by when you get to our age.'

'Oi, enough of that sort of talk. Our age indeed. We're still bright young things.'

'Yeah, sorry, Marian,' he said. 'I was talking about myself. Obviously you'll be young forever.'

She laughed. 'Of course, but this time next year I shall be an old married woman.'

'And I shall be the happiest man in London,' he said.

'You'd better be, after wanting it for so long.'

'You want it too, though, don't you?'

'Of course I do,' she said, slipping her arms around him. 'You know me. I only do things I don't want to in dire circumstances. And marrying you is not one of them.'

They sat for a while talking until they were interrupted by a knock on the office door. When Marian said, 'Come in,' they were both astonished when Wilf appeared.

'You're needed at the hospital, Marian,' he said, looking pale and worried. 'It's George; he's been beaten up and is in a bad way.'

'Oh my God,' she cried.

'Flo is with Emmie, but I reckon Polly will want some female support,' said Wilf.

'I'll come right away,' she said shakily. 'Archie will see everybody safely off the premises and lock up for me, won't you, love?'

'Course I will.'

'Come on then, Wilf,' she said, heading for the door.

'You might need this,' said Archie, going after her with her coat. 'It's cold out there.'

'Thanks,' she said absently, too eager to be on her way to care about her own comfort.

'It doesn't make sense, Auntie,' said Polly in the early hours of the next morning, after George had lost his battle for life and slipped away. 'He was a young man. How can he have died?'

'Someone must have beaten the living daylights out of him,' said Marian. 'It doesn't matter how young you are when your body takes that sort of punishment. And as the doctor told you, the prison camp had taken its toll.'

'I don't know what to do, Auntie,' she said.

'You don't need to do anything for the moment except have a cup of tea with me, if I can find anyone to make one at this time of the morning.'

The police had other plans for Polly, but they did arrange a cup of tea for her while she was talking to them in the matron's office.

'I can tell you anything you want to know about my husband's life with me, but I know nothing about the people he mixed with outside, in the pubs. Except that they were unsavoury types.'

'Why do you say that?'

'He was beaten up once before,' she said. 'He came home one night in a right state. I didn't like him mixing with those types, but he wasn't the sort to take orders from a woman. He kept that part of his life separate from me.'

They asked a lot more questions and she told them everything she knew. Nothing could hurt George now.

'Sorry to put you through all this at such an awful time, but we want to find whoever is responsible for your husband's death.'

'I understand,' she said. 'I want them brought to justice too, but I don't have any idea who it might have been.'

The day continued with everyone being kind and wanting to help her. She was surrounded by people who were worried about her being alone when that was all she wanted, especially as she'd only had a short sleep when they got back from the hospital.

Somehow she got through the awful job of telling Emmie that her daddy was in heaven with the angels. She gave him the benefit of the doubt on that one for her daughter's sake. Now, in the evening, all she wanted was to be on her own to clear her head.

'You're not staying here,' declared Flo. 'You and Emmie are coming home with us.'

'It's nice of you, Mum, but—'

'Surely you don't want to be alone tonight.'

'I do, Mum,' she said, looking towards her daughter, who was fast asleep in the chair. 'Emmie needs to go to bed too. I don't want to drag her out now.'

'I'll stay the night with them, Flo,' suggested Marian. 'You go home with Wilf.'

'You look tired, Mum,' said Polly truthfully. If she was to be forced into having company, her aunt was her first choice, because she had always found her easier to talk to than her mother.

'Are you sure?' asked Flo.

'Positive.'

'I'll be around first thing in the morning, then.'

Polly thanked her parents for everything and saw them out, certain that they would be glad of a break from the drama even though they would never admit it.

'So, Auntie,' began Polly later when Emmie was in bed and the two women were sitting in the living room. 'Now I have to grieve for my husband for the second time. When I was told he'd died at Dunkirk, I was heartbroken. Absolutely beside myself. I thought he'd given his life for his country. I'm very sad now, of course, but also angry, because it need never have happened if only he'd stuck to plumbing instead of hanging around the pubs with dodgy types.'

'That was George, though, wasn't it?' said Marian. 'He enjoyed that sort of thing, the wheeler-dealing. You can't change someone just because you marry them.'

'No, but he was a husband and a father. You'd think he would have thought about me and especially Emmie before putting himself in danger. I don't think it's properly sunk in with her yet, the fact that she'll never see him again.'

'She's young,' said Marian. 'She'll get over it.'

'Yes, she will, but she shouldn't have to.'

'Plenty of kids lost their dad in the war and they manage to survive somehow.'

'That's the ironic part,' said Polly. 'He got through the war and then put himself at risk. The whole thing scared me, though I never dreamt it would have such a tragic outcome. When he came home that night covered in bruises, I said I wouldn't have the stuff in the house because I didn't want him mixing with those types.'

'People who dabble in the black market aren't all violent,' said Marian.

'Do you know any, then?'

'Not personally, but I know it goes on,' she said. 'There's a grocer I've heard of who's involved, and some market traders too. They're not evil; just willing to take a risk to make a few shillings. Being angry with George isn't going to help.'

'I know,' Polly sighed. 'Anyway, I seem destined not to have a man in my life, don't I? First there was George, then James, then George again, and now nobody.'

'You'll be all right,' said Marian. 'You're made of strong stuff and you've got all of us around you.'

'I'm glad of that, Auntie,' she said. 'Somehow I know I'll get through it. I know that because I've already done it once.' She looked into space. 'I have no idea about the practical side of things yet. I'm certain George wouldn't have had life insurance. It isn't something you think about when you're in your twenties, is it?'

'Not usually, no,' Marian said.

'I doubt if he would have had any money put by either,' said Polly.

'Didn't he keep you in the picture about that?'

'No, he held the purse strings completely. He gave me what I needed whenever I wanted it and never quibbled. He lived from week to week and I don't think he'd ever been inside a bank. When he came home from the war and started working, he insisted on being in charge of the money. It's not a nice thing to do, but I shall have to go through his things to find out what he's left me with.'

'Of course you need to know your financial position.'

'It's so damned sordid, Auntie. When I thought he was dead before, I was living with Mum and Dad anyway, and working.' She waved a hand towards the nicely furnished room. 'Now there's all this.'

'Don't worry about any of that now,' Marian advised her.

'I shall have to go to see his gran to tell her,' said Polly.

'I'll do that for you if you like,' offered Marian.

'Thanks, but I'd better tell her myself. I think it's the least I can do.'

'If you go in the morning, when I'm not at work, I'll go with you,' she said. 'And Archie and I will help you with the funeral arrangements.'

'I have to find some money before I can even think about that,' Polly said.

'We can help out if you're pushed for cash.'

'Thanks, Auntie, but I'm hoping that won't be necessary. George was always splashing money around, so I'm hoping to find some in his wallet and pockets.'

'You know where we are if you need us.'

'Yeah, I do,' she said. She was grateful for Marian's offer, but she was determined to try and do things herself. She'd been in charge of her life before George had come back and she would be again somehow.

'But he was as right as rain at Christmas,' said Bess shakily when Polly told her the awful news.

'He seemed to be, I know, but the prison camp had taken its toll and he wasn't up to a beating,' said Polly. 'It was the company he kept that was the problem.'

'What was he thinking, putting himself at risk like that when he had a wife and child?' said Bess, dabbing at her eyes with a handkerchief. 'I told him to be careful.'

'I know you did.'

'But would he listen? Not him!'

'I'm sure he didn't mean to cause us any trouble,' said Marian, who had gone with Polly for support while Flo was looking after Emmie.

'Oh no, George would never knowingly have done that,' said Polly. 'He took his family responsibilities very seriously, which was why he was mixing with such types in the first place. He wanted to make money for us, but I don't think he realised how dangerous these people are.'

'Are the police trying to find out who did it?' asked Bess.

'I believe so,' replied Polly. 'They've asked me lots of questions, but I'm not much help because I don't know anything about the people George mixed with outside of our immediate circle.'

'They have ways of finding these things out, I expect,' said Marian.

'Anyway, Gran, I wanted to come and tell you myself,' said Polly. 'I expect you'll want to come to the funeral, but I can't organise that until the police release his body.' As she spoke, a shiver went up her spine. Words like 'murder' and 'death penalty' came into her mind, things that had never had any place in her life until now. She didn't want to think about the manner of her husband's death, because she could feel the pain as he must have.

'Anyway, shall I put the kettle on?' suggested Marian, noticing Polly's sudden pallor.

'I'll do it,' said Bess. 'What am I thinking, not making you a cup of tea?'

'Shocked by it all, like the rest of us, I expect,' said Polly. 'I haven't been able to think straight since I had the news.'

Polly and Marian stayed with Bess for a little while longer. When they left, the elderly woman went to see her friend and neighbour next door.

'I'll ask Archie if he'll come and collect her for the funeral,' said Marian as they were heading home. 'Maybe he could drive over in George's van. She's getting on a bit to be coming across London on the tube.'

'Good idea,' said Polly, but she felt isolated, in a world of her own. Arranging George's funeral was the least of her worries.

*　　*　　*

Having been through all of George's things, a necessary but unpleasant task, Polly realised that her way of life was about to change dramatically yet again. George had some cash stashed away in various places: his wallet, his pockets and a tin in which he kept his plumbing earnings.

There was enough for a simple funeral with a little over, but not enough to pay more than two weeks' rent. So as soon as she had given George a decent send-off, Polly would have to sit down and work out what she was going to do. There was no time to mope when you had responsibilities.

The day was cold and so was Polly, inside and out. She was still angry with George, and this distanced her from the solemn words being spoken in all their dark beauty as she stood at the graveside. Why hadn't he been content with what he'd had instead of entering into a world he didn't really understand and making her go through this terrible ordeal? A husband and father in his twenties being buried. It was all wrong.

It was when the coffin was lowered into the ground that the grief finally registered, replacing the anger with a horrid knot inside her. Poor George, he had meant well and now he was gone. His life taken in an instant by some unknown thug.

Tears fell and she was aware of people either side of her taking hold of her arms reassuringly. She knew without looking that it was her mother and her aunt. Her father was comforting George's grandmother.

Polly was very glad she had left Emmie in the safe hands of a neighbour. This was no place for a young child. It was bad enough that she had to lose her adored father. The least Polly could do was spare her the burial.

Finally the ordeal at the graveside was over and the proceedings moved to Polly's house, where she went through the motions expected of her, supported by her mother and her aunt. The worst thing was knowing that this sad and punishing event was only the beginning of her problems.

Emmie was her priority now. Naturally the child was upset by her father's death and they had tried to soften the blow with euphemistic talk of heaven and angels. Because children lived in the moment and didn't have long memories, Polly hoped she would soon forget the drama of the last few days and just have fond thoughts of her dad. For all his faults George had been a good father to her.

Now, somehow, Polly herself had to be a good single parent. She'd done it before and she would again. But she had got used to sharing the responsibility and the joy. All that was over. Emmie, love, she thought, it's just you and me again.

A few days after the funeral, Polly had a courtesy visit from the detectives who were dealing with George's murder. They told her that according to witnesses at the local pub, George had been escorted forcibly from the premises by two men, strangers to the staff and clientele. The police believed he had been taken to the Paddington pub against his will, probably to see whoever the men were working for.

So he hadn't betrayed her on New Year's Eve after all. He had just gone to the local for a pint as he'd promised. But somehow this news made her feel even sadder.

Chapter Thirteen

Having faced up to the dire reality of her circumstances and considered her options, Polly went to see her mother one morning soon after the funeral.

'I'm here to ask a favour, Mum,' she said.

'Don't look so worried about it,' urged Flo. 'If I can help, I will.'

'George has left me flat broke and I need to ask if Emmie and I can move back in with you and Dad, just until I get back on my feet.'

Flo was visibly shocked. 'Of course you can, but I thought George was doing really well. He always seemed to have plenty of money to splash around.'

'He was doing all right but not well enough to have anything put by, and he had no life insurance. Obviously he wasn't expecting to die so soon. He didn't have time to build up any savings.'

'I suppose not.'

'Whatever he earned he spent from week to week. There was enough to cover the funeral expenses, and to feed and house Emmie and me for a week or two, but that's it. I can't afford the rent for any longer than that.'

'I'm so sorry, love,' said Flo. 'I know how much you love your house.'

'Yes, I'm very disappointed that we can't stay there, but it can't be helped,' Polly said briskly. 'I shall get a job as soon as I can, but I won't be able to earn enough to keep the house on. At the moment I'm skint, though I will be getting a widow's pension, which you can have as rent.'

'Don't be ridiculous,' Flo objected. 'As if I'd take that off you. When you're earning you can start paying your way, but not until then.'

'Thanks, Mum. This is a big step backwards for me, having to come home with the begging bowl after having had my own place, and it's important to me to pay my way as soon as I can. Emmie is at school now, so I can look for a full-time job. There are usually vacancies for typists around. I shall hate to go back to that, but needs must.'

'There are often advertisements in the local paper,' said Flo, who was delighted that her family would be back together but angry with George for mixing with villains and getting himself killed, causing Polly such distress. 'There's no hurry, though.'

'Oh but there is, Mum,' Polly said. 'I need to get back out there looking for work right away. You lose confidence when you're at home.'

'I suppose you would do,' said Flo, who had no personal experience of such things. 'Meanwhile, you can move in as soon as you like.'

Still feeling vulnerable from her bereavement and her drastically reduced circumstances, Polly threw her arms around her mother in an impulsive gesture of gratitude. 'Thanks, Mum,' she said emotionally. 'Dad won't mind, will he?'

'Of course he won't,' said Flo. 'We both love having you and Emmie here. Surely you must know that.'

'It won't be forever, I promise.' Polly had no idea how she was ever going to get enough money for her own place, but she was determined to do it somehow. Her parents needed some peace and quiet at their time of life.

'So will you sell your furniture?' asked Flo.

'I shall have to,' she said. 'I can't afford to put it into store. I'll be glad of the money, anyway.'

It was all very sad for Polly, losing her home as well as her husband. She'd loved being in her own place, caring for it and making it special. Now it all had to go. Still, that was the least of her problems.

'It will be nice having you and Emmie home again,' Flo said. 'Breathing a bit of life into the place.'

Polly smiled. They both knew that the time for her to be living at home permanently had passed. She should be well established in her own place by now, though the housing shortage meant that plenty of other young people were in the same position. She counted her blessings that home was still an option for her. Many people had lost their parents and the family home in the war.

Rationing and shortages showed no sign of abating as the new year got under way. Everything was scarcer than ever, which meant long queues everywhere. There was even horse flesh for sale at the butcher's, available without coupons, and there was never any shortage of takers. But Flo couldn't bring herself to join that particular queue.

The weather didn't help to lift the general mood.

Temperatures dropped and Londoners awoke one morning to find a blanket of snow covering everything. As well as general chaos, this also caused a fuel shortage, as coal deliveries couldn't get through to power stations, factories or homes. But life went on even though the population crawled around their freezing homes wrapped up in their outdoor clothes.

Flo was in a long queue at the greengrocer's one bitter morning, chatting with the other women to pass the time. Most of them had known each other for years.

'You've got your daughter back at home then, Flo,' said one woman who lived nearby. 'I saw her with the nipper the other day. She said she'd moved back in.'

'Yeah,' said Flo, instinctively on the defensive.

'How's that working out?'

'Fine. Why wouldn't it?'

'Well, it's nice to get them out from under your feet when they grow up and leave home, isn't it?'

'I enjoy having them around, as it happens.'

'Just as well, love. I don't expect you had much choice in the matter,' said the woman. 'I read about your daughter's husband's death in the local paper. What a shocking thing.'

'Yeah, we were all very upset.'

'But I suppose you have to expect that sort of thing when you get mixed up in the black market; it said in the paper that that was what was behind it,' said the woman. 'Thugs, the lot of them.'

'My son-in-law wasn't a thug,' Flo objected, her cheeks suffused with pink. 'Far from it. He was a good husband and father. A decent man.'

'All right, keep your hair on,' said the woman. 'I'm just repeating what it said in the paper.'

'No one knows for sure what happened,' said Flo.

'So we'll all draw our own conclusions until the truth comes out,' said the woman.

'If it ever does.'

'Mm. Anyway, you've two extra mouths to feed, then?'

'No, not all,' Flo came back at her quickly. 'My daughter has a job, so she's able to pay her way. It was just the high rent on the house she couldn't manage.'

'Oh, I see,' said the woman, suitably deflated. 'What does she do?'

'She works in a typing pool.'

'Good for her.'

'Yes, I'm very proud of her,' said Flo. 'She didn't mope around. She was out job-hunting soon after the funeral.'

The gossip wasn't going well, and the woman craned her neck to see what was happening ahead of them in the queue. 'At last there seems to be some movement,' she said. 'Looks as though we might get served sometime this year after all.'

'Thank Gawd for that,' said Flo. She wondered why she had had such a strong reaction to the criticism of George, as she had never approved of his dealings with the black market even though she'd sometimes taken his treats and turned a blind eye. Maybe she'd become fond of him in her own way.

Polly's days in the typing pool seemed endless now that she was working full time. The work was repetitive – all typing, with no other jobs such as filing or doing the post – but she needed the money, and now that Emmie was at school there was no reason why she couldn't work a full day. She was concerned about not being there for her daughter during the school holidays, but there was no way around it.

She was determined that her parents wouldn't be out of pocket because of her and Emmie. Her situation wasn't likely to change any time soon, so she made sure she paid her mother generously from her pay packet as soon as she got home from work on a Friday night.

By early March the weather was still bitter. Emmie sometimes cried with the cold at night, and Polly often felt like doing the same. During this harsh spell they were sharing a bed for warmth. Cuddled up together, it didn't seem so bad. Then, in the middle of the month, a violent storm swept the country and the thaw began. But as the snow melted, the rivers overflowed, causing disruption countrywide. The water supply was cut off because of damage, and the family had to queue at a tap at the end of the street.

'It's like the Blitz all over again,' Polly remarked to her father as they were waiting with their buckets.

'It is an' all,' agreed Wilf.

Eventually things got back to normal and spring was welcomed with gusto, everyone's spirits lifted by the sight of daffodils and tulips. It was good not to be permanently cold, too.

Emmie came home from school with a letter one day, a notification of a parents' open evening. Polly was pleased, because she took a keen interest in her daughter's progress.

'I shall find out if you've been behaving yourself, Emmie,' she said laughingly.

'Can I come with you?'

'No. It's grown-ups only,' she replied. 'You can stay with Gran, if she doesn't mind.'

'Of course I don't,' Flo assured her.

Emmie's teacher was young and enthusiastic, and had nice things to say about the little girl.

'She makes a big contribution to the class,' she said. 'She's always cheerful and keen to join in, and she seems popular with the other children.'

Polly was delighted to hear her daughter being praised.

'She's particularly admired by the other children for her ability in the gym class. Her cartwheels and backbends are the envy of all the girls,' said the teacher.

'Yes, she's always been very good at that sort of thing,' said Polly. 'But her other lessons are more important. Her reading at home seems to be coming along quite well.'

'She's a bright child,' said the teacher, and Polly swelled with pride.

'She lost her father earlier in the year, as you know,' said Polly. 'Did that affect her at school?'

'She was rather subdued for a while, but she seems all right now,' said the teacher. 'I think children forget about home to a certain extent when they're with their friends.'

'Yes, I suppose that's true.'

Polly was feeling very positive about her daughter when the interview drew to a close and she got up to go.

'By the way,' said the teacher, 'I must apologise for the handwritten note telling you about the parents' evening. Our school secretary left unexpectedly and we haven't been able to find a replacement yet, so we are all having to write our own correspondence. It's driving us mad.'

Polly smiled politely and assured her that it didn't matter, whilst feeling excited by what she'd heard. By the time she got home, she was buzzing with an idea.

'There's a secretary's job going at the school,' she told her mother when Emmie was in bed. 'That would suit me down to the ground because of the hours. I'd be home during the holidays and when Emmie finished school every day. It would be more interesting for me too, because it wouldn't be eight hours solid typing and I'd get to use my initiative.'

'So are you going to apply?'

'I hope to, though the salary will probably be less than I get now because it's not such long hours.'

'Can you manage on less?'

'Not really, but I've thought of a way to top it up if I need to,' she said. 'If I do a few evenings at the Cherry, I'll have enough, but it would mean you looking after Emmie while I'm out.'

'That's no problem for me, but will Marian have a job for you?' asked Flo.

'Maybe not right away, but I'm prepared to do anything. I'll wash up in the cafeteria, take the coats, whatever.'

'You need to have a chat with Marian about it.'

Polly hugged her mother. 'Oh, Mum, it would be such a relief to be out of the typing pool.'

'Why don't you call in at the Cherry on your way home from work one day?' suggested Flo. 'Just find out if she could give you a few shifts if you do get the school job.'

'I can't go for one without the other, so I'll go and see her tomorrow.'

'Well this is good news, Polly. Of course I would love to have you back.' Marian frowned. 'I can't offer you your old job because I have someone doing that at the moment. But I can give you a shift in the cafeteria a few nights a week. Evening staff don't usually stay very long, so something else will probably come up soon.'

'The cafeteria will be fine for me, but it will depend on my getting the school job,' Polly said. 'I can't take on anything else with the job I've got at the moment because I'll never see Emmie.'

'I understand that,' said Marian. 'We'll sort something out when you're ready. It will be lovely to have you back on board again.'

'Thanks, Auntie.'

'I hope you're not so wrapped up in all this that you forget about the wedding next week.'

'As if I would.'

'I'll be taking my holidays then and there will be a relief manager on duty. So you should wait until I'm back before starting here.'

'I haven't even got the school job yet,' Polly said. 'There will probably be masses of applicants and some of them might have shorthand, which I don't. I don't think it's essential, but I suppose it could be an advantage.'

'The hours might not be enough for a single woman, and most married women went back to being housewives after the war, so I reckon you'll stand a good chance.'

'That's true. In fact, I'm quite a novelty in the typing pool. All the women in the office are younger than me and single, so there's a lot of talk about boyfriends and dances and nights out at the pictures.'

'Do you feel a bit out of it, then?'

'No. Not at all. I enjoy hearing about their adventures. They keep me up to date with things. Not that we get a chance to talk during working hours. The supervisor has eyes in the back of her head and everywhere else too. If she spots someone so much as glancing at the next girl, she's down on them like a ton of bricks.'

'So the school job is an escape route for you?'

'I'll say,' Polly confirmed.

'You need to make enquiries as soon as you can, then,' said Marian.

'I shall call there in my lunch hour tomorrow and find out what the procedure is.'

They moved on to other things and Marian said, 'I've been thinking about your George just lately.'

'Really? Why?'

'I'd have been after him to get me some clothing coupons for my wedding outfit. You can't get anything decent with the amount the government give us.' Realising she could have been a bit more tactful, she added quickly, 'Whoops. Sorry, love. Me and my big mouth.'

Polly felt a reaction at the casual mention of George's seedy sideline but then smiled with the sheer relief of hearing him being spoken about normally, as he really was. Since his death, everyone had either been afraid to mention him at all or talked about him as if he'd been some sort of a saint.

'Don't worry about it, Auntie,' she said. 'If he was around

I'm sure he'd have helped you out with that. That was what George did best: get things people wanted and didn't mind paying for. He was a wide boy, a spiv. We all know that. I don't mind if people mention it. He can't be hurt and he wouldn't be anyway. He enjoyed the dodgy part of his life better than the legit part. He was even proud of it in his way. I know it might seem awful, but that's the way he was.'

'Yeah, I know, love,' agreed Marian. 'I didn't want to hurt your feelings.'

'You could never do that, Auntie,' said Polly.

Marian wasn't so sure about that, but she said, 'I'd always try not to.'

'The secretary is at the heart of our school,' said the headmistress, sitting across the desk from Polly at her interview. 'Myself and all the teachers rely on her. It isn't just a matter of typing and filing. You would deal with phone calls from parents feeling aggrieved about some issue concerning their child; teachers asking you to arrange to get a pupil collected in the event of sickness, and other unexpected emergencies, as well as doing all the typing and general school admin, including keeping the records up to date. The hours are attractive for someone like you with a child at the school, but the job is no easy option.'

'It sounds very interesting, though,' said Polly. 'And I enjoy a challenge.'

'I know that you're a typist, but have you done any general office work?'

'When I was learning to type and getting my speed up, I worked as a general clerk, mostly filing and looking things up. But I've never run my own office as is required for this job.' She glanced at a large machine in the corner with a metal roller on top. 'At least I know how to work a Gestetner copying machine, though, and I think I would soon pick the rest up.'

The headmistress, a stout woman with bosoms like pumpkins and her hair taken back into a bun, nodded and asked Polly some more questions. Then she said she would be in touch when she'd seen all the other applicants and made a decision.

'Thank you for seeing me,' said Polly rising. She tried to hide her disappointment as she left the headmistress's office. It didn't seem likely she would get the job, not if there was plenty of competition. Having heard more about it, she really wanted it. Not just because of the hours, but because it sounded so interesting.

Oh well, she had plenty to take her mind off it, with Auntie Marian's wedding to look forward to on Saturday.

Despite the restrictions of clothes rationing, Marian managed to look stunning for her wedding in a light beige suit with an emerald-green blouse and accessories, the outfit finished with a wide-brimmed hat in cream with a green satin bow. The colours were perfect with her auburn hair. She was clever with make-up, which completed the look beautifully.

'Well, we finally did it,' said Archie during his speech at the small reception at a local hotel. 'At least we managed it before we hit old age.'

'Oi, speak for yourself,' Marian chipped in. 'I'm still just a young thing. In my head, anyway.'

A cheer went up.

'Anyway, folks, I just want to thank you all for being here and tell you how proud I am to have Marian as my wife at long last. Being a part of this family means a lot to me too. I haven't always been popular with you, which makes it all the more special.'

Laughter and jokes were flying around.

'And finally,' Archie continued, 'I'd like to thank our lovely flower girl, Emmie.'

They all cheered, Emmie smiled and Polly swelled with pride. Her daughter had been disappointed that it wasn't going be a church wedding with her as a bridesmaid, so Polly had made her a basket of flowers and a headdress so that she could be a flower girl in her best party dress.

Now Wilf got to his feet.

'Well, what can I say about my sister-in-law Marian?' he began.

'I'm sure you'll think of something,' his wife cut in. 'I've never known you lost for words before.'

There was a ripple of laughter, then he continued.

'As you all know, Marian has never been one to be conventional—'

'I'm going to Bournemouth for my honeymoon,' Marian interrupted. 'You can't get much more conventional than that.'

Everybody laughed.

'You'll have to behave yourself,' said Wilf. 'They're very proper down there.'

'I know how to behave,' said Marian, pretending to be outraged. 'Bloody cheek!'

'I rest my case,' he laughed. 'You'd better not swear in Bournemouth. Posh people go there.'

'Maybe we should have booked to go to Margate or Brighton then,' she retorted.

'Pipe down and let me finish my speech,' urged Wilf.

'That's no way to speak to the bride,' she joshed.

'It is if she won't stop yapping.'

'All right, Wilf, carry on . . .'

'As I was saying, folks, if Marian thinks something is right, she'll not be afraid to say so or to act on her initiative, and I admire her for that.'

There was a roar of communal agreement.

'She's been in my life since I first got to know Flo,' he continued. 'Marian was the annoying little sister who wouldn't go away when we were trying to be alone together.' He grinned. 'I'm sure you all know what I mean.'

'Don't be disgusting, Wilf,' admonished his wife, while the others laughed.

'Of course, we've all got a few miles on the clock since those days. Marian's had her problems but she's worked hard and made a good life for herself. She had to wait a while but she's finally found happiness with the love of her life, a good bloke who I'm honoured to be related to at last. So welcome to the family, Archie, and all the best to you both.'

Glasses were raised and the conversation resumed; everyone was happy.

'What were these problems that Auntie had when she was young?' Polly asked her mother, who was sitting beside her. 'I've heard that mentioned before.'

'Oh, nothing more than anyone else has when they're growing up,' replied Flo.

'What, boyfriends, that sort of thing?' suggested Polly. 'Unrequited love?'

'Something like that,' said Flo.

'Why hasn't it all been forgotten, then?' asked Polly. 'Like everyone else's youth.'

'It's a wedding, Polly,' said her mother. 'They drag anything up for the speeches.'

'Mm, I suppose so. But there's always been some kind of mystery about Auntie,' said Polly thoughtfully.

'It's the first I've heard of it,' said Flo.

'I've often sensed that something happened to her. Did she get in trouble with the police or something?'

'No she most certainly did not,' snapped her mother. 'Honestly, what a thing to say. I suggest you get any such daft ideas out of your head.'

'Yeah, all right.' Polly thought for a moment. 'I bet she was a cracker in her day. She must have led the boys a right old dance.'

'She was a very pretty girl,' said Flo. 'She always made the best of herself, too.'

'Still does,' said Polly. 'She looks really lovely today, don't you think?'

'Yes, she does look nice,' said Flo, who wasn't given to hyperbole.

Archie tapped a spoon against a glass to get their attention again.

'Just one more toast, folks, if you don't mind,' he said. 'Can I ask you to raise your glasses to the missing members of the family, Ray and George.'

Polly realised that in the happiness of the day she had forgotten all about poor George. How awful! He'd hardly been gone any time and she wasn't thinking about him. Still, she supposed you weren't meant to have someone on your

251

mind all the time when they'd died. Were you? It wasn't the sort of thing she could ask anyone.

She raised her glass with everyone else, but she was consumed with guilt.

Emmie had been sitting quietly beside her mother, but now she was beginning to get restless.

'Are we going soon?' she asked.

'Yes, it's coming to the end now,' said Polly. 'We'll wait to see Auntie go off on honeymoon, then we'll go home.'

'Can I go out to play?'

'When you've changed out of your nice dress.'

'Can't I wear it to go out?' she asked.

'Not likely,' said Polly. 'That's your best dress. You only wear it on special occasions.'

'I want to show it to my friends.'

'All right, you can show your friends, but then you come straight in to get changed. I'm not having you going over the bomb site in it and ruining it.'

'She'll be grown out of it before you can look around,' said Flo. 'So you might as well let her wear it.'

'It's a taffeta party dress, Mum; not made for the street,' Polly reminded her. 'She can wear it for her birthday party.'

'That's a couple of months away yet. I doubt if it will fit her by then.'

'I am not letting her wear it to play out,' said Polly determinedly. Her mother did tend to think she knew best about everything. 'Jumping off walls, climbing trees, raking around on the bomb site. It will be torn to shreds and filthy within ten minutes.'

'All right,' said Flo. 'There's no need to snap.'

'Sorry, Mum.' She was irritable because she was angry with

herself for forgetting George, but she couldn't tell her mother, or anyone, that.

One day the following week, Emmie came home from school with a note for Polly asking her to call in to see Miss Haywood, the headmistress, as soon as possible.

'Has something happened at school, Emmie?' she asked her daughter, her maternal instincts swinging into action.

'No.'

'You weren't ill or naughty or anything, were you?'

'Of course not.'

'She wouldn't be naughty, would you, love?' said her adoring granny.

'Did all the children get a letter?' asked Polly.

'I don't know, but my friends didn't.'

'Perhaps it's about the job,' suggested Flo.

'They wouldn't send something like that in a note with a child,' said Polly. 'It would be more official.'

'Maybe not, seeing as they don't have a secretary,' said Flo.

'Mm, that's a point,' said Polly, but she was still more inclined to think it was about Emmie, which worried her. Perhaps some ailment had been noticed by the teachers.

'I'll call in at the school before work tomorrow morning,' she said, frowning.

'Thank you for responding to my note so quickly,' said Miss Haywood. 'I apologise for the rather unconventional means of contact, but it was urgent and of course we have no secretary.'

253

'What's happened, Miss Haywood?' asked Polly. 'Is there a problem with Emmie?'

'No, no, nothing like that,' she said. 'I'd like to offer you the job as secretary, but I need you to start as soon as possible.'

'I have to give a full week's notice,' Polly explained. 'But I can start immediately after that, so that would be a week on Monday.'

'Good,' said the headmistress. 'I'm sorry, we're not usually so disorganised. Do you have time to do the official paperwork now?'

'I'm on my way to work and I'm already late. I could come in my lunch hour tomorrow, if that's convenient.'

'Yes, that will be fine. We'll see you tomorrow then.'

Polly went on her way feeling terrified, because running an office was new and she didn't want to make a mess of it and have it reflect on Emmie in any way. But she was also excited, and very much hoping to make a success of it.

'Are you going to be a teacher, then?' asked Emmie on hearing the news that evening and not seeming too happy about it.

'No, love. I'm going to be working in the office.'

'Children's mothers don't usually work at the school,' she said, sounding worried.

'I know of at least two mothers who are dinner ladies there,' said Polly.

'But they're only in the kitchen and the hall where we get our dinner.'

'And I'll only be in the office. Don't worry, Emmie. I won't be spying on you. You won't even know I'm there.'

'Oh, that's all right then.'

Polly was reminded of how sensitive children were, and how they liked to be exactly the same as their peers.

'Aren't you going to wish me luck?'

The child nodded. 'It will be good if I fall over in the playground and hurt myself because you'll be there,' she said. 'But not so good if I'm playing with my friends and you're watching me.'

'I'll be far too busy to be watching you,' Polly assured her. 'I'll be tucked away in my office.'

The child thought about this for a moment. 'I'm glad you're going to be working at the school, Mum,' she said, with an apparent change of heart. 'It makes me feel nice inside.'

'I'm glad too,' said Polly.

To say that Polly felt out of her depth on her first morning in her new job was beyond an understatement. She was utterly lost. The phone didn't seem to stop ringing; everyone from anxious parents demanding to speak to teachers, to educational book reps wanting an appointment with the headmistress and the education authority also wanting to speak to Miss Haywood. Polly had a list of typing jobs, including a notice about the sports day that had to be typed on to a stencil and reproduced for the parents. She had to notify the caretaker about a repair that needed doing to one of the sinks in the toilets, and she hadn't even had time to open the post. Somehow she had to get through it, though, because she knew that on the other side of the terror of newness was an interesting job.

★   ★   ★

In contrast to her despair at her day job, Polly felt as though she had come home when she started back at the Cherry. There was nothing glamorous about selling cups of tea and sticky buns, which was all they had to offer because of the shortages, but the magic was still here. The music, the lights, the aching familiarity of it all, and of course the memories. This was where she had met the two men who had changed her life. George had been her first love and she had been very fond of him until the end. James had been her passion and her impossible dream, which hadn't ended for her when he'd gone back to Canada.

She had just finished serving a customer and put the money through the till when a familiar figure appeared in the cafeteria.

'Hello, Auntie.'

'I just thought I'd pop across to see how you're getting on,' Marian said.

'All right, I think. A damned sight better than my day job, anyway. But serving cups of tea and coffee wouldn't be too difficult for anyone.'

'You wait until the good times come and we can widen our menu,' said Marian, laughing. 'That'll make you think. We'll have lemonade and fancy cakes and all sorts of goodies. Lots of different prices to remember.'

'I can't wait,' smiled Polly.

'Finding the other job a bit hard, are you?' asked Marian.

'Interesting but impossible at the moment,' Polly said. 'I've been used to doing one thing at a time.'

'And you don't at the school?'

'There are interruptions,' she said. 'Phone calls, children being taken ill, messages to be delivered to teachers, all

256

sorts of things to remember, never mind the actual clerical work.'

'Are you sorry you changed jobs?'

'Oh no, not at all,' she said. 'I enjoy being a part of everything, and when I get the hang of it, I know I will love the job as well.'

Marian laughed. 'You're like me, you'll never be a quitter,' she said.

'I suppose I would be if I simply couldn't do something, but not before I'd given it my very best shot.' Polly smiled. 'It's funny about the atmosphere of a school. I think I'm probably as scared of the headmistress as the kids are. She's got a certain air about her even though she's very nice.'

'Our school days, and how we felt then, stay with us, don't they?' said Marian.

'They certainly do,' agreed Polly.

The bandleader announced the interval.

'Brace yourself for the rush,' said Marian.

'I'm ready,' said Polly. 'And, Auntie . . .'

'Yes, love?'

'It's good to be back.'

Chapter Fourteen

Polly was a few weeks into the job at the school and feeling much more confident. She was learning how to cope with sudden dramas and general interruptions. Her working day was busy, but the atmosphere was much less austere than the typing pool.

It was a Monday morning and she was checking the dinner money and getting it ready for the bank. As she did so, she reflected on the fact that the children always complained about school dinners – 'Swede, ugh . . . cabbage, yuck' – but the parents knew that the meals were nourishing, which was especially vital with food still being so scarce.

Having finished that task, she typed a notice on to a wax stencil, then rolled off lots of copies on the Gestetner machine. Turning the handle and watching the pages come through, she thought what a clever invention it was.

Pleased that the day was progressing nicely, she was then unexpectedly called upon to take a sick child home because his mother couldn't be contacted by phone. So much for getting on top of things, she thought, as she headed off with the tearful boy, who was in the reception class so only little.

But it was all in a day's work and it was a job she now enjoyed, especially as it felt so worthwhile.

There was great excitement at the Cherry cafeteria because Marian had managed to get hold of some ice cream to sell. It was in the form of small, rather uninspiring vanilla bricks wrapped in flimsy greaseproof paper, but there was a touch of magic about them because it was such a long time since anyone had seen an ice cream.

'This is the first time we've had any sign of an improvement,' Marian said to Polly. 'Let's hope it's the beginning of better times.'

They both suspected that the journey back to normality would continue to be a slow one. Still, an ice cream was a lovely treat and a reminder of what they had to look forward to.

'They'll be snapped up in no time, but it's lovely having something nice to offer the customers for a change,' said Polly.

'It certainly is,' Marian agreed.

'Do you think the Cherry will start selling alcohol at some point in the future?' Polly asked casually. 'That would give people more variety to choose from.'

'Never in a million years would we be granted a drinks licence,' said her aunt. 'Dance halls are meant to be wholesome places catering largely for young people. Selling alcohol would be seen as a corrupting influence. The powers-that-be are very strict about that sort of thing.'

'I didn't realise that,' said Polly. 'I was just thinking that I don't have much to offer people.'

'You will when the good times come,' said Marian. 'Just you wait and see.'

It was Emmie's seventh birthday party and the house was swarming with children. They'd had tea, played pass the parcel and musical chairs and were now all going a bit mad, the boys fighting and the girls alternating between giggling and crying.

'We need to calm them down somehow,' said Flo.

'We've more chance of stopping the Thames from flowing,' said Polly.

'How long do we have before they go home?' Flo enquired hopefully.

'An hour,' said Polly.

'Blimey, doesn't time fly when you're enjoying yourself,' her mother said drily. 'Let's get them all to do a turn. Sing a song or do a magic trick. That might calm them down.'

Polly thought they would probably need something chemical to do that, but it was worth a try. There was a lot of laughter and prevarication, but they finally persuaded one of the boys to recite a poem, and after that they were all clamouring to have a go.

'I think the birthday girl should be next to do something,' suggested Marian encouragingly. 'What about some of your lovely cartwheels, eh, Emmie?'

'No, I don't feel like it,' Emmie said with an unusual lack of enthusiasm.

'I'm sure your friends would enjoy it,' said Polly to a chorus of agreement from the youngsters.

'I'm not doing anything,' said Emmie fiercely and started to cry.

Polly comforted her while Flo and Marian persuaded one of the girls to sing the popular song 'Give Me Five Minutes More'. It was a fairly tuneless rendition but the kids approved, and it inspired more of them to join in with the impromptu entertainment. Emmie recovered from her tears only to be upset again by one of the boys.

'Charlie said I've got spots, Mum,' she wailed. 'Tell him I haven't.'

'Of course you haven't,' Polly said rather absently. 'He's just having a bit of fun.'

'No I'm not,' denied Charlie. 'She has got spots. On her neck. Have a look if you don't believe me.'

'It'll be time for you all to go home soon, so you need to calm down,' said Polly, dismissing the boy's claim because she was feeling harassed and had a lot on her mind. 'I'll go and get you something to take with you.'

There was great excitement when she returned with the party bags, even though they were a pale copy of those of Polly's childhood. Unable to buy any paper bags, she had used curls of newspaper, filling them with sweets, a jam tart and a small toy she had managed to find in Woolworths. There really wasn't very much available, and she couldn't help thinking that they would have had something a bit more inspiring if George had still been around. However, having known only hard times, the children were all thrilled, and bounded out of the house smiling and chattering when their parents came for them.

'Phew, I think we deserve a cup o' tea and a sit-down after that,' said Flo.

'Definitely,' agreed Polly. 'I'll make the tea, Mum; you and Auntie go and sit down.'

'Thanks, love.'

'Is it safe to come in?' asked Wilf, putting his head round the door. He and Archie had escaped to watch a local game of cricket.

'Yeah, they've all gone,' said Polly.

'What's the matter with Emmie?' asked Archie. 'She doesn't look her usual cheery self.'

'Oh, some boy told her she has spots and it really upset her,' Polly explained.

'I hope you gave him a good telling-off,' said Wilf.

'Not much of one,' admitted Polly. 'There was too much going on.'

'Could be insect bites,' said Archie, looking at Emmie. 'They do sometimes cause a rash.'

'What are you talking about?' asked Polly, who was busy filling the kettle.

'The spots on her neck,' he explained.

Polly left the kettle and hurried over to her daughter. 'Oh no, there does seem to be some sort of rash,' she said worriedly. 'How come I missed it?'

'Busy with other things,' suggested her mother.

Emmie started to cry.

'It's nothing to worry about, love,' Polly said kindly. 'Just a bit of a rash.'

'Charlie was right, though, wasn't he?' Emmie said tearfully. 'I do have spots.'

'Yeah, but it doesn't matter. We all have a few spots from time to time.' Polly gave her a cuddle. 'There's no need to upset yourself. I'll keep an eye on it, though.'

Emmie seemed comforted, but Polly castigated herself for not noticing, especially as the child had seemed a little off colour these last few days. She supposed that was the price she paid for being a working mother. She tried to devote all her energies to her daughter when she was at home, but there was always so much to think about. Anyway, it was only a few spots, and they would probably have cleared up by tomorrow, she consoled herself.

Far from clearing up overnight, the spots had multiplied by the morning and Emmie wasn't at all well. She was feverish and said she hurt all over.

'Measles,' declared Flo. 'No doubt about it. I recognise it from when you and Ray had it.'

'Should I get the doctor?'

'Of course not,' Flo declared. 'You don't need to pay a doctor to tell you what you already know. She was bound to get it sooner or later; at least this will get it over with.'

'I won't be able to go to work.'

'Why not? I'll be here to look after her.'

'It's infectious, Mum.'

'It's measles, love, not scarlet fever or the plague,' Flo pointed out. 'It isn't dangerous as far as I know; just a necessary evil of childhood. Anyway, Emmie will have caught it from someone at school, and the kids who were here yesterday will probably already be infected. These things do the rounds. Some people deliberately expose their children to it to get it over and done with.'

'Mm,' said Polly, who had heard about that. 'I don't want to leave her today while she's so poorly, though.'

'It's up to you, but you've only just got into the job. You don't want to seem unreliable so soon. Not when I'm here to look after her.'

Polly was torn. The thought of leaving her daughter while she was ill was almost a physical pain. But she needed to keep the job at the school.

'I'll go to the phone box as soon as school is open and tell Miss Haywood the situation, and if she's worried about us having measles in the house I won't go in. Otherwise I'll go as normal.'

'That's settled, then,' said Flo.

'There are quite a few children away with measles today,' Miss Haywood told Polly at school later. 'It's obviously starting to do the rounds.'

'Emmie isn't well at all,' said Polly, still feeling bad about leaving her.

'Some children can be really ill with it, apparently,' said the headmistress. 'Hard to believe it's only measles in some cases. Others have it very mildly.'

'I'm hoping like mad that Emmie's will turn out to be the milder variety.'

'Indeed,' said the older woman before turning her mind to work. 'I need a letter to go out to parents of year four about a show they're putting on and to which the families are invited; and one to all the parents about the children bringing the correct dinner money. Monday mornings are a nightmare for the teachers trying to find change.'

'I'll get on to it right away, Miss Haywood.'

The other woman departed and Polly applied herself to her work, but her thoughts were at home with her daughter. Still, as Mum said, it was only measles and nothing to worry about. Not very nice for Emmie, though.

* * *

'I don't feel well, Mummy,' said Emmie when Polly got home from work that afternoon to find that her mother had made a bed up for her daughter on the sofa downstairs.

'Oh, love, I'm so sorry,' said Polly. 'Where does it hurt?'

'Everywhere; my skin hurts.'

'Poor you,' she said, then, hoping to cheer her up, added, 'some of the other children from school have measles too, so they've had to stay home as well.'

But Emmie was beyond being cheered by such news. 'I don't want to have it, please make it go away, Mummy,' she wailed tearfully.

'It will go soon on its own, and meanwhile we'll all try to cheer you up,' said Polly.

She held Emmie's hand, noticing that she was now covered in spots, but it was her temperature Polly was most worried about. She was burning up.

'I've been putting a cool flannel on her forehead,' said Flo, handing the flannel to Polly, who held it gently against her daughter's brow. It seemed to soothe her a little.

Taking her mother aside into the kitchen, Polly said, 'Mum, I shall have to call the doctor. This can't be normal for measles.'

'She's poorly, no doubt about it,' said Flo. 'But it is just measles and it has to take its course.'

'I suppose so, but she seems so ill.'

'Some children are with measles. It's a well-known fact. But it isn't anything to worry about.'

'Was I as ill as this?'

'You were pretty sick as far as I can remember,' said Flo. 'Look, love. It's hard when your child falls ill, but you have to stay calm for her sake.'

'I know, and I'm trying not to show my feelings in front

of her,' Polly said. 'I'll have her in bed with me tonight. She might find some comfort in that.'

'Good idea.'

Polly was woken with a start by violent movements beside her. Slipping out of bed to turn the light on, she was horrified to see that her daughter was having convulsions. Apart from making sure that Emmie couldn't hurt herself, she could do nothing more than watch, trembling with fear. A girl she'd been at school with had had epileptic fits and they'd always stopped quite soon, she remembered. But it was very distressing to see your own beloved daughter in such a state.

Polly was too involved even to call her mother and when it ended, Emmie was as still as death. Polly had never prayed harder, every nerve in her body rigid. Quite soon, the little girl stirred and the relief was so strong Polly's legs almost buckled.

Emmie didn't seem aware of anything untoward having happened and she seemed to want to sleep, so Polly turned her on to her side and put a pillow behind her head. Then she spent what was left of the night lying awake in fear that something else would happen.

'A fit?' said Flo anxiously the next morning when Polly told her. 'Oh, Polly, you should have woken me.'

'It was already in progress when I woke up and it didn't last long so I didn't disturb you. Anyway, there was nothing you could have done,' Polly said. 'She seems to be all right now and is sleeping. I was so scared, Mum. It was awful.'

'I bet. It would have been caused by her high temperature, I expect,' said Flo.

'I'm going to get the doctor in,' said Polly. 'I want her checked over. It's really shaken me.'

'It would do, love. I don't think it's anything to worry about, but it's best to let the doctor have a look at her under the circumstances.'

'I'll go over there as soon as the surgery opens and ask for a home visit. I won't be going to work. I'm not leaving her while she's like this.'

'I don't blame you,' said her father, also worried. 'But I'm sure she'll be fine.'

The doctor confirmed Flo's suspicions. After examining Emmie thoroughly, he said that the fit was almost certainly caused by the fever.

'I know that a fit is frightening to watch, but in itself it's of no real medical significance,' he said. 'It's what it's an indication of that we worry about. In Emmie's case I am satisfied that the cause was her high temperature.'

'That's a relief,' said Polly. 'But how can she be this ill with measles?'

'It's a very underrated illness and some children do have it more severely than others,' he said. 'Unfortunately Emmie seems to have drawn the short straw over this. You can give her half an aspirin to make her more comfortable. Other than that, carry on as you are. Keep her in bed for the next few days; put a cool flannel on her face when she's burning up. It's just a matter of letting it run its course, I'm afraid. Let me know if you're worried, but I think she'll be all right now.'

Polly thanked him and paid him, and he went on his way.

'Oh, Mum, I feel so much better now,' she said.

'Yeah, the doctor does give you confidence,' Flo said. 'Works out a bit pricey if you have to call him too often, though.'

'Fortunately it's a just a one-off, but I'd find the money somehow if Emmie needed him again.'

'Of course,' agreed Flo.

A few evenings later, Wilf hurried through the streets to the doctor's to ask him to come and see Emmie again. The little girl seemed to have taken a turn for the worse.

'She's been screaming in pain on and off all day,' explained Polly when he arrived. 'It seems to be her ear that's troubling her.'

'Let's have a look at you then, young lady,' the doctor said kindly.

'Please make the pain go away,' Emmie begged him. 'It hurts so much.'

'I'll do my best to make you more comfortable,' he said.

After another examination and a conversation with Emmie, he said to Polly, 'She has an ear infection caused by the measles. She will need half an aspirin every four hours for the pain.'

'How long will she be like this?' asked Polly. 'The poor child is in agony.'

'The aspirin will help,' he said. 'The infection should clear up in few days but the actual measles will take a little while longer. Another couple of weeks and she should be back at school.'

* * *

The ear infection dragged on intermittently for several days, and even when it finally eased off, Emmie was far from well. She was very quiet and seemed weak. Polly went back to work because she needed to earn a living, and felt blessed to have her mother there to stand in for her.

Eventually Emmie was well enough to go back to school, but she was a different child from the effervescent little girl she had been prior to the measles. She seemed strange; quieter than before.

'Is everything all right at school, Emmie?' Polly asked one afternoon when they were walking home together. 'Have you settled back in?'

No reply.

'Emmie,' she said, looking down and giving her a nudge. 'I said is everything all right at school?'

The little girl stared at her mother rather oddly, then said, 'Yeah, the same as usual.'

'Are your friends being nice to you?'

Again the strange, rather intense look. 'Yeah, of course,' she replied.

'Can you hear me, Emmie?' Polly asked.

She didn't answer, so Polly repeated the question. There was a pause, then Emmie said crossly, 'Yeah, course I can.'

'That's all right then,' said Polly, but she was worried.

'She seems so listless, Auntie,' Polly told Marian during her evening shift at the Cherry. 'You know how exuberant she usually is, always doing cartwheels and handstands. She does none of that now. And she's very quiet, quite unlike her old self.'

'It must be the after-effects of the measles,' suggested Marian. 'She was very poorly and it's bound to have taken its toll on her. People do get down when they've been ill. I'm always depressed after I've had the flu.'

'It isn't that she's miserable exactly,' said Polly. 'More that she's in a world of her own. The only thing that brings her out of herself is the kittens next door. Their cat has had a litter and Emmie adores them. She's been begging me to let her have one. The neighbours are looking for homes for them, and Emmie is scared that they'll drown them if they can't find people to take them.'

'Why don't you have one?'

'I'd love to, but it isn't my house and Mum doesn't like animals,' she said. 'She'd have to look after it while I'm at work, and that wouldn't be fair.'

'It won't need much looking after once it's grown into a cat,' said Marian. 'They're very independent creatures, going off and doing whatever it is that cats do. As long as you put food and water down for them and make a fuss of them every now and again, that's more or less all they need.'

'But it will need to be house trained, and I can't ask Mum to do that. If I had my own place, I would definitely get one. I think it's good for children to have a pet. Ray and I never had one because Mum doesn't like animals. We always wanted one, though.' Polly paused, mulling something over. 'There's something else worrying me, Auntie. I'm wondering if Emmie might have lost some of her hearing. She doesn't always answer me, and when she does, there's a pause before she speaks.'

'She must be able to hear you or she wouldn't answer at all,' said Marian.

'Mm. She watches my lips before she responds, though.'

'Oh, I see. It could be that she has a bit of catarrh or something. That can affect your ears. I wouldn't worry about it at this stage. Give it time to clear up, and if it doesn't, you'll have to get her checked out at the doctor's. I know it's a bit pricey, but it has to be done if necessary, and I can help you out with that.'

'Thanks, Auntie,' Polly said as a customer came up to the counter. 'You always manage to cheer me up.'

'I try to,' said Marian and headed back to her office. But she wasn't as calm as she seemed, because Polly and Emmie meant the world to her.

'No, Marian. Absolutely not! I would do most things for Emmie, but I'm not having a cat.'

'It would be company for her and would cheer her up.'

'She has plenty of company: the kids at school and those in the street,' said Flo.

'But Polly said she isn't mixing with the other children very much at the moment.'

'A cat won't change anything,' declared Flo. 'An animal is no substitute for human beings.'

'Not necessarily. Animals can be very therapeutic,' Marian persisted. 'Children often find them a comfort. Might be just what Emmie needs.'

'She needs time to get over her illness. She doesn't need a flamin' moggie,' said Flo. 'They're full of fleas and make a mess.'

'I think you can probably get something for the fleas, and they only make a mess when they're kittens. Grown-up cats are very clean animals.'

'You have one then if you're so keen on the idea.'

'I wouldn't mind actually, but Emmie doesn't live with me so it would be of no benefit to her.'

'She'd see it when she comes to visit.'

'That isn't the same thing at all,' insisted Marian. 'If you had one here it would be hers. You could make her responsible for feeding it and so on.'

'And when it makes a mess she's going to clear it up, is she?' Flo said. 'Don't make me laugh. It'll be muggins here who'll have to do all that.'

'It won't make a mess once it's trained.'

'All animals make a mess; they can't help it because they're animals and don't know any better. I'm not having one in this house and I don't want to hear another word about it.'

'All right, Flo, you win,' said Marian sadly. She so much wanted Emmie to be happy again.

There had been a time before Emmie was ill when she preferred to walk home from school with her friends. These days she stayed close to her mother's side. It was breaking Polly's heart to see her distance herself from the other children. Working at the school gave her a chance to keep an eye on things, and as far as she could see, Emmie wasn't being bullied. She just didn't seem to want to play, and immersed herself in a world of her own. Of course this would probably lead to problems, because she was making herself different and therefore a target for bullies.

'Hello, you two,' said Flo as they came in the front door after school one afternoon. 'Had a good day?'

'Yeah, not bad,' replied Polly.

'What about you, Em? Did you get your sums right today?' Flo asked.

The usual pause, then the little girl said, 'Most of them, Gran.'

'Good girl,' she said. 'Now, I have something for you.'

Emmie looked at Flo carefully, then said, 'Is it a present?'

'Yes, it is, in a way.' She took her granddaughter's hand and led her into the kitchen.

Polly knew she would never forget the moment when Emmie first caught sight of the tiny black-and-white bundle of fluff that stared at her with luminous green eyes. For the first time in weeks she saw her daughter react to something.

'Is it ours?' Emmie asked, gently picking up the kitten and kissing it, whereupon the fluff ball purred.

'She's yours, darling,' said Flo. 'But she'll be a part of our family so we'll help you to look after her. The first thing you need to do is give her a name.'

Emmie was silent for a moment, then she said, 'Can I call her Suki?'

'Yes, I think that's a good name for a cat. Suki it is.'

Emmie was the happiest Polly had seen her in ages.

'There are things that have to be done for her and I want you to help,' Flo told her granddaughter. 'She'll need food and fresh water on a regular basis and I want you to see to that when you're not at school.'

'All right, Gran,' Emmie said. 'Shall I do it now?'

'Not yet,' said Flo, who was cursing herself for allowing Marian to persuade her. It was bad enough trying to feed a family in these hard times. Now they had a blasted moggie to cater for too. She'd try to get some fish for it tomorrow. She'd heard that cats liked that. She'd have to queue for it, though. Damned animal. What had she let herself in for?

'She's the best kitten in the whole world, Grandma,' said Emmie effusively with the cat cradled in her arms. 'Thank you for getting her for me.'

'You're very welcome, darlin'.' If the wretched creature was going to bring such a smile to Emmie's face, Flo would put up with anything.

'I presume you've been got at by Marian,' Polly said to her mother later on in the kitchen, while Emmie was playing with the cat in the other room.

Flo nodded. 'Bloody woman,' she said. 'I swore I wouldn't let her talk me into it. Then the next thing I knew I was in next door telling them that I'd take one if they had any females left. I'll live to regret it, I know.'

'Thanks, Mum.' Polly was wet eyed with gratitude. 'I haven't seen Emmie smile like that since before she was ill.'

'Mm, well,' said Flo gruffly; she wasn't good at accepting praise. 'Just don't expect me to be kind to it if it makes a mess.'

'It's a she, Mum.'

'It's an animal,' was her reply.

'The kitten is the love of Emmie's life,' Polly told Marian in her break at the Cherry. 'She's absolutely besotted!'

'Has it brought her out of herself at all?'

'Not completely. She still seems to be in a world of her own, but the cat is in there with her. So maybe she feels less lonely.'

'That's good,' said Marian.

'I still suspect that the measles damaged her hearing to some degree,' said Polly. 'But I'm hoping it will only be temporary;

it was just measles, after all. As you say, it might just be that she's blocked up with catarrh. If it doesn't improve I shall take her to the doctor, but I'll see how it goes for a bit longer.'

'I think you're wise to let nature take its course for a while,' said Marian. 'The poor little love.'

'She was always so energetic, Auntie,' said Polly. 'Who would guess what measles can do?'

Polly was actually a lot more worried about Emmie than she had admitted to. She'd kept it to herself because she didn't want to worry other people; also because she was afraid that if she articulated her fears it would give them credence. But suddenly the weeks of anxiety reached a point where she could hold back no longer and she burst into tears.

'That's it, love; let it all out,' said Marian, putting her arms around her.

'I'm so worried about her, Auntie,' Polly sobbed. 'She just isn't my little girl any more and I don't know how to make her better. She can't hear properly, so she finds it easier to withdraw. It must be very frightening for her, but she won't admit that she can't hear. She gets upset if I ask her.'

'She'll come through this,' said Marian. 'And if she isn't showing signs of improvement in a week or two, we'll take her to the doctor. I'll come with you to give you a bit of support.'

'Thank you, Auntie. I feel so alone,' Polly confessed. 'George was reckless and irresponsible but he was there and now he's dead, and James is on the other side of the world and probably married to someone else by now. It isn't that I mind being a single mum, but sometimes you just need that someone special by your side to share the responsibility and help make the decisions. I know I'm very lucky to have you and Archie and Mum and Dad, and you're all wonderful, but . . .'

'I know exactly what you mean,' said Marian, remembering all those lonely years before Archie had come back into her life. 'But you're still a young woman, you might meet someone else at some point in the future.'

'No thanks. I'm done with men. It's far too painful,' Polly said. 'I cared for George but I wasn't in love with him when he died. Those feelings were all in the past.'

'James?'

She nodded. 'Head over heels, but that was doomed from the start because of the geography of the situation. I always knew in my heart that it wouldn't be forever, and when George came back it was scuppered completely.' She sighed. 'What a mess!'

'Most of us have a mess in our lives at some time or another,' said Marian.

'I doubt if Mum and Dad ever have,' Polly said. 'They're the most straightforward people I've ever come across.'

'They've had their troubles though . . . Losing Ray went deep with them both.'

'Yes, of course,' Polly agreed.

Marian said, 'Anyway, things can change for the better, remember. You just have to keep going.'

Polly nodded. 'Thanks for the chat,' she said, drying her eyes. 'I'd better get back to work.'

'Off you go then.'

As Polly hurried back to the cafeteria, feeling a bit better, she wondered how it was that her aunt always had such a calming influence on her. Mum was very supportive and couldn't do enough for her and Emmie. But Auntie had a special empathy somehow. Whatever the problem, she seemed to understand.

Chapter Fifteen

A shriek of terror filled the house. 'Mum . . . Mummee! Help me . . . please . . .'

It was Saturday morning and Polly was making the beds when she heard the anguished cry and tore down the stairs to find her daughter sitting in an armchair in the living room, hanging on to the arms as though her life depended on it, ashen faced with fear.

'Whatever's the matter, love?'

'The room's going around, Mum!' Emmie cried, her voice contorted with terror. 'It won't stop. Oh, Mum, I feel sick. I'm scared I'm going to fall.'

Polly dropped to her knees and put her arms around her daughter, holding her firmly. 'It's just a feeling, love, and it'll go away in a minute,' she said, taking a wild guess to calm her and trying to hide her own anxiety. 'I've got hold of you.'

Flo swept on to the scene. 'What on earth is going on here?' she asked anxiously. 'I heard the screams from outside at the washing line.'

'Emmie's feeling giddy, Mum,' said Polly.

'Oh, you poor little love.'

'I'm falling,' said Emmie, terrified. 'Oh no, please make it stop.'

'I've got hold of you, darlin',' said Polly soothingly. 'You're quite safe.'

Eventually the dizziness passed and Emmie said she felt better, but she still looked very pale and nervous.

'Have you had this before?' asked Polly.

The little girl nodded. 'A bit, but not as bad,' she said weakly.

'Is that why you stopped doing your cartwheels and handstands?'

She nodded. 'I was afraid it would come on,' she said.

'Why didn't you tell me?' asked Polly.

'I don't know.' She looked very forlorn. 'It wasn't so bad before and usually happened at school. I tried to forget about it once it had gone.'

'Well now that I do know, I can try and get something done about it.'

'The measles has left some damage to the right ear,' said the doctor, having examined Emmie. 'That will have caused the dizzy spells as well. Measles can be a very vicious illness. People don't realise.'

It was a huge relief for Polly, who had been bracing herself for something as dire as a brain tumour. 'What can be done to stop it happening again?' she asked, looking at him across the desk in his surgery. 'The poor kid was terrified.'

'I can give you a tonic for her,' suggested the doctor. 'She's probably still a bit run-down. It will help with her general health and make her feel more able to cope.'

'But it won't cure anything?' Polly asked.

278

The doctor tapped his pen against the desk. It was awkward. He knew that these were ordinary people and they probably didn't have any spare cash. It would be expensive for Emmie to see a specialist, and treatment would almost certainly be beyond their means. But it was his duty to mention the option. 'I can get you an appointment with a consultant if you wish,' he said. 'As a general practitioner I don't have sufficient specialist knowledge to advise you in any great detail.'

'How much will that cost?' asked Polly.

'We'll find the money somehow,' Flo chipped in.

'I'll make some enquiries,' said the doctor. 'If you call in tomorrow, I'll have the information for you. Then if you want to go ahead, I'll arrange an appointment.'

'Thank you,' said Polly. 'I want my daughter to get better, and as soon as possible.'

'I don't think there's a magic cure,' he warned. 'But there might be things you can do to help her. You need to speak to an expert in that field.'

'Please go ahead and arrange it, Doctor,' Polly said. 'I'll find the money somehow.'

'I'll see what there is in my savings book,' said Flo as they walked home. 'Emmie is going to get the help she needs somehow.'

'He didn't sound hopeful of a cure, though, did he?' said Polly, feeling dismal. 'I got the impression he thinks she'll just have to live with it.'

'Maybe he was just being cautious so as not to get our hopes up,' Flo said.

'Could be.'

'Let's concentrate on finding the money for the specialist for the moment,' suggested Flo. 'Your dad might have a bit in his post office account.'

Never had Polly felt more helpless. She lived from week to week on the money she earned and there was never anything left over. Maybe she could do some extra shifts at the Cherry to get the cash they needed. It would probably take a few weeks to arrange the appointment, so she might have time. It was worth a try. With renewed hope she decided to ask her aunt about it that evening.

'No, Polly, I will not give you any extra shifts here at the Cherry,' said Marian when Polly went to her office before she started work.

'Oh, Auntie,' she said, devastated. 'I really need to earn more money to pay for Emmie to see a consultant. I wouldn't ask for myself.'

'I won't give you any extra shifts because I think you work hard enough already. I will pay for Emmie to see the consultant myself.'

'I can't let you do that.'

'Why not? I wouldn't offer if I couldn't afford it.' Marian knew she didn't have the resources to pay if Emmie had to see the specialist on a long-term basis, but now wasn't the time to worry Polly with that. One step at a time.

'I'm very grateful for the offer, Auntie.'

'Archie and I both earn decent money and we don't have kids of our own to spend it on. So I will be happy to pay for Emmie and I know that Archie will agree.'

'It will take me ages to pay it back,' said Polly.

'I don't want it back,' she said. 'This will be a chance for Archie and me to show our appreciation for all the pleasure Emmie gives us.'

Polly was full of emotion and gratitude. For her daughter's sake she must accept the money graciously. 'Thank you ever so much, Auntie,' she said.

'A pleasure, love,' said Marian. 'You let me know how much you need when you find out, and I'll make sure the money is available.' She paused, smiling. 'Meanwhile, perhaps you can go and open up the cafeteria.'

Polly had put all her faith in the consultant, so was disappointed by his verdict.

'The ear is a very delicate organ,' he said, somewhat unnecessarily. 'There is no instant cure for her condition, I'm afraid.'

'Are you saying there is nothing at all you can do to help her?'

'No, I'm not saying that,' he said firmly. 'I can give you some drops that should help, and advice on how to manage the condition.'

'I was hoping you could offer something more positive,' Polly said.

'Not at this point,' he confessed. 'I am not going to recommend that you incur the expense of surgery. But there are things that can be done to help her, and she's already begun to help herself by learning to lip-read. The dizzy spells are frightening for her, but they are not life threatening.'

'They could be; if she had an attack while crossing the road, for instance. She could get knocked down.'

A look of unbridled disdain headed Polly's way. 'Obviously

281

I meant that the condition in itself is not a threat to life,' he said.

Polly nodded, properly put in her place. 'But it's so miserable for her.'

'Indeed. But when she realises that the feeling will pass, she will be less afraid and better able to cope.'

'She's only seven.'

'Yes, it's a pity she has to deal with this at such a young age, but the condition is manageable. She will get stronger and more able to handle the episodes as she gets older, and she may have long periods without any. I know it is very frightening for her, but if you help her to stop fearing the attacks it will make a big difference. On the practical side of things, it's important that she doesn't get water in her ears, so she must wear a swimming cap in the bath and any other time she is exposed to water. You will need to cover her ear when you wash her hair. I will give you a list of other things you need to be aware of. And possible solutions.'

He wasn't the sort of man who invited discussion. Anyway, Polly knew that they couldn't afford any type of surgery or treatment that might be available now or in the future. At least she had the comfort of knowing that the condition wasn't a threat to her daughter's life, which was a huge relief as that had been a constant worry.

'Thank you,' she said. 'That will be very helpful.'

'I suppose I was hoping for some sort of instant fix,' Polly said to her aunt as they waited for the bus. 'But at least we now know what we're dealing with.'

'I think the appointment was very worthwhile,' said Marian,

who had gone with Polly for moral support. 'At least Emmie doesn't have to have an operation.'

'We wouldn't have been able to afford that anyway,' Polly reminded her, speaking quietly so that Emmie couldn't hear. 'But she's going to have her life blighted by deafness and dizziness.'

'Not necessarily,' said Marian. 'The doctor just said that learning to cope with it is the best option for now. Later on they might be able to do something if we can somehow find the money.'

'I suppose so.'

'Emmie is a tough girl; she has shown that already in the way she copes. I know the giddiness scares her and she doesn't mix as much as she used to, but she never complains because she can't hear properly.'

Polly looked down at her daughter, who was hopping happily from foot to foot. She was so proud of her it brought tears to her eyes. 'You're right, Auntie, and between the lot of us we're going to make sure she has the support she needs.'

'I'll go along with that,' said Marian. She would never let Polly know how upset she was about Emmie's condition, because it was important that she stayed positive for both of them. Marian was a strong woman and coped with everything that life threw at her. But although she tried never to show it, she had her vulnerable side, and Emmie's illness had hit her hard. For Polly and Emmie, though, she was always strong, and that was how it would stay.

'I can't wait to get home to see Suki,' said Emmie. 'Do you think she's missing me? I hope she isn't too sad.'

'She has your gran for company,' said Marian. 'She'll make sure Suki isn't lonely.'

'Yeah,' said Emmie, watching Marian's lips.

Marian smiled inwardly. She couldn't imagine Flo inter-rupting her housework to make a fuss of the kitten, who she called 'a bloody nuisance' when Emmie wasn't around. But who would have thought she would take a kitten on at all, and she was very kind to the little thing. You just never knew with people. One thing Marian was sure of, though. Polly would move heaven and earth to help Emmie cope with her problem. For herself she was a fighter. For her daughter she would be an absolute trouper.

Polly was no stranger to a challenge. She had grieved twice for her husband, said goodbye forever to the man she loved and come through the war with all its hazards. But dealing with Emmie's problem was much tougher. It was very hard to stand back and let her daughter deal with it herself, but that was the only way Emmie would take her place again among her peers. But it was almost physically painful for Polly to do nothing when her maternal instincts were crying out for her to help.

Emmie's teachers were all aware of the problem and inter-vened if they spotted any bullying. Because Polly worked at the school, it would be all too easy for her to cast a constant motherly eye in the direction of the playground, but she knew that wasn't the way forward.

Some good did come from the situation, though. At the next parents' evening, Polly was told by her daughter's teacher that Emmie's schoolwork had improved dramatically. Polly wondered if she had engrossed herself in her work to take her mind off her social problems. Whatever the reason, she was very proud of her daughter and made sure she knew it.

The whole situation was very draining for Polly, though, because she was constantly worried and emotional, and struggling not to show it to Emmie.

'Polly is absolutely worn out from worrying about Emmie,' Flo said to Marian when she called one morning for a chat. 'Always manages to keeps cheerful, though.'

'Yeah, I had noticed,' said Marian.

'It's at times like this she must miss George,' Flo continued. 'She has us, but it isn't quite the same as having your partner by your side, is it? George was a bit of a rascal and would probably be alive today if he hadn't been such a scallywag, but he loved young Emmie and he would have been a good support for Polly. You know yourself there are times when only your other half will do.'

Marian knew exactly what her sister meant. Sometimes the only person she wanted around her was Archie.

Now that Polly worked in the cafeteria at the Cherry, which was inside the ballroom itself, rather than in the foyer, she could feel the atmosphere more strongly: the music, the special lighting and that air of vibrant expectancy as people came looking for fun and excitement and maybe to meet that special someone.

She wasn't short of offers herself, especially in the interval, when the punters poured into the café. 'How about the last waltz?' she was often asked by some young man. Or 'I bet you do a mean jive. Come and jitterbug with me when you've finished here.' It was just banter, light hearted and fun, and it took her mind off her troubles.

One night towards the end of her shift, when she had just finished cashing up, a man came up to the counter and asked if he was too late for a coffee.

'No, that's all right,' she said, barely glancing at the customer and inwardly cursing because now she would have to alter the figures.

'You're just as lovely as I remember,' he said, and she looked up swiftly as the Canadian accent registered.

'James!' she said in glorious astonishment.

'It sure is.'

'But how?' she said, lifting the flap to go to his side of the counter and hug him in greeting. She felt physically weakened by the shock of seeing him.

'I'm visiting for a month,' he explained. 'Staying at a hotel here in London.'

'Ooh, posh,' she said, still feeling shaky.

'It isn't the Ritz,' he said. 'Just a small place, but it's quite comfortable.'

Now that the shock was wearing off, Polly was filled with a feeling of pleasure and excitement at seeing him again. It wasn't the rapturous reunion she had occasionally allowed herself to fantasise about, because she was so worried about other things. But she was very glad to see him. He looked a lot different to the soldier she had known; she had never seen him in civvies before, and his clothes were lighter and more colourful than those worn by an Englishman. But he still had the warm eyes and lovely smile she was so fond of.

'I've almost finished here,' she said. 'You sit and drink your coffee and I'll close up and be with you. We don't keep the cafeteria open as late as the dance, so I can go when I've taken the money to Auntie.'

'Okay,' he said, smiling at her broadly.

'So what brings you all the way over to England?' asked Polly in a late-night café across the road from the Cherry.

'I came to see you.'

'Blimey, James, it's a long way to come to see an ex-girlfriend,' she said. 'I'm very flattered, but it must have cost a small fortune. It takes a long time too, doesn't it?'

'I came by plane, Polly.'

Her eyes widened. This sort of thing was completely outside of her experience. 'Good grief,' she said. 'That's a bit pricey for a farm worker, isn't it?'

'Yeah, it is, but I'm not just a farm worker. Sure I help to run the place, but it's the family farm and it's pretty darned big. We've just sold some land and my siblings and I were given a large sum of money by our father, so I can afford a holiday in England.'

'Why didn't you tell me you were well off?'

'You didn't ask,' he said. 'I told you I worked on a farm and you came to your own conclusions. Anyway, I was a soldier back then, not a farmer, and civilian life seemed to belong in another world. They were different times.'

'They certainly were,' she said. 'I thought you'd be married by now, but obviously not if you came halfway across the world to see me.'

'Aren't you pleased that I did?'

'Of course I am,' she said, reaching across and covering his hand with hers. 'I'm more than pleased; I'm delighted and very flattered. But a lot has happened in my life since I last wrote to you.'

'I know that your husband died,' he said. 'Marian and I have been in touch quite regularly. So I'm pretty much up to date.'

'Oh! I was aware that you were pen pals, but Auntie and I have never discussed it. I've had a lot to deal with so I've been in no position to go down memory lane and think about the marvellous times you and I had together. But that doesn't mean I have forgotten them.'

'I know you've had a hard time, Polly,' he said. 'What with George dying, and then Emmie getting sick.'

'Oh!' she said, shocked and more than a little miffed. 'My aunt *has* been busy.'

'I asked her,' he said. 'I wanted to know how you were doing, so I pestered her for news of you. You weren't just a wartime girlfriend to me. You were so much more than that. Please don't be angry with Marian.'

'You mean the world to me too, James, but nothing has changed,' she said. 'We still live in different parts of the world. I could never take Emmie away from here, especially now that she isn't on top form. She needs her relatives around her.'

'I would never ask you to take her away from here,' he said. 'Surely you know me better than that.'

'Yes, I do know that. And neither would I want to be responsible for you leaving your family, if that is what you are about to suggest,' she said. 'The fact is, James, I am committed to Emmie and all my energy is going into caring for her and trying to get her back on track. So there isn't really any left over for my own personal feelings.'

'I was hoping I might see something of you while I'm here,' he said, somewhat deflated.

'Of course,' she said, squeezing his hand. 'Do you think I would let you come all this way and then not spend time with you? Mum and Dad will want to see you too. They're very fond of you.'

He smiled, and it still had the same magic for her. Oh why was everything so difficult?

'I'm gonna do some sightseeing while I'm here,' he said in his Canadian drawl. 'Places I didn't get to see in my army days. So I won't be around all of the time. But it would be nice to spend some time together.'

'Of course,' she said. 'I'd be very disappointed if we didn't.'

'Good.'

He'd had no intention of sightseeing when he'd decided to come to England. All he wanted was to be with Polly again. But she seemed worried by his presence, almost afraid, so he thought it best to give her some space. It was disappointing, though, especially as he had new plans, though he probably wouldn't even mention them if she didn't warm to him once she'd got over the shock of seeing him so suddenly. What had he expected? A hero's welcome? A lot had happened to her since those golden times they'd spent together, and people changed.

'I always knew that we were from different worlds, James, in that we live such a long way from each other,' she began. 'Now it turns out that we are separated in other ways too.'

'What do you mean?'

'Well, I have two jobs to keep myself and Emmie from week to week, and I'm back living with my parents in their small rented house. It now transpires that you are a wealthy farmer and probably live in a whopping great farmhouse. So distance isn't the only problem.'

'I'm not rich, Polly.'

'But you are comfortable,' she said. 'I have never known that feeling. I'm not ashamed of my background. Quite the opposite. Mum and Dad have always worked hard and I'm proud of them, but we can't compete with you.'

'Compete?' he said, astonished. 'Who said anything about competing?'

'It's only natural.'

'Not to me it isn't,' he said. 'And you're not the only one from a hard-working background. My grandparents grafted so that we could have what we have today. And farming isn't an easy life. We don't just sit around all day.'

'Don't you pay people to do the work?'

'We do employ people, yes,' he said. 'But we still take a very active part in the farm, and there's always some sort of emergency that needs dealing with.'

'So that's me properly put in my place,' she said with a wry grin.

'You do seem to have things out of proportion.'

'Sorry.'

'No need to apologise,' he said. 'Just stop acting as if you're fresh out of the workhouse and I'm some sort of pampered millionaire.'

They both laughed and the atmosphere lifted. 'I really am pleased to see you, James,' Polly said warmly. 'Despite all the complications, it is very good to have you here.'

He leaned across and kissed her, and all the problems seemed to disappear.

'A hotel,' said Flo, when Polly had got her up to date the next morning over breakfast. 'James is here in London and he's staying at a hotel, when he could bunk down here with us like he did during the war and save himself a lot of expense.'

'He isn't short of money, apparently, Mum,' said Polly. 'He doesn't just work on a farm. His family owns it and it isn't small. He'll be more comfortable in a hotel. Anyway, it might be a bit awkward for him to stay here now that he and I are no longer together.'

'I suppose so,' Flo agreed. 'I hope we're going to see something of him while he's here, though.'

'Definitely. He's keen to see you.'

'So what's happening about you and him?' asked Flo in her usual outspoken way. 'You're free to be with him now if you want to.'

'Nothing is going to happen,' Polly said quickly. 'I'm sure you wouldn't be best pleased if I told you I was moving to Canada, would you?'

'No I would not,' Flo confirmed. 'But I wouldn't stand in your way if that was what you really wanted.'

'And drag Emmie halfway across the world, away from people who love her? No chance.' Polly looked at her daughter, who had the cat on her lap and wasn't paying any attention to the conversation. 'Come on, Em. Finish your breakfast, then brush your teeth and collect your stuff for school.'

'Okay,' she said.

Polly smiled. She was such a darling child.

Polly had a shift at the Cherry that night, and she got to work early because she wanted a few words with her aunt, with whom she wasn't best pleased.

'I'm not happy, Auntie,' she began.

'Oh?' said Marian, looking worried. 'With the job?'

'No. The job is fine. I am not happy about you sending my personal business across the Atlantic.'

Marian seemed surprised. 'I've never made any secret of the fact that James and I correspond from time to time.'

'You didn't mention the fact that you were telling him everything about my life and the struggles I've had recently, though, did you?' Polly blasted.

'He wanted to know about you,' Marian explained.

'But I didn't want him to know,' said Polly. 'It makes me feel vulnerable. You know, "Poor old Polly. She's having a hard time." He feels sorry for me and I hate that.'

'He's come all the way from Canada to see you,' said Marian. 'I don't think he did that out of pity, do you? He absolutely adores you, Polly.'

'I can't deal with any of it,' said Polly, overwhelmed by her responsibility to her daughter. 'My priority is Emmie and I can't let myself be distracted by an old love affair. I just don't have the energy.'

'James would help you, I'm sure.'

'He lives in Canada, Auntie,' she said, almost screaming in her state of heightened emotions. 'How can he help me from there? It isn't his responsibility. It's mine.'

'Calm down.'

'How can I calm down when I'm not in control of my own life? I was just about managing when you stuck your oar in and James appears and turns everything upside down.'

'I didn't tell him to come,' said Marian.

'You made me seem so needy that he felt he ought to,' she said, beside herself with rage.

'No I didn't. I would never do that.'

'Maybe you didn't mean to, but that is the end result,' rasped Polly. 'What makes you think you have the right to discuss my business with strangers?'

'He isn't a stranger,' Marian pointed out. 'He's a dear family friend and he thinks the world of you.'

'But it isn't your place to tell anyone about my private business, is it?' Polly was becoming almost hysterical. 'Even my mother wouldn't humiliate me in such a way. How dare you do that, Auntie, how dare you?'

Marian was very tense, her cheeks flushed.

'Lost for words, are you?' said Polly, completely out of control. She had never spoken to her aunt in this rude way before, but the words were rolling off her tongue almost of their own volition. 'I should bloody well think so.'

'Keep quiet for a minute and let me speak!' Marian almost shouted, bringing Polly to silence. 'I *am* your mother, that's how I dare. That is why I would do anything to make your life better. Anything at all!'

'What . . .'

'I am your mother, Polly,' she said in a quiet, sad tone. 'And in telling you that, I have broken a long-term promise to my sister. I hope you're pleased with yourself, goading me like that. Now, we have a ballroom to run here, so I suggest you go and open the cafeteria and do the job you are paid for.'

Polly was trembling as she left Marian's office.

'I was sixteen when I fell pregnant with you,' Marian told Polly in her office after the ballroom had closed. 'Flo was married by then and had your brother Ray. There had been complications during his birth that had damaged her womb, so she knew she couldn't have any more children of her own. Our parents were very strict and they put me through hell for getting myself into trouble. They made me feel like the lowest form of life and I have had to fight that feeling ever since.'

'You always seem so confident.'

'It's a defence mechanism I perfected long ago to keep going. But they almost destroyed me.'

Polly was feeling traumatised by this revelation but she managed to appear normal for Marian's sake.

'It was my mother's idea for Flo to take you and bring you up as her own. They sent me away to an aunt in Essex when I began to show, and after you were born, Flo brought you back as her own, a system widely used in cases like this.'

'You just gave me away, then?'

'Well, yes, but it wasn't as heartless as you're making it sound. It was the last thing I wanted but it was for your own good, and I was living in the same house so I saw plenty of you.'

'What about my father?' asked Polly. 'I suppose he was some irresponsible yobbo who didn't want to know when you got pregnant?'

'Not at all,' Marian replied. 'He was, and still is, the love of my life. Archie is your father.'

It was as though Marian had thrust her fist into Polly's face, such was the impact. 'So why didn't he stand by you?'

'He wanted to, but he had nothing to offer. He was just a penniless boy. My mother banished him from the house and forbade me to see him again. She said my baby would have a good upbringing but Archie was to keep away or the deal was off. We were powerless. It broke both our hearts, I can tell you, but at least this way we knew you would be all right.'

'So you didn't see him again?'

'Not until years later, when he came to find me. He kept his promise and stayed away for all that time. You were grown up and married by then, so it didn't matter as far as you were concerned. But both Archie and I regret the years together we were deprived of, and the fact that we lost you. Neither of us is the type to dwell on things unduly, outwardly anyway, but we are both really sorry. We would have loved to have brought you up ourselves. But that's the way it was for girls like me. Attitudes haven't changed much either. It's just as bad these days.'

Polly nodded.

'Have you never felt my deep love for you, Polly?' Marian enquired.

'I've always felt very close to you,' Polly said. 'We've always been mates.'

'Sometimes my feelings for you were so strong I thought you would guess.'

'It would never have occurred to me,' Polly said. 'It wouldn't, would it?'

'I suppose not.'

'You were always a very special aunt, though. I knew I could turn to you.'

'I tried to always be there for you,' Marian said. 'When I left home, I always came back often. I was keeping an eye on you even though you didn't know about it.'

'So you and Archie are Emmie's real grandparents, then,' said Polly, thinking things over.

'Yeah, but I don't think we should tell her yet,' said Marian. 'We'll have to see what Flo has to say about it. She's going to be livid with me for blurting it out.'

'I'll tell her it was my fault,' said Polly. 'I'll make sure she knows that I'll always think of her as my mum. How can it be otherwise when it's all I've ever known?'

'Of course,' said Marian, still hurt even after all these years. It had been very hard watching her daughter grow up as someone else's child.

'My whole life has been a lie, hasn't it?' said Polly, still reeling from the shock.

'I suppose you could say that. But you were loved and looked after and I was never far away,' said Marian.

'I appreciate all that, but I'm still not who I thought I was and it may take some time to get used to it.'

'I understand,' said Marian sadly.

Chapter Sixteen

'The truth had to come out some time, love, so try not to be too upset,' said Archie sympathetically when Marian arrived home in tears. 'Not unless you were thinking of keeping the truth from Polly indefinitely.'

'I didn't have any plans, Archie,' said Marian. 'I was just letting things carry on as they were, as we agreed with Flo all those years ago. I've always wanted Polly to know, of course, but I certainly didn't intend to blurt it out like that. The poor girl is shocked to the core.'

'She's bound to be until she gets used to the idea,' he said. 'Personally, I'm glad she knows. I think it's long overdue. I hope she'll be happy to have us as parents when she's had time to think about it.'

'It's too late for that, Archie.'

'She can be pleased to know who really made her, though.'

'Or angry and hurt that we gave her up,' said Marian. 'Flo will be livid with me for telling her.'

'I expect she will, but surely she must be able to see that Polly needs to know who her real parents are. Everyone has that right, don't they? Even if things carry on as they are.'

'It was an arrangement made before Polly was even born and it hasn't been discussed since,' Marian reminded him. 'It's always been the unmentionable family secret, and as the years passed, we were all so used to the way things were, it got to be almost as though Polly was Flo's real daughter.'

'But she isn't, so it's high time that was put right. It was a solution to the problem meant for Polly's childhood, not her whole life,' he said.

'She said that Flo will always be her mum, though.'

'Which is only natural, but I suppose you were hurt by that,' he guessed.

'I was, yeah,' Marian admitted sadly. 'But how can it be otherwise? Flo's been a good mother to her.'

'Exactly,' he said. 'You have always been very close to Polly, though, so hopefully that will continue and you can build on it. Without taking anything away from Flo, of course.'

'I'm not so sure if it will work now, Archie,' she said. 'Polly might turn against me for giving her up.'

'We did what we had to do at the time. There was no choice but to do as we were told, and it was the best thing for her,' he reminded her. 'We were too young, and powerless to consider problems so far into the future.'

'I'll take what comes,' she said. 'But I hope she doesn't think badly of me.'

'I'll be very surprised if she does.'

'It all sounds so cold, us giving her up. She has no way of knowing how deeply painful it was for us. And if I try to tell her, it will seem as if I'm making excuses.'

'Maybe we'll just have to let her come to terms with it and see what happens.'

'Yes, I'm afraid so.'

'You're a bit quiet this morning, Polly,' said Flo the next day over breakfast. 'Are you all right?'

'I'm fine.' She had promised Marian she wouldn't say anything to Flo until Marian had had a chance to talk to her herself.

Now that Polly knew the truth, it seemed obvious. She even looked like Marian, which she had put down to a general family resemblance. Her aunt had always been good to her, closer than usual for an aunt, and Polly had always adored her. But what was she supposed to do and feel now? This revelation had been foisted on her when she already had more than enough for her emotions to cope with.

Feeling a sudden rush of affection for Flo, who she now knew had taken her on out of the goodness of her heart and not because she had given birth to her, she got up and hugged her.

'What's all this?' asked Flo. 'Have you got a guilty conscience or something?'

'Can't a daughter give her mother a cuddle without there being an ulterior motive?'

'Well yeah, of course she can,' Flo said, pink with pleasure. 'It's just that we're not that sort of family.'

'We could be,' said Polly. 'It's never too late to start.'

Flo was furious later on when Marian told her what had happened the night before.

'You had no right to tell her,' she seethed.

'I think I probably have more right than anyone,' Marian riposted.

'But you gave your word.'

'I didn't mean to blurt it out, and I'm sorry.'

'I should think so too.'

'Anyway, it's time she knew, Flo,' said Marian. 'Unless you were planning on never telling her the truth.'

'I hadn't really given it much thought, to be honest,' Flo admitted. 'I'm so used to the way things are, and I always think of Polly as my daughter. There is more to being a mother than just blood.'

'I know that, of course, and nothing will change as far as that's concerned,' said Marian. 'She isn't going to suddenly start calling you Auntie Flo. You've done a good job and she will be well aware of that, as I am. It's important she knows the truth, but you'll always be her mother.'

Flo was obviously relieved, but she said, 'I suppose that will be up to her.'

'She has more important things on her mind at the moment anyway,' Marian pointed out. 'Emmie primarily, and now James has come back, which must have affected her in a big way.'

'Sure to have done,' agreed Flo. 'All we can do is be there in case she needs us.'

'Exactly,' said Marian.

'It's just like old times,' said James as he and Polly left the Cherry together that night. 'Me walking you home from work.'

'Such a lot has happened since then, but it seems as though we are just carrying on where we left off.'

'Yeah. Back then it was wartime so everybody was working long hours,' he said. 'It hurts me that you still have to work at night as well as during the day.'

'Those are my circumstances and there's not a lot I can do about it,' she said. 'Anyway, I get Sundays off. Which reminds me, Mum has invited you for Sunday lunch. It will give you a chance to see everybody.'

'I'd like that very much, Polly,' he said.

'Good. I'll tell her.'

On Saturday morning when Marian called at the house, Polly took the opportunity to speak to her and Flo together in the hope of putting things straight.

'Look, you two, I don't know how I'm supposed to feel now that the truth has come out about who I really am, so I'm going to carry on as I always have, loving you both as my aunt and my mother. Nothing will change as far as Dad and Archie are concerned either. It isn't as though I'm some little kid who needs looking after.'

'You're not angry with me for giving you up, then?' ventured Marian.

'Of course not. You all obviously did what was best for me at the time, and I've had a good upbringing, so can we get rid of the awkwardness and go back to normal?'

'Suits me,' said Flo.

Sensing some disappointment in Marian, Polly said, 'Come on, Auntie, we might not be such good mates if we try being mother and daughter at this late stage.'

'I suppose that's true,' she said. 'It's just that . . .'

'I'll always know who you are here,' said Polly, pointing to her heart. 'But I don't want to lose my very special auntie, so let's keep things as they are, for now anyway. Obviously, at some point, Emmie will need to know.'

'That's fine with me,' said Marian, realising that she did actually mean it. She and Polly had a good, solid relationship; why change something that worked so well?

'I'll put the kettle on,' said Flo predictably.

'Sorry it isn't more of a banquet, James,' said Flo on Sunday when they all sat down at the table for lunch. 'The war's been over for more than two years but the rationing and shortages are as bad as ever. Gawd knows when things will get back to normal again.'

'Please don't apologise,' he said. 'I'm just so happy to be here with you all again.'

'And we're glad to have you here, which is why I would have liked to put on more of a spread,' said Flo. 'We didn't expect to see you again, but we're very glad that we have.'

'Hear, hear,' said Marian, and there was general agreement.

'Emmie,' said Flo loudly, to make sure the little girl heard her.

'Yes, Grandma.'

'Put that cat on the floor now, please. I know you've got her on your lap hidden under the tablecloth.'

'She doesn't like being on her own,' said Emmie.

'She's a cat, darlin', and they are independent creatures,' Flo reminded her. 'Anyway, the Sunday dinner table is no place for an animal.'

James laughed heartily. 'You should try telling our cats that,' he said.

'You've got more than one?' said Flo in astonishment.

'We have half a dozen,' he said.

'Blimey,' said Flo. 'Your mother must be a nervous wreck. Our little thing drives me nuts, and there's just one of her.'

'You need cats on a farm,' he explained. 'To keep the rats away.'

'Oh my Gawd,' said Marian. 'It's a different world.'

'It sure is,' said James.

'I wish we could have a lot of cats,' said Emmie.

'You're all right with one,' said James, looking at her so that she knew what he was saying.

'And that one is going on the floor while we have our dinner,' said Flo.

'Do as your gran says, please,' said Polly firmly. Her daughter was a much-loved child but she wasn't spoilt, or not often anyway. Polly made sure of that.

Emmie lifted the animal down and the conversation resumed, everyone talking at once at times. The warmth of the atmosphere touched James's heart. He was so glad to be back.

'Are you going to let me take you out for dinner one evening soon?' enquired James later on, when Polly was seeing him off at the front door.

'A date?'

'Sure.'

'How lovely.'

'I suppose it depends on whether you can fit me into your busy schedule.'

'Are you being sarky?'

'Of course not,' he replied. 'You don't have much spare time with all your working commitments. It's a fact.'

'I'll find the time and ask Mum to babysit Emmie.'

'Good,' he said. 'Let me know when and I'll book a table somewhere. The West End if you fancy it.'

'Sounds lovely.'

'I'll do my best to make it so,' he said.

'The West End, eh?' said Flo. 'I wonder what he's got in mind.'

'A good meal, I should think,' said Polly drily. 'He probably feels half starved after a week or so in England.'

'He had a good meal when he was here,' said Flo. 'I made sure of it.'

'I know you did, Mum,' said Polly. 'I meant in general. There isn't much food about and he isn't used to it like we are. I expect they have plenty of everything in Canada.'

'I expect they do,' said Flo. 'But I was thinking that he probably has more than just food on his mind if he's taking you to some swanky West End place.'

'I don't know if it will be a swanky place, but there definitely won't be a marriage proposal, if that's what you're hinting at,' said Polly. 'He knows the situation as regards that. So you can forget any ideas of shipping me off to Canada.'

'As if I'd ever do that.'

'You do seem keen on my getting together with James.'

'Because he's a good man and so right for you.'

'And he lives in Canada.'

'Mm, that is a drawback, I must admit.'

'So, can we let it go and not mention it again?'

'I just want you to have someone nice, Polly. I don't want you to be alone.'

'My priority is Emmie, Mum, you know that,' she said. 'I can't take on anything else.'

'You're being a martyr and it isn't fair to Emmie.'

Polly was astonished by this remark. 'How can you say that? Emmie means the world to me. I would never do anything to hurt her.'

'Then stop using her as an excuse and get on with your life,' Flo said.

'And go and live in Canada?'

'If that's what it takes, yes. I would hate it, of course, but people have to do what's right for them.'

'I'll get Emmie's tea,' said Polly. She wanted to bring the subject to a close.

They went to a restaurant in a side street off the Strand. Small, intimate and classy.

'Someone I got chatting to at the hotel recommended it,' James explained.

'It's lovely,' Polly said, looking around at the starched white tablecloths and silver candelabra. 'You'd have thought that all those nights in the shelter during the air raids would have taken the romance out of candles, but it hasn't.'

'That's good,' he said.

'You want a romantic atmosphere, then?'

'It's always nice to have a special atmosphere in a restaurant, don't you think?'

'I haven't been to many restaurants,' she said. 'I'm more of a Lyons tea shop sort of a girl.'

'Well you're a restaurant sort of a girl tonight,' he said, smiling at her.

'And I shall enjoy every moment.'

'I'll do my best to make sure of that.'

The atmosphere was light hearted and fun. James ordered some wine and they both became even more relaxed. So much so that Polly's tongue was loosened.

'You didn't come to England just to see me, did you, James?' she said. 'There must be another reason.'

'What makes you say that?'

'The wine probably, but it has occurred to me that no one would come all this way at such expense just to see an ex-girlfriend.'

'They might if she was very special.'

'If they had more money than sense maybe,' she said. 'And I know you're not short of a few quid but I don't think you're so rich you can afford to travel across the world on a whim.'

He looked at her with a hint of a smile. 'You're right, of course,' he said. 'But you are most of the reason. In fact, if it wasn't for you, I wouldn't be here for the other thing.'

'How very mysterious . . . Why don't you tell me what it's all about?'

'I'm here about a job,' he explained. 'With a Canadian company manufacturing farm machinery. They're expanding into Britain and they want me to join the sales team here.'

'You'd be selling farm machinery?' she said, astonished.

'That's right,' he confirmed. 'We use their machinery on our farm and there isn't much I don't know about it, which is why they've offered me the job. At least they've offered me the chance to try for the job. I've had a series of interviews in Canada, but this trip is to meet the director based here in London, an Englishman. They've told me the job is mine provided the guy here approves. The fact that I spent time here during the war has helped my application, as I would be dealing with British farmers and I do know a little about English culture and so on. Plus there's no one better to sell machinery to farmers than a farmer.'

'So it was a pack of lies about your dad giving you money, then?'

'Not at all. The company are paying my travel expenses and my accommodation for a few days. But I'm footing the bill for the extra time here, which I can afford because Dad gave us all some money.'

'So why the secrecy about the job?'

He looked worried. 'The plan was that if I definitely got the job I was going to ask you to marry me again. I know Emmie is your priority, and I'm not going to charge in and take over. I thought maybe I could get to know her better before we take things any further. But I'll be here in England, that's the important thing. My interest in the job is so that I can be here with you.'

Such thoughtfulness was typical of him. 'But James, your family, your life in Canada,' she said. 'You can't just walk away from it. You'd miss it all terribly.'

'I'd miss the family, of course,' he said. 'But the idea of a new challenge excites me.'

'How would the job work exactly?'

'I'd be based at the London office but I would travel all over the country to see farmers and make contacts in the farming world. I'd go to the farmers' markets looking for business and set up sales promotions. The company advertise in agricultural magazines, so that will bring in leads. I know this country is in the doldrums at the moment, but the good times will come and we want to be a part of it.'

'But you're a farmer, not a salesman.'

'I was born into farming so I know nothing else,' he said. 'But I love the idea of doing something different while using my experience. I'll still be involved in agriculture, just not working on the land.' He gave a wry grin. 'Some parts of that I won't miss at all, especially in winter.'

'Well you seem to have thought it all through, so all I can do is wish you luck,' Polly said. 'What's the procedure now?'

'I'm seeing the chap who runs things here next week,' he said. 'That's when I'll know if I've got the job. If I have, I shall go back to Canada to clear everything up, then come back and start work.'

'What do your family think about it?'

'They don't want me to leave, naturally, but they know I want to make my way in the world,' he said. 'They also know how I feel about you. I told them my plans and they fully support me.'

She nodded slowly. She seemed to be in sole charge of his happiness, and that was an awesome burden.

How could she take another man into her life after the havoc George had caused? Emmie had adored her father and been devastated when they had lost him. That child had been through enough. But James was so keen, so earnest and truthful. The fact that he was prepared to leave the people he loved and change his whole life for her was a huge compliment, but a responsibility too.

'You seem a bit quiet,' he observed.

'I was just thinking what a big thing this is for you,' she said. 'And I don't want you to be disappointed.'

'Keep your fingers crossed for me,' he said warmly.

'Of course.'

★   ★   ★

'It's a huge thing he's doing,' Polly said to her aunt during her break at the Cherry the following evening. 'I mean, can you imagine leaving everyone you love behind and starting afresh somewhere else?'

'Mm. It is a big thing, but plenty of people do it these days,' Marian said. 'Mostly the other way around, though. British people go to Australia and Canada in search of a better life. And who can blame them with the way things are in this country at the moment? A lot of ex-servicemen are emigrating, so I've heard, going somewhere they've never been and where they don't know anybody. At least James is coming to someone who loves him.'

'Exactly,' said Polly. 'He's doing it to be with me.'

'It's his choice and an adventure for him,' said Marian. 'So stop worrying. If he drives you nuts after a while, join the club. I could strangle Archie sometimes. It's called marriage.'

Polly laughed. She could always rely on her aunt to put things into perspective.

'That's better,' said Marian, glad that her relationship with Polly remained intact after the recent revelations.

It was dinner time at the school and the playground resonated with the high-pitched clamour of children's voices. Polly was going to do some shopping in her break and was heading for the exit along the corridor when something caught her eye out of the window.

Emmie was on her own out there, which always tore at Polly's heartstrings. But as she watched, two girls went over to her and started pushing her around. Polly couldn't hear what was being said, but she could tell it wasn't nice.

Where was the teacher on playground duty? she fumed inwardly, heading towards the door to stop this cruel behaviour. But when she reached the playground, she stopped in her tracks. Emmie had stepped forward and was pushing her attackers away. Clearly angry, she was fighting them off, giving as good as she got.

The bullies disappeared and another little girl came up to Emmie and put her arm around her. Together the two of them walked away and joined some other children. This really was a seminal moment for Polly, and she was so glad she hadn't intervened. Emmie was coping and Polly was proud almost to the point of tears as she headed for the shopping parade. She knew that she must take a step back. Always be there if her daughter needed her, but allow her to make her own way too. Emmie was stronger than she'd given her credit for, and it was Polly's job to help her build on this by letting her get on with her own life.

After school that day, Polly was informed by her daughter that she would be walking home with her friend Violet.

'Can she come and see Suki after tea?' Emmie asked.

'As long as her mother says it's all right, of course she can,' said Polly.

'Thank you,' said Violet, a bright-eyed, smiling child with her brown hair tied back in bunches. 'Mum won't mind but I'll make sure I ask her.'

'We'll see you later then,' said Polly, and walked on ahead, leaving the girls to indulge in their childish chatter. She was smiling all the way home.

★   ★   ★

A few evenings later, when James appeared at the Cherry beaming, Polly knew he had got the job and was absolutely delighted for him.

She was in the process of closing the café and the band was playing 'Sentimental Journey'.

'Shall we have a celebratory dance?' she suggested.

'Why not?' he smiled.

It was being played as a slow foxtrot and they smooched around the floor.

'I'm so happy you're going to be around,' she said.

'Are you sure?' he said. 'I had the feeling that you were a little worried by the prospect.'

'I was at first,' she admitted. 'Because of my responsibility towards Emmie I thought I had no room for anything else in my life. But I seem to have got that into perspective now, and I know you will be a great support to me, as I will be to you.'

'Really?' he smiled, leaning back to look at her.

'Yes, really,' she confirmed, tightening her arms around him. 'Welcome to England, James.'

'I sure am glad to be here,' he said softly. 'Especially if you agree to be my wife.'

'Try stopping me,' she said.

One day in the summer of 1948, Polly and James were in the doctor's surgery with Emmie.

'Well, young lady,' said the doctor, after he had read Emmie's notes and examined her ears, 'I think we'll make you an appointment with a consultant to see if we can get something done about this problem of yours.' He looked towards Polly and James. 'Things have changed since she last saw someone, and it won't cost you anything for specialist advice and treatment now.'

'Yes, isn't it marvellous,' Polly said. Thanks to the new National Health Service, which had been introduced recently, she could at least get help for her daughter now even if the condition couldn't be completely cured. James had been a strong support in this and had proved to be a good and loving stepfather to Emmie.

They had had a Christmas wedding and lived quite close to the family. James had settled well in England and earned a decent salary, so they could afford the rent on a small house and Polly no longer had to work evenings at the Cherry. When they went there now, it was to dance, and they loved it. James was a broad-minded husband and didn't object to his wife working, so Polly had kept her job at the school.

Life was good for them and they were hopeful of better things for everyone. They had waited a long time for the end of austerity, but it seemed that at last it was on its way. They could be patient. The war had taught them that.

'Grandma is here,' said a smiling Emmie, leading Flo into the living room, where Polly and James were waiting, dressed up and ready to go out.

'Hello, Mum, thanks for coming to sit with Emmie while we have a night out,' said Polly, giving Flo a hug.

'A pleasure, love,' said her mother.

Indeed, Flo enjoyed nothing more than babysitting Emmie so that Polly and James could go out of an evening now and then. It was such a relief to her that nothing had changed since Marian's dramatic revelations. She had maintained her position as mum to Polly and gran to Emmie, while Polly and Marian were still the good pals they had always been.

'We'll get off then,' said Polly, and turned to her daughter. 'Be a good girl for your gran.'

'She always is,' said Flo, noticing that Emmie was already setting out a board game on the table, something they both enjoyed. 'Go and have a good time.'

Flo closed the door behind them and headed back to join Emmie in the living room, imbued with a sense of well-being so strong it brought tears to her eyes. Family had always been at the centre of her life, and now it had expanded to include James as well.

'Come on then,' she said to Emmie. 'Let's get playing, and no cheating.'

Emmie giggled. 'I never cheat, Gran,' she said. 'But I'll be keeping my eye on you.'

'Cheeky madam,' said Flo, and the room resounded with their laughter as Emmie threw the dice.

Marian was expecting them, so was in the foyer to meet them when they arrived.

'Welcome to the Cherry,' she said, hugging them both.

'It's good to be here,' replied Polly, the buzz of the place sending excited shivers up her spine.

'You've arrived at the right time for your favourite,' said Marian as the upbeat sound of 'In the Mood' drifted out from the ballroom. 'No need to get tickets. This one will be on the house. But hurry up, or you'll miss it.'

'Come on, James,' said Polly, taking his hand and smiling. 'Let's get dancing.'

'Try stopping me,' he said.

Happy and excited, they went through the swing doors, leaving Marian looking after them fondly.

Polly was buffeted by the music, the lights and the exhilarating roar of people having fun. Her reaction was so strong it was almost physical as memories poured in. But tonight wasn't for looking back. It was about the present, and their enjoyment in each other. They were both smiling as they threw themselves into the dance he had taught her – their beloved jive.